FOR *Always*

Now & Always Duet
Book Two

AMANDA BENTLEY

Cover Design: Crowe Abbey Covers

ISBN (paperback): 979-8-9868923-7-5

For Always (Now & Always Duet Book 2)

Amanda Bentley Books LLC

amandabentleybooks@gmail.com

Contents

This one's for the badasses who've ever felt like they needed someone.
How great did it feel when you realized you didn't?

Content Note

Dear Reader,

For Always is the second book in the Now & Always Duet. If you haven't read For Now, go read it first. This series **must** be read in order (unless you want to be confused with a bunch of spoilers). This is a new adult, romantic suspense series and features mature themes and content that may not be suitable for all audiences. The content warnings for this book are different than those of For Now, so if you need to, please check the author's profile links @amandabentleyauthor.

You must be enjoying the rollercoaster if you're reading on. We've still got some twists and turns ahead, but I think you'll be happy you rode by the end of the story.

♡ Amanda Bentley ☺

Playlist

Listen on Spotify!

1. "Circles" by Post Malone

2. "I Blame The World" by Sasha Alex Sloan

3. "DEVIL" by Shinedown

4. "Sucker" by Jonas Brothers

5. "Addicted" by Saving Abel

6. "Falling Slowly" by Vwillz

7. "Big Man, Little Dignity" by Paramore

8. "Inside Out" by Eve 6

9. "Friends Don't" by Maddie & Tae

10. "River" by BRKN LOVE

11. "Stay" by Post Malone

CHAPTER ONE

February 18th

KATE

I've never doubted my ability to read until this moment. My eyes squeeze shut, my face scrunching along with them. There's no way I read that right.

Why would Brad Atkin's name be on a police report in Santi's guest bedroom?

Is Lorenzo really stalking me? It seems to be the only explanation. Why the hell else would there be a report for Brad in Santi's house?

Better yet, why is it in his guest bedroom?

It dawns on me—Lorenzo mentioned Santi having a roommate. Everyone has left except for Lorenzo.

Is this his room?

I force my eyes open and scan the room haphazardly. I need to read the rest of the report. I need to know what it says.

Recovering the paper from the floor, I straighten it and read the narrative.

```
Dispatch received call from anonymous witness
advising that a car was seen crashing into a
```

```
tree on highway 135 (see page 2 for location
details). Arrived at the scene of collision at
2001 hours. Ambulance (requested by dispatch)
arrived at approximately 2003. Victim stated
unknown V2 was attempting to get in V1's lane
but did not see V1. Victim swerved to avoid
collision and hit a tree. V1 is extensively
damaged (see detailed report on page 3).
Victim described feelings of dizziness and
nausea. Victim's hands showed lacerations over
knuckles and fingers. Victim advised he did
not see the license plate of V2 but described
it as a black coupe. Victim is unsure of V2
make and model. Victim could not make out
features of V2 driver. Paramedics dictated
that medical assistance should be utilized and
Victim accepted.
```

The door knob turns as I finish reading. I choose not to hide the paper. I choose not to shut the bottom drawer of the nightstand. If *he's* stalking me, *I'm* allowed to snoop.

"Where do you live?" I demand the second Lorenzo shuts the door behind him.

Still in just his boxers, I watch his muscles tense as his eyes flick to the paper in my hands then back to my face. His eyes widen, almost imperceptibly. I wave the report for emphasis.

"Why were you digging through my shit?"

My shit. I knew it. "Why do you have a police report with *Brad's* name on it?" I counter, my low and lethal voice unfamiliar to me.

He doesn't answer and he doesn't move, his wary eyes analyzing.

"You *are* stalking me, aren't you?" I ask, recalling the night he stormed in on my date with Brad. A range of emotions flicker deep in his irises, settling on reservation.

"Stalking is extreme."

"Extreme? I'll tell you what's extreme. Finding out that you have a police report for a guy I went on *one* date with! How? Why? I—"

I've started babbling because I'm at a loss, trying to wrap my head around the facts here. Why in the hell would he be so obsessed that he's stalking me, yet not want to be more than friends with benefits?

"I wanted to make sure you weren't going to see a crazy man."

"What, so this was for protection?" I scoff and toss the paper. "This was some heroic gesture? How can you expect me to believe that?"

He takes a hesitant step towards me, as though I'm a growling dog that's prepared to bite. "I care about you, Kate."

"You care about me?" I laugh mirthlessly. "This feels like *way* more than caring. This is creepy. This is—" I glance at the fallen piece of paper. "How did you even get this report? Why is there only one page?"

The questions are coming to me faster than I can spew them. This feels dirty, disgusting, out of control. Out. Of. Control. It's too much. This is too much. Too much for so little.

"Kate." He's in front of me now, though I'm not sure when he moved. I'm sinking into the depths of this chaos like quicksand.

"Hey." His tone is soft. He pulls my trembling chin up with a finger. I stare into his eyes but I'm not seeing anything; the ringing in my ears is too loud. The pounding of my heart is too distracting.

"Why?" I whisper. I zero in, staring deep into his eyes. I see desperation, I see yearning, I see... pain.

"I was trying to protect you," he whispers, a crack in his voice. He places his hands on my waist tentatively, and for a moment, I let him.

But his touch doesn't provide the comfort I need.

I take a step back, his hands sliding off. I shake my head. "You make no sense to me."

"Let me try," he says. He looks so earnest, so sincere, it confuses me more.

"Why are you so desperate to protect me yet you don't want anything more?"

"You said you weren't looking for a boyfriend."

"What, so this is my fault now?" The shock is melting into puddles at my feet.

"That's not what I meant. It's just—"

"Tell me. What did you mean?"

"I thought this was a mutual agreement!"

"It is!" I let out a grunt of frustration. "But I wouldn't call stalking me on a date 'casual.'"

He looks away and his jaw ticks, but he turns back and bores his eyes into mine. "I ca—don't—want anything serious. It has nothing to do with you."

"Have you ever had a girlfriend?"

He starts to shake his head but stops, looking down.

I laugh humorlessly. "I'm her, aren't I? I'm that stupid, idiot girl who gets strung along, hoping she's different. That she can be enough."

His eyes snap to mine. "Don't say that. Of course you're enough."

"Don't *fucking* lie to me!" My voice is getting louder.

"Just because I don't want anything serious doesn't mean I don't care about you!"

We're back to screaming, just like Valentine's Day. My head is spinning. This doesn't feel right. None of this feels right. I take a few deep breaths, my eyes fluttering shut. Thankfully, Lorenzo stays silent, allowing me a moment.

"You haven't answered the first question," I say evenly. I know the truth but I want to hear it from his mouth.

"Which?" he replies coolly. I'm certain he knows exactly which I'm referring to, but I humor him anyway.

"Where do you live?"

He hesitates. His shoulders sink, his chest deflates. "Here."

"This house?"

He nods and tosses his hands out. "This room."

"Why?" My voice is a broken whisper.

"Because," he answers, not feigning ignorance this time. "I don't like to show people where I live. I don't like others knowing about my personal life."

"Are you telling me all your friends tonight don't know you live here?"
His silence cracks my slowly freezing heart.

"I'm leaving." *Fuck* not running away; I should have left earlier.
But then you wouldn't have found the report.

"Kate, please," he says, wrapping a hand around my wrist. There's a deep rooted plea to the way he says it, like his heart will replicate mine if I walk out that door.

Like all my choices surrounding this man, I make the wrong one. I don't move.

"I've known them all for years. Santi and I both. It's different. I haven't known you that long, I haven't... I wanted to keep this as casual as possible."

"So you achieve that by lying to me? By stalking me?"

"I fucked up," he says. His eyes belong to a traitor. Yet I want to believe that the remorse I see in them is genuine.

"Look, I get that people lie. But you have to understand that this is all so fucking weird. We're hooking up in a room I thought was your friend's guest room, only to find out it's actually your room. Then, you have an incident report for a guy I went on *one* date with in your drawer."

I see his dark depths shift, like the bricks for the wall are being cemented as we speak. Call me a dumbass, but I still hold hope that some explanation he provides will change this, will reverse the damage.

"You're not just some chick. I invited you to the New Year's party for a reason."

He's trying to convince me, to make it seem like his intentions were pure.

"You're driving me insane."

"You've been driving me insane for months! Join the *fucking* club!"
He has the nerve to actually look irritated by that fact, and I'm not sure why, but it's what makes me believe him.

I inhale deeply, trying to clear my thoughts. He doesn't reach for me again, despite the pulsing need to feel him.

"How can you not care if I date Brad again?" *If I'm going to get any answers, now's the time.*

"Of course I care, Kate. I want you to be mine." He runs a hand through his hair. "But I know that's not fair. It's not fair of me to ask you to be with me at arm's length and expect you not to date."

He's giving me serious whiplash.

"I'm so confused..." Trying to calm my racing thoughts is like trying to douse a fire with oil. It only causes it to burn brighter. "You keep me at a distance yet stalk me. You stormed in on my date yet tell me to let you know if I do continue to date him."

"Fuck!" He claws at his chest. "You think I want to feel like this? You think I want to think about you constantly? To feel possessive over a person for the first time in my life? To feel like I need you?"

My stomach drops, tingles spreading down my arms. I'm not sure if I should be enamored or afraid.

I settle somewhere in the middle. "This is only confusing me more."

His jaw ticks. "I'm sorry. I wish I could be clearer."

"What does that even mean? Just *be* clearer."

I've never felt so pathetic. I'm basically begging him for answers. Basically putting my entire emotional self on the line for someone who's only filling me with doubt. I hate being so pushy, so nosy, but I can't help it.

I made my peace with being friends with benefits, with this never being more. But he keeps making these strange, cryptic confessions that rattle my brain and have me thinking about more when I know I shouldn't.

"Answer me this first, princess." The use of my pet name doesn't make me feel any better. "Why don't you want a boyfriend?"

"I—" The vulnerability of the truth feels too painful. "I don't want to get hurt."

His brows pinch together as he searches my eyes. "I don't want to hurt you. I'll walk away right here, right *now*, if I'm hurting you."

"I'm not hurting. I meant what I said—I'm down for friends with benefits. But at this point, you're making no sense to me. I feel like I've been clear on what I want. I haven't lied."

He bows his head for a moment before meeting my eyes again. "I know."

"I know that I'm annoying with my constant questions, demanding answers. But it's for a reason—I don't want to leave room for misunderstanding. And at this point, I don't understand you at all."

He nods, his eyes volleying between mine.

"Honestly, you've never told me once why you don't want to be my boyfriend. *Why* you only want to keep things casual."

He sighs and looks out the window. Time passes slowly and all too quickly. "Because I'm not capable of loving you properly."

I literally bite my tongue to refrain from asking why. My eyelids feel so heavy. This is exhausting.

I nod. "We can figure this all out. We can just see where things go, like you said."

He slowly turns back to me, his steely eyes full of resolve. "There is no we. There is you. There is me. This is fun."

His words stab into my heart, cracking the newly formed ice. I wonder if he can see the shards in my eyes. I refuse to cry so I ball my fists tightly at my sides.

"What am I supposed to do with that?"

"Make a choice." He's calm, too calm. If he cared so much, if he needed me like he says he does, then why wouldn't he take all of me? Let me have all of him?

"I need to think about all of this," I say. My eyes sting from the effort it takes to resist the tears pricking them.

Lorenzo nods his head, then picks up the report. He tosses it back into his drawer and closes it.

It's symbolic, really, what opening a drawer can result in. This is why I like having boxes mentally shelved. I can pretend they don't exist.

But this box is wide open and I have to decide what to do with it.

"Do you want me to drive you home?" he asks. He has my clothes in his hand and passes them to me. I take them, holding them close to my chest.

I should take an Uber; being around him is too intoxicating. But every fiber of my being wants to be near him, to share the same air.

I let out a heavy, mangled breath. "Sure."

He nods, retrieving a pair of black jeans from the dresser tucked in the closet. I tear my eyes from him and we put our clothes on in silence. He sits at the edge of his bed while tugging on a long-sleeved black shirt, keeping his face down. Once I'm redressed, I realize my shoes are still by the pool.

"My shoes..." I can't form a coherent sentence. My mind is racing a mile a minute.

"I'll grab them." He stands up and walks to his closet, quickly opening and closing a drawer. "Here." He turns around and tosses me a pair of keys. They bounce off my open palm but I catch them when they fall back down.

"I'll meet you out there."

I nod and follow him out of the room. He breaks left to the patio and I turn right towards the front door. When I step outside, the cool breeze blows on my exposed skin, and I suddenly feel the weight of my wet hair. My feet absorb the coldness of the brick walkway.

My teeth begin to chatter, so I run to his black Audi, unlocking the doors with the fob. My fingers touch the cold metal of the car, and I rush inside. I look for the key to insert into the starter but I don't find one. I glance behind the steering wheel and locate a button that says 'start engine stop'.

I forgot they'd made those.

I drop the fob into the cup holder and press the button, but it doesn't start. Something flashes on the screen between the speedometer and tachometer. I lean over the center console to look at the words above an image of a foot over a line: Press brake pedal to start engine.

It takes me a moment to comprehend that I need to press the break with the button. I debate waiting for Lorenzo, but my bones are rattling from the cold. I crawl over the center console and sit in the driver's seat, placing my foot on the break. My shaking becomes more intense from the nerves of having my hands over a steering wheel, even if the vehicle *is* off. The amount of anxiety I have just from being in the driver's seat is ridiculous, I know that.

But that's the thing about fear. Once you let it take control of you, it grows into an insurmountable reality, no matter how false it is.

I take a deep breath, my ribs expanding with the oxygen I force in, and press down on the brake pedal. I uncurl the fingers of my right hand that were gripping the leather wheel and slowly drag my pointer finger to the start button. As my finger touches it, the door opens and I jump in my seat.

"Oh my god!" I yelp, my hand flying to my racing heart.

"Just me, princess." Lorenzo says with an amused grin, my shoes in one hand. He takes in my leg, still extended with my foot on the brake pedal, before meeting my wide eyes. "You want to drive?"

"God, no. I just wanted to turn the car on!" I release my hold over the car parts and clamber into the passenger seat. Lorenzo drops into the driver's side as naturally as rain dropping into a body of water. He drops my shoes on the floorboard beneath me and presses his foot into the pedal without a thought, holding down the press to start button and letting the engine purr on.

"Where's the key?" he asks, tossing his hand onto the gear shift and glancing in his rear view mirror.

"Right here," I say, pointing to the cup holder. He reverses out of the driveaway, pops the gear into drive, then reaches into the cup holder.

"Cool feature in this car," he says, placing the fob into a discreet pocket within the cupholder. I meet his eye and my favorite twinkle is there. It's clear he has a fascination with this damn machine.

"Cool," I say, but it's probably the uncoolest thing I've ever seen. Cars are purely utilitarian to me, serving the purpose of getting us from point A to point B. I see no pleasure to seek from it.

"You could have driven if you wanted. I don't mind." Lorenzo speeds up quickly, and it only just occurs to me that I'm surprised this thing isn't a stick shift.

"Ohhh, no. No, no, no." I let out a sort of maniacal laugh, and he pegs me with a curious stare. "No, I don't drive."

His eyebrows shoot up into his hair. And then, he belts out a full belly laugh.

"What?" I say, frowning. He continues cackling into the enclosed space, the car steadily increasing in speed. I force my eyes to stay on him and not on the speedometer. I grip the car seat to hold in my nerves.

"A control freak that doesn't drive? You continue to surprise me, Kate," he finally says when his laughter settles.

"Excuse me? A control freak?" His eyes leave the road yet again, cutting me with a look that screams, "Don't kid yourself". I can't help it, my eyes shift to the speedometer and my jaw drops.

"Slow down!" One hand flies over my chest while the other claws at his upper arm. He immediately lets off the gas, but he doesn't hit the brakes. My eyes are still glued to the dash and my breathing slows when the arrow drops from ninety to sixty miles per hour, which is *still* over the speed limit.

"Sorry, babe," he says, putting his eyes back on the road. He flexes his muscles, reminding me that I still have him in a vice grip. I don't release him immediately, liking the physical connection. He seems to like it, too, because he doesn't move at all, even though his hand dangles awkwardly near his thigh.

But I do eventually release my grip, slowly but surely. He adjusts his arm, placing his hand over the gear shift knob.

"Why don't you drive?" he says conversationally. I pull on my flats as I ponder how to answer him.

"I can admit that it's a bit of an irrational fear," I start. He hardly slows down near a stop sign before blowing past it. I squeeze my eyes shut for a moment and tell myself to calm down. "When my parents were teaching me to drive, I backed into my dad's car in the driveway."

He waits for me to continue, but I don't. There's really nothing more to tell.

"That's it? You hit your pops's car and called it quits?"

"I had a full blown panic attack, it was a whole thing. My dad swore up and down that it was fine, which I know it was. But I asked to stop for the day. The next few times my mom or dad asked if I wanted to practice again, I'd say no." The shame seeps into my tone, embarrassed from the amount of power I've given to this silly fear. "I just kept thinking, what if that had been a person? Or an animal? I could have hurt someone. I *did* hurt that car."

I expect Lorenzo to laugh at me, or call me something insulting, but it never comes. He slowly nods his head as he turns onto the main road. "Yeah, okay. I can understand that."

My jaw drops but I close it quickly. "You understand?"

"I get not wanting to hurt people, even if the fear behind it is irrational."

"What, so you're some sort of hero?"

"I told you once, and I'll tell you again, Kate. I'm not going to save you."

This time, his words force goosebumps to erupt over my skin. I meant what I said, that I don't need saving. What does that really even mean, anyway? But it's his tone, filled with regret and sorrow, that has me reacting.

It forces the memory of everything I discovered not even an hour ago to seep to the forefront of my mind. Not that it's forgettable, but it's so easy—*too* easy—for me to get lost in him.

As though he senses where my thoughts have gone, Lorenzo asks, "You've never wanted to learn?"

It takes me a moment to remember what he's referring to. "I mean, I feel pathetic not driving. Letting this thing have power over me." He grins at that, mumbling, "Control freak." I ignore him. "But it's been so many years at this point. You know Azalea Pines doesn't require you to have a car. And I've placed myself in a position where I won't need one."

He nods pensively, turning down the street towards my apartment. It's quite impressive that he remembers where I live so well. He's a mental map.

"What do your parents do?" he asks.

I'm a bit surprised that he's asking about my family. "Um, my dad's actually a cargo truck driver. My mom studied finance but she stayed home when I was born. Then when my dad made enough money, she decided not to rejoin the workforce. She does a lot of side stuff though, helps in the community and such. She'll bookkeep temporarily during tax season, too."

"And your dad never forced you to learn to drive?"

"He's not the pushy type, really. He kept asking, but I kept saying no. He never pushed further than that."

Lorenzo pulls up to my complex, directly in front of a parallel parking spot that he could have easily slid into. My eyes shift from my building to him, his eyes already on me.

There's no twinkle, there's no amusement. There's no malice, either. He looks more resolute than I've ever seen him.

"Thanks for the ride," I say quietly. The emotions of earlier have returned with the realization that once I leave this car, I don't know what will happen.

"Of course." Fire begins to burn behind his pupils, but the rest of him remains stoic. He doesn't want it to show.

I decide not to engage. It won't help either of us.

"See you at work?" I try to be light-hearted, though I'm anything but.

"See ya at work."

I put my hand on the door handle and pull, but he calls my attention when the door opens swiftly.

"Promise me something."

His voice is croaky, like when you're about to start crying. But his eyes are dry and I know his heart is stone cold.

"You demand a lot of promises for a man who doesn't give any."

He's undeterred, the fire turning into an inferno before me.

"Whatever you do, whatever you think... please *know* that I do care about you, Kate."

My lips part with the rush of electric shocks. That's not what I was expecting. My heart picks up speed with the implication of his words.

I nod while blinking furiously, then shut his door and turn on my heel.

Staring into his eyes with the aftermath of his proclamation would make me stupid again.

But it's time to get smart.

CHAPTER TWO

February 24th

KATE

I t's been a week since I left his house. Well, basically. It was like 1 am when he finally dropped me off. I'd like to say I've fully processed everything he revealed, but I'd be lying. Or maybe I have processed it but haven't accepted it. Something hasn't sat right with me since leaving. I want to believe his words, but I have a nagging feeling that I'm missing something.

And he's obviously had no problem lying, so I can't just take his word at face value.

We saw each other everyday at work in the break room. I kept up our usual greeting, but I didn't seek him out for more. He didn't, either.

I'm not sure how to feel about that.

On the one hand, it's a good thing, really, that he's respected my requests for space. Well, except for when he intruded on my date with Brad. But on the other hand, I wish he'd reach out. Even just a message, so I know he cares.

Please know that I do care about you, Kate.

His words have played on repeat in my mind like a broken record. I want to believe them oh-so-badly.

That's the part that stumps me the most. Does he actually care? His words oppose his actions. I have to be missing something. This must be why doctors can't operate on their own family—emotions get the best of you.

And what about the stalking? Am I supposed to be okay with him constantly looking into the things I do? I'm starting to doubt he overheard someone about my impulsive job search. I think he looked into it purposely.

Why, though?

That's the question, isn't it? Why be so involved in a woman you claim to only want a casual, friends with benefits arrangement with?

I'm torn from my train of thought when Char walks through the door. We're meeting at Slooshed, an older bar in town. I canceled brunch last Sunday, too down from the events of that night to find the energy to be social.

"Hey, toots," she says, swinging her purse onto the table and plopping herself down in the chair. Her long, cherry tinged hair is fanned across her shoulders. She looks as content as ever, the freckles peppering her nose bringing out her beaming hazel eyes.

"Hey," I respond flatly.

"Uh-oh. Trouble in paradise?" she asks as she flips open the menu. It's another contrast in our friendship—she changes her order based on mood, while I stick with the same thing every time.

"Paradise," I scoff. I sip my lemon-infused water but don't add anything else.

"Well? Are you going to spill it, or do I have to pull teeth? The end result is the same." She peers at me over her menu. This is the only time she ever resembles anything like stern. One brow is arched, and I know she won't let it go.

"Fine, but let's order first. It's a long one." The server passes by so we place our drink orders. I get a vodka-cranberry, and Char orders a raspberry margarita with a sugar rim instead of salt.

"I need something sweet if I have to hear something sour," she explains. The server takes my menu; Char holds onto hers when he tries to take it.

I jump right into it, sparing only the details I don't want to share. I don't tell her about the way Lorenzo's dick tasted in my mouth and how much I liked it. I don't tell her how much prettier Larissa is than me. I don't tell her how nervous I was to get into the pool in only underwear.

She listens silently, the only reactions I get being her facial ones. When I finish, she blows out a breath.

"First of all, I want to meet Larissa. She sounds dope. Second"—she pauses to lick the sugar rim and take a sip of her margarita—"that's a lot of shit."

"Yeah, tell me about it."

"How do you feel?"

"I feel... confused. It doesn't make any sense! Why do all this shit behind my back when he doesn't want more?"

"Hmm," Char says, her eyes hazing as she loses herself to thought. "How did he get a hold of the police report, anyway?"

This is why I love Char. She's as curious as I am. My emotions have put me in an unfortunate position, because I should have thought of these things myself. "Great question."

"You're certain it's the same Brad? It's not that uncommon of a name."

I pin her with an exasperated look. "What are the chances he has a report with the same name as the guy I went on a date with? A date he *ruined*, by the way."

"I don't know if I would call it ruined. From the sounds of it, he saved you with incredible car sex."

"Yeah, well, he 'won't save me', remember?" I snide. "What in the fuck does that even mean?"

Char chuckles. "Keep it down, *princess*. We're in public."

I glance around but no one's paying any mind to my incredulity. "Anyway, I read the narrative on the report. It's exactly what Brad told me happened."

"Yeah... that still doesn't explain how he got the report."

"He'd need to know his last name, at least." I sift through my memories, but I can't think of a time I said it aloud, let alone for Lorenzo to hear.

"Maybe he searched my phone?" I offer, deep in thought.

"When, though? You guys hadn't hung out since New Year's."

"That's true." Char is doing so much more for me than being a shoulder to lean on. She's grounding me, bringing me back to myself. Removing the emotion so I can properly assess this.

"What does your gut say?"

I sip my drink. "Something's not right."

She nods. "Trust that."

We sit in silence for a few moments, each of us reviewing the facts mentally. Eventually, Char speaks.

"Well, the way I see it, you have two options."

"Only two?"

"Only two. You fuck off from him. Leave his strange, stalky tendencies behind you."

I know she's pausing for effect, but I implore her. "Or?"

"Or, you keep seeing him. Learn what you can. Solve this."

That's a tempting option. Being totally and completely honest with myself, I'm not ready to let him go. He makes me feel something, and I like having sex with him. Not to mention, he's fucking hot. I can't deny that crucial point.

But where will this lead me? I can't continue hoping, even on a subconscious level, that I have some sort of chance with him. I don't. He's made that clear at every opportunity.

"I don't know, Char," I finally say.

"The right thing to do, probably, is to leave it behind you."

My brows rise as high as they can go. "I'm shocked by your... reasonability."

"Unexpected, I know. But I can't really see how this ends well. If you wanted to be with him long-term, it could be worth figuring out before making a decision. I mean, it's kinda hot that he'd feel that strongly about protecting you. *If* that's the truth."

"It is *kinda* hot," I admit.

"But, he's made it clear over and over that he doesn't want anything serious. He's not waving a red flag. He's wearing the damn thing."

I remember his words, and a detail about them makes me question more. "It was weird. It seemed like he was about to say he *can't* be with me... then he switched to don't."

"He may have misspoken. Or maybe he's got a bunch of childhood trauma. Who knows. But the message is clear. He doesn't want more."

"Yeah."

"Yeah."

CHAPTER THREE

February 26th

KATE

Work has always been a sort of escape for me. I'm not a workaholic by any means, but it's a place where I can put my focus on something productive. And working with numbers always improves my mood. They don't require anything from me other than logic and problem solving.

Our audit results came in, so Jasmine and I have a meeting scheduled with Matteo to review them. Jasmine is the lead underwriter, UW for short. While the audits span across our whole company, Rowan has each department review them to ensure we're scoring well.

I finish putting together an estimate for a new client when the clock changes to 10:59. I head over to the small office towards the back of our cubicles. Jasmine is already there, but Matteo is not. I walk in and put my laptop on the desk before taking my seat.

"Hey, Kate," Jasmine says, hardly looking at me before continuing to clack away on her keyboard.

"Hey," I reply. Matteo walks in a moment later and we dive into the results. We quickly realize that we've excelled in all areas we're in control of. We work on the lender loans for mortgages. A separate team works on Rentals, and it seems they were dinged a significant amount of points.

"That's really strange, Rentals has never been dinged before," Matteo says, chewing on his pen top.

"That we know of. Maybe it happened before we started here," Jasmine responds. Jasmine was hired at the same time that I was brought in as an intern. Matteo has only been here a few months.

"Well, not our circus, not our monkeys, right?" I say lightheartedly. Matteo laughs but Jasmine doesn't.

"Rowan wanted to stop by," she says solemnly. "Maybe it has to do with this."

"Oh, he's in town?" Matteo says. While Rowan is co-owner of the company and boss of our branch, he's often away on business trips or visiting other branches. Broker owners aren't required to be licensed, so he really only manages the business side of things.

Sometimes I wonder if he really even does that. He's the exact opposite of a micromanager, trusting us as employees to do our jobs correctly. So I'm equally surprised that he's popping in today.

"I guess so. He pinged me a few minutes before our meeting and asked us to wait for him," Jasmine responds.

"I wonder if something bad happened," I muse aloud. Jasmine shrugs, but Matteo stares at me warily, apparently sharing the sentiment—something is off.

"They were dinged for submitting incorrect documentation," Jasmine says, reorganizing the papers and tapping them on the desk to straighten the stack. "I don't know what, exactly. I wasn't sent their analysis."

"Hmm. I wonder why Rowan wants to discuss it with us," I say.

"*If* that's what he wants to discuss. He didn't say. I've been telling him for years to let me help him with Rentals," Jasmine says with her chin lifted. Come to think of it, I don't know who manages them. I don't know anything about Rentals, other than people love renting from Valeri Financials because we offer the lowest rental rates.

"Why doesn't he?" Matteo asks.

Jasmine shrugs. "He says he can handle it and doesn't want to overwhelm me. But it's two employees."

"Who are—" I cut myself short when Rowan raps his knuckles on the door as he opens it.

"Team! How are we doing this fine morning?" He beams at us, his crinkled eyes shining on our guilt ridden faces.

"G–Good morning, sir," Jasmine stammers.

"Please, call me Rowan," he says, just as he always does. Jasmine's always been a pecking order kinda gal. No matter how insistent Rowan is on keeping things casual and informal, she can't help herself. I'm certain that she regrets every moment of her chastising criticism before he walked in.

"How are you, Rowan?" I say, feeling comfortable with his informality. There's always that added layer of pressure when you're speaking to a higher up, but I let the rigidity in me fall when I learned that Rowan preferred the casualty.

"I'm well, Kate, thanks for asking. Let's jump right into it, I don't want to waste anyone's time." He pulls out the chair from the head of the table, comfortably and naturally taking his place as lead. Matteo is on my right and Jasmine is in front of me. There are a few chairs between us and Rowan, but he doesn't seem to mind.

"I reviewed the audit results. I am aware that Rentals was dinged." He pauses for what seems to be emphasis, glancing at each of us before continuing. "I have already spoken with them, and they'll be combing over documents to ensure this mistake doesn't occur again."

"Sorry, sir," Jasmine squeaks. "What was the issue?"

I hold my breath, unsure if that's information we're privy to. When Rowan speaks, I let out an exhale.

"Someone dropped the ball." Again, he pauses. "They sent the wrong lease agreements in."

His expression darkens, his obvious distaste for the mistake evident.

"Do you need anything from us, Rowan?" Matteo addresses our boss in a professional manner, his hands clasped on the desk in front of him.

"Thank you, Matteo, but no. While it cost us on the audit, it's not a difficult correction. They're already working on it. Come the next audit, we should have no issues."

"Sir, I've offered before, but—"

"Thank you, Jazz, but I will continue to lead rentals." Jasmine frowns; she *hates* being called Jazz. Or, quite frankly, anything that isn't her full name. She eventually nods, reaching for the papers on the long table in a sort of dismissal. Rowan nods back, then turns to Matteo and I.

"I realize this all could have been sent in an email, but I wanted to address this in person." He shifts in his seat and a look crosses his face too quickly for me to catch. "I request that you keep this ding to yourselves. You all know how important it is to score well on audits, and I don't want bad-mouthing to start."

I had no intention of talking to anyone about this, but a strange feeling settles into my stomach with his request for secrecy.

"I prefer to stay behind the scenes and have full trust in my employees. Please don't give me a reason to get involved," Rowan adds, standing and tapping the desk. "Keep up the hard work team, I appreciate you all."

And then he's gone.

The rest of the work day flew by. When I got back to my desk, there were five new online loan requests and that ate up the rest of my afternoon. I still have one more to finish, but I'll get to it tomorrow. As much as I despise leaving work for another day, that's the nature of the beast at times. I also really wanted to figure out who works Rentals, but I put it on my to-do list for tomorrow. My pilates class was at 5:30 pm, and I don't like to be late.

After working out and showering, I sift through my closet, trying to plan my outfit for the morning. I wish I still had that long-sleeved blouse Lorenzo ruined the buttons on. My skin burns at the thought of him thrusting into me, my head banging into the car. God, I wish I could be back in that moment. To feel him deep inside me over and over again.

I shake my head to bring me back to the present moment. Lorenzo remains a mystery, but a part of me has settled into it. I want answers, and I won't be getting them from him. That much I know. But what he said just isn't sitting right.

Trust that.

I have to trust my gut. I need to get more answers. But right now, I need to pick my outfit for tomorrow. While the memory of his car turns me the hell on, the fact that he ripped the buttons off my pretty new blouse ticks me off. Who does he think he is, claiming that outfit for himself? He doesn't own me. He says I'm his, but I'm not. We're friends with benefits, nothing more.

I'm pretty sure the department store where I bought that blouse closes at 9. I glance at the simple silver clock on the wall above my desk and quickly realize the battery must have died; I know it's not 3:32. I step onto my chair and pull the clock off its nail, pulling out the AA battery from the back. I pad over to the hall closet to put a new one in. Once secured, I return to my room and pull my phone off the desk to check the time. There's a message from Char, but I turn the dial on the clock first. I put it a minute ahead of 7:06, because I want the time to be accurate, down to the second. I watch the seconds tick on my phone. At 7:05:59, I push the dial back in.

Once the clock is back on the wall, I swipe open the message from Char.

Char: it might be time for me to join pilates with you

I giggle and reply.

Me: changed your mind? Not a waste of time after all?

Char has been anti-exercise for as long as I can remember. In PE, she would always walk instead of run, and she'd cheer both teams on from within the game because she had to pretend to participate.

Char: I had to walk up five flights of stairs to see the new apartment and I was dying

Me: we need to work those muscles. It's good for you!

Char: ugh

Me: what are you up to? Wanna run to Reno's with me?

Char: is that even a question? What are we buying

Char: be there in 20

Char: make that 10, they close soon

Me: they close at 9, we have over an hour

Char: there's never enough time for shopping

CHAPTER FOUR

February 27th

KATE

I t's a crisp morning, the cool air nipping my skin as I walk briskly to the office. I'm certain I'm imagining the smokey scent in the air until Lorenzo steps out of the alley near our building, stomping on a cigarette.

We haven't had a real conversation since I left his house, even though we have remained cordial. But I don't need to play games. I've got my new-old blouse on and my confidence back. I don't need to be rude.

"You know smoking kills," I say. *Okay, maybe a little rude.*

He glances over his shoulder, does a double take, then stops dead in his tracks to fully face me. His eyes roam over the blouse, lingering on the perfectly sewn in buttons. While I paired it with the same black waist-hugging skirt I wore for my previous date—*dates*—with Brad, I swapped the knee-high boots for simple black heels.

"Smoking *can* kill," he amends, his lips twitching with suppressed amusement.

I shrug. "Semantics."

There's a pause, and I take a moment to appreciate him. He looks delectable in his trademark black slacks and black dress shirt, the sleeves rolled up to his elbows. We're eye fucking each other not five feet from our office entrance.

"Nice shirt," he comments finally, breaking the silence.

"Thanks!" I beam at him, showing him every tooth in my mouth. I'm buzzing with the power my choice in shirt is providing me. Or rather, the choice to buy and wear the shirt. "I really love this blouse."

"Hmm," he purrs. He glances around and waits for a guy to walk into the office before adding, "I was fond of that shirt, too. But I'm having trouble understanding how it's back in working order. Unless you're a professional seamstress."

I chuckle and take a few steps forward, patting his chest. "Wouldn't you like to know?"

I wish I could take a photo with my eyes so I can forever remember the expression I landed on his face. This new energy I'm expelling is what I want to own forever. Maybe he was right all along. I *am* a badass.

"It's getting late, we need to get in," I say, sliding my hand down his chest to his stomach, which has tightened from my touch. I walk past him and into the building, resuming my brisk pace. I'm not sure if he's behind me, and I refuse to turn around and give him the satisfaction of knowing I want to find out. Just in case, I make sure to sashay my hips with more enthusiasm than I normally would.

Nothing wrong with flaunting what you've got.

As I pass the break room, his hand circles my wrist and pulls me into it. My immediate impulse is to tear myself from his grip, highly aware of our public setting. But he maintains his grasp and pushes me into the wall that's shared with the hallway.

"You look absolutely fuckable," he murmurs into my ear. His hard body is pressed into my back. I arch my ass into him, feeling him bulging through his slacks. Somewhere in the recesses of my mind are the shady things that came to light and the reminder that I have investigating to do. But my pussy heats with the all consuming desire to feel him deep inside me, so those thoughts remain suspended for the time being.

His head is still tucked into my neck, his breath tickling my sensitive skin. I inhale deeply, breathing in the cinnamon and smoke. It's more smokey than usual, and while I should be disgusted, I'm that much more intrigued.

"We're at..." The denial is begging to slip from my tongue, but I know *very* well that something about public secrecy turns me the fuck on. We've already done it in Rowan's house, why not his office building, too?

I feel Lorenzo smirking on my skin because he knows damn well what I'm thinking. I glance around me before giving in. "Where?" I breathe. He takes a step back and grabs my lunch bag, stuffing it into the fridge with his own.

"Follow me." As if he's been waiting for this moment his entire life, he stalks out of the break room and down the hall. I follow, as instructed. Why should I deny myself what I so desperately crave?

He tugs on the knob of what I've always assumed is a broom closet. It opens and he grabs my wrist, pulling me in with him.

My assumption was correct. There's a broom and mop bucket in the corner of the tiny space we're in. There's no table, chair, shelf—nothing to get on top of.

"How are we supposed to do anything in here?" I shout-whisper, dropping my gym bag.

Lorenzo's hand slides up my neck and digs into my hair, pulling me toward him. With his lips over mine, he whispers, "Don't doubt my creativity, Kate."

His mouth swallows my reply, his tongue claiming every inch of my lips before plunging into my mouth. I moan into him and he shoves me against the solid, concrete wall, tearing his lips from mine to claim my neck.

"Be quiet, princess, or I'll have to leave you panting and wanting for more." He proceeds to suck on my exposed skin, fisting my hair to hold me in place. I breathe heavily in place of any audible sounds. My clit pulses and my pussy surges, dampening my panties.

Lorenzo hasn't stopped assaulting my neck with his mouth, only adding his teeth in a painfully perfect way. My hands claw at his shoulders, equally begging for mercy and more. I feel him smirk before he pulls away slowly.

"You think you're cute, huh? You like getting a rise out of me?"

It's my turn to smirk. My outfit choice had nothing to do with getting a rise out of him, but I can't say it's not enjoyable. There really is something to embracing your bold side; I don't think I'll ever turn back.

"Princess might be too tame for you. You... you're a fucking brat."

In an instant, his free hand is on my throat, applying so much pressure that I lose my breath instantly. My eyes pop open but it takes no effort to keep quiet this time—I couldn't cry out if I wanted to.

"You know what happens to little fucking brats, Katherine?"

It's too dark to make out his eyes but I don't need to see them. I know they're filled with lust and greed and malice. He wants to hurt me and I want to let him. If I could gulp, I would, but his palm against my throat makes it impossible. I open my mouth to speak but no words come out.

He loosens his grip enough so that I can whisper throatily, "Why don't you show me?"

He groans so quietly, but it's enough for me to hear it. He presses his dick into my pelvis and increases the pressure on my neck again.

"You've only had a taste, princess. You have no idea what I'm capable of."

The blood rushes in my ears, my heart races, but I'm not afraid. I'm *exhilarated*.

He releases my neck and I draw in a sharp breath.

"Smart of you to wear this at work... I can't rip it to shreds," he spits. "I'll have to start keeping spare clothes for you."

He runs a finger down my collarbone and past the buttons on my blouse. I puff my chest out, taunting him intentionally this time.

As excited as I am about his implication that this will happen again, I toy with him. "You sound so sure that this isn't the last time."

He chuckles darkly. "You don't need to be my girlfriend for me to know you're mine."

His lips crash over mine in a bruising kiss as his hands grip the back of my thighs. He hoists me up and shoves my back into the wall, forcing me to wrap my legs around his waist. His dick pokes my ass and I rub into it, asking him, *begging* him, for what I want. For what I *need*.

He pulses his hips before shifting a thigh between my legs, my ass resting on it. He brings a hand to his belt buckle, quickly maneuvering it out of the loop. His tongue is swirling with mine, but I pull back in the inch or so that I have. I bring my hands to his zipper, lowering it as he pops the button.

"Tell me, Kate," he whispers. "What should your punishment be?"

Fuck, this is really happening. My pussy is so slick with desire, the walls pulsing with only one thought in mind—fuck me, now. I stroke his dick before pulling it out through the slit in his boxers.

"Fuck me hard," I whisper back, a bit nervous and a whole lot desperate. His dick throbs in my hand and he pulls his wallet out of his pocket. My back starts sliding down the wall but he shoves his thigh up, supporting me and making me so fucking needy for him.

He holds his wallet out to me. I hesitate for a moment before taking it. "Left." That's all he says as he returns his hand to the back of my thigh. He doesn't move his leg, which I'm eternally grateful for because my pussy is resting right on it. The warmth and firmness of his body is putting a cap on the overflowing desire I have for him.

I open the folds and see foil sticking out of the left side of the cash holder. I pull out the condom and fold the wallet back up, handing it to him. He grabs it with his teeth and whips his head, the wallet crashing into the wall before falling limply onto the floor.

"Open it," he growls. My shaky hands fumble with the wrapper for a moment, but I successfully tear it open at the corner. I pull out the latex and follow his lead, dropping the foil onto the ground.

That seems to please him because I can hear the satisfaction in his tone. "Roll it on, princess."

And just like that, my nerves sky rocket, shaking the confident foundation I've built. He wants me to roll it on? I've never done that before. I'm back to feeling like a novice around him, but I refuse to let it show.

I think back to my sex ed classes, remembering the teacher rolling the condom onto a banana. I quickly *stop* thinking about that, because it's the biggest turn off in existence. Instead, I grab the tip and bring the opening to his head.

"You got this, baby. Get me ready for you." I can't tell if he's aware that I don't know what the fuck I'm doing, but either way, his support helps my confidence flourish. I roll the condom down to the base and squeeze instinctively. The vein in his dick throbs and I'm certain I'm at least doing *something* right.

Just like in his car, he hikes my skirt up, but one handed this time. He's still impressively able to hold me up, and I wonder just how he's come to be this strong.

He slides my panties over, having the good grace not to rip them this time. It's one thing to return home after a scandalous sex act. But having to work with shredded underwear? Hard pass.

He slowly removes his thigh from under me, my pussy aching with the loss of contact. He fixes it quickly, though, holding me up by my thighs and bringing his wrapped cock to my opening. His lips hover over mine and I inhale his essence as my eyelids droop.

"Keep your mouth shut, no matter what. Got it?"

I nod, pressing my lips together tightly. He enters me slowly and I wonder what all that was for if he wasn't going to ram into me. He slides in and out slowly, my abs tightening as the pleasure courses throughout my body.

He finally places his lips on mine lightly, and he moans as I kiss him back. Our tongues taste each other slowly, provocatively. I move my hips to match his movements and we breathe heavily into each other's mouths so as not to make noise.

"I love being inside you," he murmurs into my ear. "It's too bad I have to ruin this sweet moment."

He cracks his hand down on my ass like a whip and I grit my teeth together with all my might to keep quiet. Although, it seems totally pointless because that was *loud*. Tears prick my eyes.

"Shhh," he soothes over my lips. I whimper oh-so-quietly, unable to contain myself. "Consider this time a warning." His lips are over mine again, distracting me from the throbs and stings that his palm caused.

I'm for sure going to have a mark.

His lips feel so damn good, though, moving with mine in a steady rhythm. My hips stop moving but his keep tempo with my heart beat. He doesn't make any indication of slapping me again, his breath increasing in depth and sound.

The speed of his hips increase as our hearts and breaths do. His skin is rubbing against my swollen, desperate clit. My legs tighten around his hips, pulling him closer, deeper. His thrusts become quick and shallow, unable to pull out because of my vice grip on him.

I bite down on his lip when the intensity becomes too much, a quiet way to exert all the stifled screams and moans. He reacts by increasing his speed even more and gripping my hips so tightly that his short nails dig into my skin.

He lets out an involuntary groan that I swear erupts from his chest, and that's my undoing. We come at the same time, his cock deep inside me and my ankles trying to mold into one from the amount of pressure I'm exerting.

His hold on me weakens as we both pant heavily, my back sliding down the wall a few inches. He rests his head on my shoulder, his chest heaving on mine. As our breathing returns to normal, my ankles loosen their hold and he releases his vice grip on my hips. I slide off him, pushing my skirt down.

Lorenzo removes the condom, ties it, and shoves it into his pocket. I watch as he becomes colder and colder with every waking breath. He steps back and recovers his wallet from the ground. I adjust my blouse so the hem sits properly on my stomach, which is currently quivering with the aftermath of my orgasm.

"We can't do this again." My eyes shoot up to his face, but it's too dark to see clearly. "Too risky," he adds.

"Right." I want to tell him how wet it made me, but I'm sure he could feel it. Something feels off again. He had no problem doing it at Rowan's house, but I can see why it's a little different at the actual office building. Personally, I don't feel sorry about what we just did. How can something that felt so fucking good be regrettable?

"It's my fault. No matter how sexy you look, I should be able to control myself."

That makes my lips tilt up, not that he can see it. Or maybe he can. Even though I have my glasses on, my vision is only so perfect.

"I really wasn't trying to taunt you," I say in an effort to exude my independence.

He chuckles, fixing his pants and buckle. I glance around the room again, realizing just how small it is. Lorenzo pulls his phone out of his pocket and opens it to check the time. It's 8:13 am. I'm super late.

Did he always have a flip phone? I could have sworn it was a regular smartphone.

"Let me crack the door and listen," he says in a low voice. I nod and he tiptoes towards the door, pulling the knob silently. We listen and I'm certain there's no one out there.

"I'll walk out first, just in case. Give it like two minutes before you leave." Again, I nod, unsure if he can see me or not. He opens the door and slides into the hallway, leaving the door cracked.

I hoist my gym bag onto my shoulder, my mind racing with excuses in case someone catches me here. You know, because all the employees step into the broom closet in their day to day work life.

The time ticks by slowly. I fill it by staring at the second hand clock on my iPhone. Ten seconds before my two minutes are up, my phone nearly gives me a heart attack by buzzing in my hand. The message is from an unknown number that's not saved in my phone.

Unknown: all clear

What the fuck? I know I have Lorenzo's number saved in my phone. I pull up my contacts quickly and confirm he's in there, but the number doesn't match the one he's texted from before.

Weird.

I pocket my phone and listen again. When I'm about to make my move, my eyes catch sight of the condom wrapper on the floor. I quickly pick it up and shove it into my waistband, then do another sound check of the hall. Once I feel confident enough that there's no one out there, I dash out of the closet and let the door snap shut behind me. I walk at a rushed pace to my cubicle, not wanting to be a second later than I have to be.

Once I'm at my desk, I load up my computer, login, and let my typical apps autoload. Victor's got his headphones on, seemingly oblivious to my late arrival. I'm about to write to Lorenzo on Teams when I remember that everything is monitored. I pull out my phone and shoot off a text.

Me: new number?

Unknown: obviously

I save the number into his previous contact. I could reply, but I'm not going to. I've got an ass ton of work to handle today, and starting off nineteen minutes late has me at a disadvantage.

I decide to work through lunch to make up for the time I missed this morning. I'd work through lunch everyday if it meant that's how I'd start my mornings. As my coworkers filter back to their desks, my phone vibrates.

Lorenzo: you okay?

Me: Yeah, why?

Lorenzo: you werent at lunch

Me: Needed to makeup for lost time.

I watch the screen but he never types back. I was pretty proud of my innuendo, but either it went over his head or he didn't want to respond to it.

I get back to work to reduce the amount of loans sitting on my desk. Fifteen minutes to quitting time, I realize I've forgotten to look into Rentals. The note I scribbled on my paper to-do list reminded me, so I pull up the work database. Working through lunch today helped lessen the load, which I wouldn't have needed if I hadn't been late.

It was technically time theft, but fuck if it wasn't worth it. I'm a little bit afraid of the fact that I don't feel a morsel of remorse. I mean I should, shouldn't I? Maybe Lorenzo is a bad influence on me.

Or maybe I really did have it in me all along, just like he said a few months ago.

Once the database loads, I roam to the search bar and type Rentals. No results populate, so I clear the search and scroll through the columns to find positions. A quick scan, because it's in alphabetical order, confirms rentals isn't listed. I search for Underwriters but I know everyone listed.

Hm. That's weird.

I shift in my seat, wincing from the soreness on my butt cheek caused by Lorenzo earlier. I read through the different positions until I land on UW Support. I didn't even know we had a support team, but UW has to stand for Underwriter.

There are only two names listed: Carter Wright and Dwayne Buchannon.

Carter and Dwayne...

It can't be Lorenzo's friends. Can it?

I type Santi into the search bar, but nothing pulls up.

It could be a coincidence, but something tells me it's not. I *know* something isn't right. Him having Brad's police report is too strange, and while his explanation fits, something feels amiss.

And he obviously has no problem lying.

I should heed Char's advice and fuck off from him. The image of him pounding into me earlier flashes across my mind and my pussy aches.

Fucking off from him is easier said than done.

I glance at the clock and hop out of my seat, realizing it's a few minutes after five. I rush to throw my stuff in my bag and race to pilates.

I'll sweat this out and see what comes back to me.

CHAPTER FIVE

February 28th

KATE

I know it's the wrong thing to be doing. I *know*. But I want to keep seeing Lorenzo. The decision was made for me when we saw each other outside of the office yesterday morning. All I could feel was an inexplicable pull to him, and our closet escapade solidified that fact.

I knew then that I wasn't prepared to let this go.

You need to get answers.

I know I do. But I'm almost... afraid of what I'll learn. It could lead to me being unable to have sex with him. To no longer feeling him all over me and bringing me to the best orgasm of my life. Whatever the female version of blue balls is was what I experienced after leaving his house that night after I found the police report.

Once I'm tucked into bed with Felix curled up on my pillow, I pull up the web browser on my laptop. No matter how afraid, I have to learn what I can.

I first go to Glenmar County's Police Department and walk through the steps for ordering a report. I confirm what I was certain of—you need a first and last name or a case number. And that's just to search for it. In order to obtain a copy, you have to send a request via email or go into the station. If you're not listed on the report, you must be authorized to obtain a copy.

So how Lorenzo had either of those things... that's the question, isn't it?

Next, I run a search on the house that he and Santi live in through the county appraiser site. The information I find there is shocking. The house is owned by none other than Rowan Valeri.

They're renting the house from our boss?

I make a futile attempt at locating Lorenzo on some social media platform, but the result is still nil. I search instead for Rowan, only finding his professional business information. The only social media site I find him on is LinkedIn.

Probably because he has to be.

I rub the skin around my thumb nail, pondering this information. Seems I wasn't off the mark when I thought Lorenzo knew Rowan at the holiday party...

The question is, why is Lorenzo living in a house Rowan owns?

Could this explain why Santi doesn't like me? Maybe he's hell-bent on HR policies of no internal dating. If Rowan even has that rule. Plus, I know from my earlier search that Santi doesn't work there. Unless... is Santi his real name?

I set a reminder on my phone for tomorrow morning so I can review the handbook. Then I hit call on Char's contact.

"Princess," she says after the second ring.

"Seriously?"

"What, I can't play around?"

I giggle but stifle it quickly. "No time. I have an idea."

"Oooh, I can tell this is going to be good! Hold on, let me grab my glass of wine from the other room."

"How's the packing going?" Char is in the process of moving apartments. She's staying in the same building but getting a bigger place to accommodate her working from home. She's going to use the extra room to run her interior design business, Live in Style. "Are you sure you don't need help?"

"I've been packing slowly for the last month. All I've got left is the kitchen. And no offense, toots, but you're organizational crap will freak me out. I like to just do my own thing, blast some Fleetwood Mac, and get it done."

"I like Fleetwood Mac!"

"Not the point. Okay, I've got my sauv, now spill it."

"We want answers, right?" I snuggle into my sheets, Felix purring peacefully on the pillow.

She chuckles. "Sure, yes."

"Let's go PI on his ass."

She lets out a hearty laugh and there's a pause I attribute to her taking a sip of wine. "Ladies and gents—Kate the Badass!"

"You know," I muse. "Maybe he wasn't wrong, after all."

"Of course he wasn't. Do you really think I'd be friends with anyone less?"

"We're getting off track. Answers. Something's not right, and I need to know what."

"I'm all in, girl. But"—she takes a gulp of wine—"are you sure you know what you're getting into?"

"What do you mean?"

"Are you sure you want to spend your energy jumping down this rabbit hole? Why not just leave this behind you? No man is worth that much effort."

A flash of his hand around my neck passes through my mind, followed by the sound of his palm on my ass.

I sigh. "I know."

"Let's fucking do this! What do we want to know?"

"I made a list." I pull the yellow legal pad filled with my scribbled notes off the nightstand. "First things first—how did he get that police report?"

"Yes. I can scour the county's website, figure out—"

"Already done." I fill her in on my searches.

"So he had to know the case number *or* his last name. Or both."

"Right. And he would have needed authorization to pull it. His name wasn't on that report."

"Outright asking him is not an option, is it?"

"I don't want him to know I'm snooping. That's like, 101."

"True." We stay silent for a moment. "Okay, what else?"

"Why did he lie about living at Santi's? And why do they live at our boss's house?"

"Oh my god, yes! So suspish." Char takes another drink from her glass. "What's Santi's last name?"

"Oh, yes," I reply, shoving the phone into my shoulder and grabbing my pen to jot down 'Santi's last name?'.

"What if he's related to the boss or something?"

I feel a rush of excitement. "Yes! That would explain so much!"

"You know, I need to meet this guy. When are you going to see him again?"

A blush creeps into my cheeks. "Well, actually..."

"Kate! You dog."

I recount the events of earlier in the office. She whistles, laughs, and gasps, egging me on to spare no detail. When I finish, she tsks.

"You, my friend, are royally fucked."

"He's not royal, Char."

"I *mean* that you don't stand a chance. You're in too deep."

"Shut the fuck up."

"Don't deny it. I mean, listen, I probably would be, too. He sounds pretty irresistible. I get why you want to go PI on his ass."

"Right, let's review." I look at my list again. "Okay—police report, living at Rowan's, Santi's last name, Carter and D working in Rentals, the convers—"

"Wait, who works in Rentals?!"

I explain my findings from earlier and the audit results that were dinged.

"This just keeps getting weirder and weirder. And who's Rowan?"

"Our *boss*."

"Jeez, sorry. I'm trying."

"I know, and I appreciate it."

"What was the last thing on your list?"

"The conversation I walked in on in the garage! That was so weird."

"Oh, that's right! He said something about sacrifices, right?"

"Yeah," I reply, reflecting back on that night. One of the most frustrating things in the world is the way our memory fades the farther away we get from what it tries to remember. Like an out of focus image that just gets blurrier and blurrier with time. "I think he said he's sacrificed enough. Santi was saying something about choices."

"We've got a lot to learn, toots."

"Exactly. So how do we go about finding all this shit out?"

"Well, for the police report, maybe the station can tell us who's gotten copies of the report. And when. You didn't notice a print date on the paper?"

"No, I didn't." I think back, trying to pull the image of the report from memory. "Maybe it was there? I don't know. I was too shocked he even had it to notice a date."

"I get it, toots. Well, let's try going down to the station."

"Wouldn't that information be confidential? They're not just going to tell us whatever we want to know."

"You called me in for a reason, Kate. I have an idea."

CHAPTER SIX

March 1st

KATE

"Okay, so we're just going in and asking for the report?" I ask Char. I grip my purse and glance up at the Glenmar County Police station. "I skipped pilates for this 'great idea'?"

"Hey, don't get snippy with me. I have a backup plan, but I figured we should try the easiest route first. They might just give it to us and then we can pry for information. Some people don't care to follow the rules."

I sigh. "Fine, let's try."

Five minutes later, we exit the station with the exact answer I expected—they can't share who's received a copy of the report and they can't give out a copy of the report to persons not related to the incident.

"Well, it was worth a try," Char says.

"Was it?" I ask sarcastically. This felt like a giant waste of time, and as much as I love Char, sometimes her optimism pisses me off.

"How the hell did Zo get a copy?" Char murmurs, ignoring me.

"Zo? What are you, best buds or something?"

"Didn't you say his friends call him Zo? I think it's cute," she says with a shrug.

"You've never even met him!" I snap.

"Kate, quit it! I'm trying to help."

I push my glasses up and rub the bridge of my nose. "You're right, I'm sorry. I'm just frustrated. I'm not sure why I care so much. I really should just let all of this go."

"Okay, but you *do* care. Sometimes that's all you need to know."

I nod and we start walking down the block toward Char's car.

"What about Brad? You could just ask him," she suggests.

"What? I'm not going to ask Brad. What would I say, 'Hey, sorry I took off like that on V-Day. By the way, can you get me a copy of your police report? Remember the guy who showed up? Yeah, he's kinda sketchy. Anyway, I'd like to look into him.' Be serious, Char."

Char laughs as she unlocks the doors to her car. "Alright, point taken."

"So, what now?" I ask after we've buckled our seatbelts and Char pulls onto the road. "I feel like we got more questions, not answers."

"Now, we really act like PI's. Let's get our hands on his report. Hopefully, it has a print date on it. I'd like to read it, anyway."

"Yeah, I'd like to reread it, too. Let's just snap a picture of it. Ugh! It would be nice if we could get a full copy, I want the other pages. You don't know anyone in law enforcement?"

"If I did, that would have been plan A."

"True..." I peer at her skeptically. "You really think we can get his copy? I don't want to get caught."

"There's only one way to find out."

"Seriously, you didn't see the look on Santi's face when I overheard their conversation in that garage. If looks could kill, I'd be looong gone."

Char's face shines with sheer determination. "Well, Santi can answer to me. My girl wants answers, so damn it, we're going to get them."

Lorenzo: im picking you up in ten

I pull my ponytail out, shaking my hair loose to get in the shower. Lorenzo's message buzzed at the perfect time, because I would have missed it had I gotten in a moment sooner.

Me: I'm sorry, did we have plans?

Who does he think he is? When he doesn't answer after a minute, I hop in the steaming shower, prepared to rinse off the day. But every fiber of my being feels alight; there's no denying that I'd love to see him.

I reach my arm out of the shower and grab my phone from the toilet tank, propping it on the shower caddy so it doesn't get wet. I lather my strawberry scented shampoo into my hair, scrubbing my scalp. I lean into the mini-massage, listening to my mellowed out thoughts.

Where in the world does he want to take me right now? I would be perfectly happy if we drove back to that bookstore. We could park in the same spot, make it a tradition. I could do without him ripping my clothes, but if it leads to—

Lorenzo: its a surprise

I hate surprises. They make my mind race like crazy. But if it involves Lorenzo... I'm willing to bend.

I rush my conditioning process, only leaving it in my hair for thirty seconds instead of the normal two minutes. I rush into my room after throwing a towel over my hair and drying off my body so I can pick out an outfit.

I prefer having more time, but I throw on a pair of skinny jeans and a loose, white blouse. I tousle my hair dry and run a comb through it, knowing I'll have to leave it down if I want it to dry properly.

He liked my hair down better, anyway. And I could use the relaxation I get from it.

Once I throw my flats on, I glance at my clock for the time. I'm right at the ten minute mark from when he texted. I scurry to my kitchen, prepare a water bottle, and throw it into a purse. Right then, my phone buzzes. I don't even check it, I rush out the door without a goodbye to Felix.

My veins are buzzing with the excitement I feel from unexpectedly getting to see him tonight. I run down the stairs rather than have to waste a moment waiting for the elevator. Once I get to the lobby, I slow my pace so I don't run out there with too much enthusiasm.

He doesn't need to know how excited I am.

I push the door open, a gust of air blowing into my hair. His black Audi is stopped in front of the cars parked parallel on the street. He's looking down at what I can only assume is his phone, so I take the moment to appreciate him in all his glory without his eyes interrupting my train of thought.

He's dressed in all black, as per usual, and his hair is unruly, sticking out from behind his ear. It's perfectly imperfectly, as corny as that sounds. As I step closer, I feel his energy exuding from the car as though it were a palpable object I could reach out and grab.

I pull the handle but the door doesn't open. His head shoots up and he peers at me through the window, a smirk pulling at his lips the second his eyes meet mine. His fingers unlock the doors without breaking eye contact, and I tug the door open.

"Always so ready for me, princess," he purrs. His innuendo is not lost on me as I settle into my seat.

"You're lucky I didn't have plans tonight," I reply, shutting the door. He peels off not a second later, causing my head to thrash into the headrest. I take a deep breath and will myself to remain calm. "Or maybe you already knew that, seeing as you're stalking me."

If I'm going to snoop, he needs to think that I believe him. I'm also bluffing. I don't plan much on weekdays, sticking to routine and the mundane. But when the guy you're hoping to see writes to you, you go. Even if he is a glowing red flag.

"I prefer the term protective," he jokes. "And you're here, so some part of you must like it."

"Or maybe I'm too stupid to do better."

"You're not stupid. I'm just irresistible." I snort but a small smile plays at my lips. He glances at me before returning his eyes to the road, one hand tossed over the steering wheel. He rolls down the windows and leans his elbow on the frame.

"Where are we going, anyway? I hope I'm dressed appropriately." I glance down at my jeans, my hair whipping into my eyes with the blowing wind. It's still early in the night, so the temperatures haven't dropped below sixty.

"You look stunning as always, Kate. And it's not because of the clothes," he says off-handedly. "Although, those jeans do hug your hips in a very fuckable way."

I'll never understand the way he can drop such sexy statements into casual conversation, as though his words don't shake my very core.

"I, um, thanks," I mumble, unsure of how to respond. I may be more confident, but his abrasive nature still isn't normal for me.

"I'm going to help you."

"Help me? With what?" I scoff. There's his arrogance again, always thinking I need something from him.

"You'll see," he says, turning to me. That sparkle I've come to love is present in his irises, and tingles shoot through my core. He turns back to the road, his foot still accelerating the vehicle. I force myself to keep my eyes on the road rather than glance at the dash to see how fast we're going.

"What do you normally do on weekdays?" I ask, deciding now's as good a time as any to get to know more about him. "Besides work, of course."

"Gym, chill," he says simply. I wait for him to continue, but he never does. He turns right at the street before the main highway, and my eyebrows pinch in confusion.

"Where are you taking me?"

"What part of *surprise* don't you understand?"

I cross my arms in a very childlike manner, regretting it the moment it's done. He chuckles.

"Gym? Chill? That's pretty vague," I finally respond. I'm not able to help myself. I know it must come off as annoying, me pestering him with so many questions. But I'm just as annoyed that he gives me so little information.

"I go to the gym every day, but other than that, I don't stick to a plan. Whatever life throws at me."

I frown, pondering his statement.

"You know, it would be nice if you would share more about yourself. Aren't we *friends* with benefits?"

"What, you feel like you don't know me?"

"Not well."

"What do you want to know? What could I possibly tell you that would make you feel like you know me better?"

"I don't know, anything... What's your favorite color?" I probably know that answer, based on his apparel, but it was the first thought that sprang to mind.

"What, you think knowing my favorite color tells you anything about me?"

I roll my eyes and huff. "Kinda, yeah! What if I wanted to buy you a present or something? How would I know what color to pick?"

He laughs heartily at that. "You want to buy me a present? Is that what this is about?"

"No! I just... I don't know. I'd like to know you better."

When he doesn't respond, I turn to look at him. His expression has darkened. Before I can ask him about it, he turns left and I glance through the windshield to find that we're in a large parking lot.

"Time to learn, Kate," he says. He throws the car into park in the middle of the asphalt road.

It takes about two seconds for my brain to catch up with what's happening. "Oh, no, no, no." My head is shaking vigorously.

"You have to face your fears sometime, princess."

"You said you weren't trying to save me. This feels an awful lot like saving!" It's a low blow, but I don't care. I don't want to do this, especially now. I've had no time to think about it, process it... there's absolutely no way.

"This isn't about saving you. This is about empowering you."

I stare into his eyes, looking as resolute as mine. This is obviously going to evolve into a fight; only one of us can win.

"It's just a parking lot. There's no one to hurt. I don't care if you damage my car on the wheelstops. The car can be fixed."

"Wheelstops?"

"The parking blocks. You know, that large piece of cement that you park in front of?" I follow his pointed finger and feel like a dumbass for not knowing.

"Oh."

"See? You don't even know the basics of driving. It's time to change that."

My resolve weakens. I stare at my hands in my lap. I'm back to choices.

I can use this opportunity to grow, or I can cower beneath the fear.

"Fine." I pull the door handle without looking at him, leaping out of the car with newfound determination. I don't close the door since he'll have to get into the passenger side. When I reach the driver's side, he's standing outside the car with one hand propped above the door frame.

My eyes finally meet his and he gives me a wide, approving grin. "Let's do this."

$$))) \bullet ((($$

An hour later, it's pitch black out and my mind is reeling. We spent the first fifteen minutes in the same position, me on the driver's side and Lorenzo on the passenger side. He explained the gear shifts (even though I pointed out that I was familiar, he insisted), the different dashboard gauges, the brake and gas pedals (again, I pointed out that I knew what they were), and how to properly set the rear view and side view mirrors.

Once he felt I fully understood and the car was set up for my use, he had me practice simply removing my foot from the brake. My anxiety started off sky-high, but it tapered after the tenth removal of my foot on the pedal. The car would inch forward, and I would resist the temptation to slam the brakes immediately, following Lorenzo's instructions as to when to start and stop.

As much as I hate to admit this, he's a great fucking teacher.

The last five minutes were spent coaxing me into simply placing my foot on the gas pedal without actually pressing down on it. My heart felt like it was going to pump right out of my chest. I left my foot on the pedal for half a second before slamming it on the brake. Lorenzo stifled the laugh I *know* he wanted to belt out, only giving me words of encouragement, though I can't recall what they were.

Now, I'm back in the passenger seat and he's pulling us out of the abandoned lot. "That's all for today?" I'm asking as though I'm sad, but really, I'm elated. An hour was more than enough. Too much, really. Being close to Lorenzo was the only thing that forced me to stay put. I love smelling him, hearing him, feeling him.

"I'm pretty sure that's all you could take for today."

"Hey!" I playfully swat his shoulder and he gives me a look like, "Don't act like it's not true."

"So are you dropping me back home?" I do my best to keep my voice neutral so the hope doesn't seep out. I'd love to hang out with him longer. But he doesn't miss a thing.

"Aw, did you want me to fuck you?" he teases. "You know I'd love to." *Do I?* "But I have to go meet someone."

"Who?" The question flies out of my mouth before I can stop it.

He hesitates, turns left in the direction of my place, then glances at me and clears his throat. "Santi."

"Oh. Okay," I say dejectedly. I get that he has plans and I'm not the center of his universe, but sometimes that feels like utter bullshit.

His hand snakes up my leg, settling on my inner thigh—*very* close to my clit. "Do you need me to take care of you?"

"What? No, I—" I stammer, a blush creeping on to my cheeks. His fingers slowly move over my pussy and he presses down.

"You sure?"

"You need to pay attention to the... the..." My words are lost to the feeling of him rubbing over my jeans. The thick fold where the zipper meets is giving an extra layer of pressure, causing my clit to pulse with raw need.

"Unzip your pants, Kate," he commands. The fire has been ignited and I don't have the materials to douse it. I quickly do as he says.

"Pull them down. We don't need to be more unsafe by making me fumble my way in there."

I shimmy my jeans and underwear down just below my ass, so my pussy is on full display. The seat is a little cold, but the heat expelling from my body makes it so it actually feels good. He slides all four fingers down my pussy and I thank all of my lucky stars that I shaved a few days ago.

"Mmm," I let out as he starts rubbing my clit with the pad of his index finger. He slides it down and dips it into my now wet pussy, then moves back up and works my clit. It throbs in appreciation.

"Don't be shy, baby. Tell me how good it feels. I do better with encouragement."

I forget where I am as he continues to work me. He's true to his word. The more I moan and curse, the more pressure and friction he applies. Within minutes, I'm panting and close to coming.

His words are my undoing. "I want nothing more than to make you come, Kate. Give it to me like the good girl that you are."

I explode, the sounds erupting from my throat and chest unfamiliar to me. He increases the speed of his finger until my body goes limp. My arm, which was pressed into the door, collapses onto my lap, and he slows down before sliding his finger down my slit.

He circles my pussy, sliding over the pool of desire for him. I peel my eyes open when he removes his finger from me. His eyes are burning and he draws his finger over his lips, painting them with my come before sucking the rest of his finger clean.

I groan, my pussy aching because I want him inside me. I glance out the window, realizing we're pulling up to my complex.

"I wanted to return the favor," I say in a raspy, just-fucked voice.

"It's not a favor, Kate. It's an honor." My eyes go wide with the implications and I swallow hard. Before I can reply, he glances at the time in the center of his car, then back to me.

"You can take care of me another time. I really do have to go." I believe he's really pressed for time because I can see the now familiar look of undiluted desire coursing through his eyes.

"Tonight was..." I start, trying to think through my orgasm haze. "Unexpected, yet wonderful."

"*You* were wonderful. You've got this, I promise." His close-lipped, joyful smile is one that I snap a mental picture of, wanting to remember it forever.

I smile back and our eyes remain locked for a moment. That strange thing happens again, where time stops and my heart beats erratically in my chest. This is a dangerous feeling.

I disconnect us and open the car door. As I'm about to shut it, he speaks.

Why does he always wait for the last moment?

"It's blue, by the way."

My eyes seek his, the only light being that of the reflected street lamp. "What is?"

"My favorite color."

CHAPTER SEVEN

March 2nd

KATE

Between the extra energy in my body from not getting in a workout yesterday and today being Friday, I'm absolutely buzzing. I've been fidgeting at my desk all morning without even finishing my cup of coffee.

At least it benefited me in knocking out the rest of the loans I had from yesterday. While new ones came in this morning, I want to spend the few minutes before lunch handling *personal* work. I peer over my shoulder to confirm no one's paying me any attention. Of course, they're not; why would they be?

Next to me, Victor looks as he always does—erect posture, eyes on his screen, hand resting comfortably on his mouse, and his headphones on. Usually when I need his attention, I have to tap him on the shoulder or ping him through our messaging system because he keeps the music on so loud.

Maybe I should try listening to music while I work. I typically find music distracting, which is why I don't end up listening to it much. It's one of those things you always do *with* something—driving, exercising, working, cleaning the house. I don't drive, and while the instructor does blast high-paced music at pilates, it's only beats; no lyrics.

I prefer to take in all that music has to offer. The sounds combining into rhythm, the words the artist chose to connect to it—it's all consuming for me. So while I could listen and work or clean, it ultimately takes away from both tasks.

I turn back to my computer and tackle the easier job—researching the employee handbook. It's a stretch, but it *could* be the reason Santi dislikes me so intensely. I'm the last person to judge someone for being a stickler for the rules. It wouldn't explain how he *learned* about the rule, unless Lorenzo told him, but it's easy enough to cross off my list.

I'm able to locate the policy quickly, which basically says it does not prohibit the development of friendships or romantic relationships so long as it does not adversely affect the work environment. The only thing that is strictly not allowed is for persons with a familial or romantic relationship to have authority over the other.

So Santi remains a mystery. Next, I pull up the database and click on Carter and Dwayne's names. It looks like they both started around the same time in May of last year. I'm not sure why the fact that they work here intrigues me. I guess it feels strange that I met them face to face and they didn't bother to mention it, even when they asked how Lorenzo and I know each other.

I'm interrupted from my thoughts when Victor raps his knuckles on my desk. "Ready for lunch?"

I glance at the time on my computer, realizing it's already 12:01. I'm usually the one that rounds everyone up but I'm all distracted. "Shit, sorry. Time's getting away from me today."

"Pshh. Today? The amount of new loans we've got coming in this week is insane."

I put my phone into the pocket of my casual Friday dark jeans and follow Victor to Alexandria's desk. "Oh good, so it's not just me?"

"Nope, not just you."

"What are we talking about?" Alexandria locks her computer and stands to join us.

"The amount of work that's come in," Victor says.

"Oh, yeah. Jasmine was telling me they're running additional ads. I guess Rowan wants to increase the amount of Rentals we're getting but the ads bring in more for all of us."

Her mention of Rentals piques my interest. "Why does he want to grow Rentals?"

Alexandria shrugs. "I don't know. Didn't ask. Oh, Matteo's out today." She steps into the lead, exiting our set of cubicles and heading towards the break room. While I normally make it in there, seated with my lunch, before Lorenzo gets in, today we ran a few minutes late. I see him a few steps ahead of us.

I wish I could call out to him. Maybe he'd snake his arm around my waist and pull me close. Or hell, we could just say hello without it seeming like anything more than friendly coworker behavior. But although the company policy allows us to carry on a relationship, I don't want all the questions it will bring in from my friends here.

I previously felt stupid for my situation with Lorenzo, which is why I didn't say anything to them. But now that I've come to terms with our friends with benefits arrangement, it's not about the embarrassment. I kind of like having this thing that's just... ours.

How would we have secret sex in the broom closet with the same amount of excitement? No one even gets to wonder about him putting his hand around my neck, or slapping my ass to the point that it leaves a bruise.

I'm so lost to the thought of our sex that I don't realize we're at the fridge. And Lorenzo's just finished pulling his lunch from it.

"Hey," he says with a head nod. His expression portrays complete neutrality but his eyes are a dead giveaway. To me, at least. They're singeing and I know with every fiber of my being he's lost in the same memory I am: the broom closet.

"Hi." I let my coworkers grab their food while Lorenzo lingers a second too long. His eyes convey a clear message—I want you, but not now.

I tilt my chin in acknowledgment and reach for my lunch. He turns on his heel and heads toward his usual table. It takes nearly all of my lunch break to come back to Earth from our interaction and remember that I still have investigating to do.

That's the problem with him. He distracts me in all the best and worst ways.

I need to stay focused. Impulsively, I act on an idea. Once I've discarded my trash and packed up my contents, I pretend to read something intently on my phone so my coworkers don't question me as they leave. When Lorenzo walks past, I step up behind him. He notices immediately because he breaks away from his group to fall in line with me.

"So, where's my present?" he says in a low, playful voice. It takes me a moment to register what he's talking about. We're walking with our arms inches apart, but I feel his energy falling off him in waves and crashing into me.

"Haha. Funny."

"You don't normally hang around, princess. I'm trying to piece together what's on your mind."

"Did you learn that while stalking me?" I joke. It might not be a joke, though, which wipes the grin off my face. "There *is* something on my mind, but it's nothing to do with presents."

He waits for me to continue, and I debate how to phrase this in the most open-ended way so I can gauge his reaction. I finally settle on, "I didn't know Carter and Dwa—D—work here."

I study him as he keeps his head facing forward as we walk. He remains... too expressionless. "Yeah, what about it?"

"I just find it weird that it wasn't mentioned when we all hung out."

"Not everyone feels the unyielding need to explain every little thing, Kate." He's become snippy, and while it may have bothered me before, it no longer does. So what if it's annoying? I'm owning it. I want fucking answers and there is nothing wrong with that.

"Well, we were—" I recall Rowan's request for secrecy, which still fills me with a sense of dread. But I redirect. "I was reviewing something and saw their names. It just surprised me, that's all."

I continue to study him but his expression remains inscrutable as he comes to an abrupt halt at the entrance to my department. "Guess the cat is out of the bag."

His tone is back to playful, and I start to doubt that he sounded irritated at all. I decide to push my luck. "How did you find this job?"

His smile falters and he checks the hall before responding. "I've got to get back to work. We can talk about this later."

He doesn't give me an opportunity to respond before walking off. I head to my desk and mentally review our conversation. Will we? Talk about this later? When's later?

I'll guess I'll have to wait to find out.

CHAPTER EIGHT

March 4th

KATE

"It's really kind of cute that he wants to teach you to drive," Char says through a bite of her omelet.

"It's actually been... helpful," I say with surprise. Lorenzo texted me yesterday in the same fashion he did the first time. We drove to the same lot and drove around for another hour. This time, I was able to put my foot on the gas pedal without immediately slamming the brakes. I even pushed down on it, accelerating a few feet before letting off. "I'm surprised how kind and understanding he is with teaching me."

"So even if he turns out to be some weird, psycho stalker, at least you're getting good dick and driving skills."

I laugh into my mimosa. "You never fail with your optimism, Char."

"It's part of my charm," she says with a wink. "But today, we're focusing on me! It's time to get into party mode."

We're going shopping for her housewarming party after brunch today. The party's set for next Saturday, and while this is Char's wheelhouse, she makes me tag along for moral support. I say she makes me, but I do it willingly and with gusto. What else are best friends for?

We map out the different stores she wants to go to. I let her dictate as I jot it all down in my travel-sized journal. I list out the different items we need and once it's all written out, she informs me of the food she already put on order.

Once our veins are swimming in mimosas and we finish eating, we go down the list of stores. We're at our third stop when we run into him. We gathered the party decorations—she's going for a rose gold aesthetic—and got in line behind no person other than Santi.

I've still got a light buzz going from brunch and he's facing forward, so I know he hasn't noticed me. I'd normally say hello to someone I recognize but his distaste for me causes me pause. His cart is full of green decorations—hats, confetti, streamers, banners, and more hidden beneath what I'm able to see.

I really don't want him to see me. Today's not the day for weird looks and hateful remarks. I motion to Char and point towards the exit, mouthing that I'm going to wait outside.

"What?" she attempts to whisper, but it comes out at full volume. *Damn mimosas.* And of course, Santi looks back to the source of the noise.

Our eyes lock and I watch the realization hit him. He grimaces, but to my surprise, he speaks. "Kate."

"Santi, hey," I fumble through my words, astonished that he's actually treating me with any ounce of respect. "Funny running into you like this." *Is it funny? Stop talking like an idiot.* "Um, what brings you here?" *Seriously? Who talks like that?*

He glances at his cart, only affirming how stupid of a question that was. "I'm prepping for our St. Patrick's Day party. College tradition we're keeping."

"Oh, that's fun."

"I'm sure you'll be there." I feel a sting in my chest, because Lorenzo hasn't mentioned any such party. But I brush it off in the next second—we're casual and he doesn't have to invite me anywhere. It's fine.

I'm about to let Santi know exactly where I stand on the matter when Char cuts in, tapping a finger to her chin. "Santi, Santi. You look so familiar. What's your last name?"

I hold back the burst of laughter. She's a genius, even if her attempt is very forward. Santi's eyes sweep over Char and a look crosses him that I haven't seen him wear before.

"I've never seen you before," he finally replies. *Why are they so good at evading questions?*

"You might think that," Char says conversationally. "But I dye my hair, like, all the time. I lost a bunch of weight, too."

My eyebrows cinch together because that's a complete lie. She's always looked exactly as she does, minus the hair dying. That part's true.

"Hmm, I'm pretty good with faces. You from around here?"

"Yep, born and raised like my girl, Kate." She throws an arm over my shoulder and Santi looks at me as though he forgot I was here. The reminder that Char is my friend places him back into a position of reservation.

"Nice to... catch you guys later." He moves up as the person in front of him leaves the register, putting his items on the counter. Char and I give each other a silent look. Then her eyebrows shoot up and she throws her arm off me.

She moves to the front of the cart and starts sifting through the plates and pack of balloons, seemingly looking for something. She keeps this up as Santi continues putting his stuff on the counter and the employee rings them up. Once it's all bagged and the noise stops, Char turns her back towards me and keeps digging through the cart.

She never actually grabs anything because she's watching Santi pull his wallet out and insert his card into the machine. Once the employee nods his head for the approved payment, Santi slides the card right out and slips it back into his wallet.

Char straightens as Santi pushes his bag filled cart out of the line. "It was nice to see you, Santi!" She waves enthusiastically.

He looks at us over his shoulder and only gives us a head nod before picking up his pace and leaving the store.

"Ugh, that was awkward. Why did you have to do that?" I mutter as we start putting her items on the counter. I regret ever thinking that was a genius move.

"You gotta take opportunities as they present themselves, Katherine."

"Yeah, well, that got us nowhere, fast." We grab our filled bags and put them in the cart. Once Char has paid, we exit.

"Well, luckily for us, I have perfect vision."

My head whips to her. "You saw it?"

She nods. "Yep. Looks like we were right. Santiago Valeri is indeed related to your boss."

CHAPTER NINE

March 10th

KATE

I pass Char the box filled with rose gold candles so she can set them on the wood grain dining table. While her apartment is limited in space, her interior design skills come in handy for party planning as well. We've spent the afternoon transforming the place to host the twenty or so people she has coming over.

"Thanks!" she says, taking the box and placing it on the table. As she takes the candles out of the box, I head to her kitchen to grab a lighter. "We're making great timing, people should start trickling in in about an hour or so. That gives us time to get ready."

I glance at the clock. "An hour? I thought you said 7 pm."

"Kate, when are you going to learn that no one arrives to parties on time?"

"Not no one. I do!" Char chuckles as I dig through her drawers. "Where the hell is your lighter?"

"Right here." She pulls it out of the back pocket of her jeans. She ignites the flame and starts lighting one of the four candles lined up in the center of the table that are surrounded by disposable plates and utensils. I push the drawer shut and return to her side.

"Great job with all of this. I think you've outdone yourself." She finishes lighting the last candle, and we both eye the living and dining room, which are a shared, open space. There are round garlands strung across the wall adjacent to the front door. Three sets of five balloons are floating in different corners of the rooms, held down by a rose gold weight. Char made a banner that says WELCOME HOME in handwritten script that you'd think came off a printer, it's that perfect.

The candles start to emit a light, fruity smell. I check the label, finding that the scent matches the name: champagne toast. I glance out at the balcony through the sliding glass door, the beige curtains Char installed held open by floral hooks.

"I really have, haven't I?" she murmurs appreciatively. Then she claps her hands together. "Okay, now for the best part! Attire!"

We head into her room and apply our makeup, then pull out our dresses from her closet. We bought similarly styled rose gold dresses, both of which end at our knees and hug our bodies. Where mine has a spaghetti strap and straight cut across the chest, Char's is a halter top that gives an extra umph to her full breasts.

She blasts pop music to set the mood, and it definitely does the job. I let the eclectic sounds fill my bones with positivity. Tonight is all about fun.

As I plug in her curling iron, she turns the volume down. "I've got a few hot, *single* friends coming tonight. Maybe someone will pique your interest?"

"What? I have Lorenzo," I say automatically. I take her brush and comb it through my hair, removing the knots built up over the day.

"And? He's not your boyfriend."

I wonder if it will ever stop stinging when that's pointed out. My eyes find hers in the mirror but she's focused on straightening her hair. "True. But I don't necessarily *want* a boyfriend, remember?"

She pegs me with an insolent look through the mirror. "Did I say find a boyfriend? No."

I consider her words for a moment. "You're right."

She mimics Lorenzo's words from months ago. *"Be that badass for one more night, Kate."*

I toss the hairbrush at her with a laugh. "How do you even remember that?"

She shrugs. I pull my hair into its typical tight bun since it'll show off my back and shoulders in this dress. I grab the curling iron to do the strands in the front. Char forced me to invite Lorenzo tonight but he said he had plans.

He did, however, invite me to his St. Patrick's Day party. He said, and I quote, "We might be shit out of luck in this world, but I'll pretend for a day." I ignored his cynical message and asked to bring Char, to which he replied, "It's a party, bring whoever you want. Except Brad."

I laughed lightheartedly because there's no chance I'd invite Brad, or any other guy. Lorenzo and I aren't serious, but when I'm with him, it's all consuming. I don't want *or* need anyone else.

But Lorenzo won't be here tonight. I had no plans of looking for another guy—there's more to life than men. But Char's suggestion did pique my interest. Maybe I can have fun tonight, just like Lorenzo's always going on about. It doesn't have to mean anything and I can take advantage of one of the benefits in friends with benefits—not being tied down.

"Done!" Char squeals, turning to face me. Her eyes light up with a twinkle, sparkling like a glass of champagne. Before I can respond, there's a knock at the door. "That must be the food!"

"Here, I'll go get it." I release the curling iron from the strand, placing it on the vanity and checking to make sure the curls are perfect before rushing to the front door. Char paid for the food ahead of time, so I take the trays and set them down on the kitchen counter. Char walks out of her room a moment later with nothing other than a bottle of champagne.

"Cheers, toots," she says, popping the cork. The sound echoes off the walls, setting the tone for tonight. I grab two of the plastic champagne flutes she bought for the party and hold them out so she can pour.

"Cheers," I say, holding my glass up. We clink and take a sip, then she walks over to the kitchen and pulls down a bottle of gin from the cabinet above the sink. She's making Raspberry Gin Champagne's for tonight, so I grab the drink dispenser and pull out the lemons to juice and slice. She mixes the various gin and champagne bottles into the container, along with simple syrup and raspberries.

Once the cocktail is mixed and the sliced lemons float lusciously inside, there's a knock at the door—time to get this party started.

))) ● (((

Three drinks and nineteen guests later, the party is in full swing. I made sure to fill my stomach with quiches and finger sandwiches before polishing off the champagne Char served us. I'm spending the night so I don't have to worry about getting home.

I've met some of her friends at parties before, but there are new people here. One of them, Gustav, definitely piqued my interest, as Char put it. He's surprisingly older, I'd say in his thirties, and has a goatee. Neither of which I've ever been attracted to. But he's got a way about him; a confidence that's impossible to ignore.

He brought a bottle of vodka and asks if I'd like to take a shot of it. The notion of shots at a party reminds me of the Fireball and Jäger shots I did with Lorenzo, which feels exciting. What do I have to lose? It's just a shot.

That led to a hell of a lot more with Lorenzo.

Gustav slides the balcony door open and waves for me to step out first. The air is cool and refreshing now that the temperatures are warming up with the near end of winter. It helps me become a little more alert through the fog I feel from my few drinks.

Gustav hands me a shot and we loop our arms to take the shot at the same time. I laugh and I feel so light and free. This is the first time in a while that I can remember feeling so careless.

Since meeting Lorenzo.

When Gustav takes the shot glass from my hand, puts both of them on the small table between the chairs, and takes a step closer to me, reality hits. It's time to make a choice. He's going to make a move, I can feel it. We haven't spent the last twenty minutes innocently chatting and flirting. This is intended to move somewhere.

Do I want it to?

I think I kinda do. When his hand tentatively touches my waist and his face inches towards mine, I inhale slowly. I watch through half-closed lids as his eyes shut and his lips press onto mine.

And I feel... nothing. Just his lip skin on mine. He starts to move his lips and I reciprocate out of reaction, not intention. Maybe I just need to get past the initial awkward phase.

You didn't need to get past that with Zo. You were into it immediately.

That was different, though. We'd had a lot of back and forth already, we'd met the night before. He's *way* more my type, which certainly helped. So why does this feel so blah? Gustav is invigorating and fun, and I certainly enjoyed the small talk. Shouldn't this kiss feel fun and exciting, too?

I want to feel that intense passion, like I do when I'm with Lorenzo. Maybe that passion only comes with secrecy and blurred lines. I had it with my ex, though. At least when we first met. Maybe it's just with assholes. Either way, when Lorenzo so much as grazes me with any part of his body, everything in me lights up like fireworks on the Fourth of July.

And then it hits me. It's not that I can't have other guys, I just only want *him*. I've been thinking about Lorenzo the entire time I've been kissing Gustav.

I slowly peel myself away from him, his head hanging forward for a second before he recovers. I give him a regretful look and he understands immediately. I'm so grateful when he doesn't ask for an explanation or push for anything more. We smile at each other and he slides the door open for me, following close behind as I walk in.

Then we go our separate ways.

The rest of the evening has been a blast. I rekindled with friends of Char's that I've met in the past, and talked to new friends. Gustav and I avoided each other amicably and while I'd expect to feel awkward, I don't. I'm at peace with my choice. I guess having sex with Lorenzo in our boss's house and office made me more secure with my sexuality.

It's getting late and most people have left the party. I'm chatting with Char and one of her business associates when my phone buzzes in my lap. I expect it to be an incoming message, because no one calls me this late, but my eyes cut to the screen when it doesn't stop buzzing. My heart skips a beat when I see Lorenzo's name.

He's never called me before. I can't explain why I suddenly feel anxious, like his call must mean that something is wrong. I jump out of my seat, which causes Char to stop midsentence and look at me.

"Phone call," I explain, waving my phone at her before rushing to her bedroom. When the door's safely shut behind me, I swipe to answer the call.

"Hello?"

His calm reply filters through the built-in speaker. "Hey, princess."

"Are you okay?" His collected voice tells me he's fine, but I can't figure out why he's calling me when he's never done so before.

"Yeah, just wanted to see how Char's party went."

"Oh," I say, surprise laced into my tone. Then I remember Gustav's lips on mine and I shudder, quickly putting it to the back of my mind. "Um, yeah, it's been fun. There are still some people here."

"Sorry I couldn't make it, had some... stuff to attend to," he replies.

"Getting ready for the party next week?"

There's a beat before he responds. "Yeah, Santi goes nuts over this holiday. I can't understand it."

I chuckle. "I don't think holidays are your thing."

"I wouldn't say they're yours, either. That's one thing we have in common."

Wherever he is, it's quiet. I can still hear the muffled sounds of music and voices past the door I'm leaning against. "That's true."

I move to sit on the edge of the bed and switch the phone to my other ear. The thirty or so seconds it takes for me to do that are filled with silence.

My heart quickens with the realization that he may have called just to... call. Which means he was just thinking about me. Which means he thinks about me. But that's... I mean that's silly, right? There must be a reason he called.

"So... what's up?" I ask.

"Oh, um"—he coughs—"I just wanted to apologize again for not being able to make it."

"Oh. Okay." When he doesn't say anything, I add, "I'll let Char know."

"Please do."

More silence.

"Can I bring anything for the party?" I offer.

"Just yourself. Everything else is taken care of."

"Okay. Don't forget, I'm bringing Char."

"Right, of course. It'll be nice to meet your best friend."

He actually sounds sincere, which nags me. This entire conversation has been more or less meaningless in terms of a reason to call. It seems like he just wanted to... talk. To me.

"Let's go for another drive before the party," he says after I don't reply, lost to my own thoughts.

Is that what this was about? It's still a week away. "That's the last thing I want to do before a party," I whine.

"You're doing great, princess. We have to keep it up if you're going to make improvements."

"Ugh. Fine."

"Good girl. I'll pick you up at 10."

"Does this mean we're not doing any lessons during the week?"

"I can't. I'll be out of town this week."

My stomach drops with the realization that I won't be seeing him. "Where are you going?"

"Family trip."

"Oh," I say, doing my best to keep the dismay hidden.

Another stretch of silence passes between us, anticipation pooling in my belly. The unspoken words hang in the imaginary space between our phones.

When he speaks, his voice is soft. "See ya then, princess."

"See you then," I reply, my voice just as soft. It gets so quiet that I pull the phone from my cheek, certain he hung up. But he didn't. I bring it back to my ear, about to say goodbye when he beats me to it.

"Later." Then the line goes dead.

CHAPTER TEN

March 17th

KATE

My driving skills are definitely improving. Although I protested after Lorenzo insisted we do another lesson before the party, like I have most days he takes me out to this lot, I'd be a total liar if I said it hasn't helped. Each lesson, the anxiety is less prominent. Each lesson, we get a little farther than we did the one before it.

Today, I did a complete circle around the wheelstops without hesitation. When I hit the brakes and threw the car in park, I literally squealed and clapped my hands together. Lorenzo smiled at me with so much pride, I had to look away to remind myself that he's not something I own or get to keep forever.

Seeing him today, after missing him all week, reminded me just how strong whatever attraction I feel towards him is. While I'd hoped he would call again, he never did. No texts, either. Breathing in the smoke and cinnamon when I got in his car reawakened my soul and filled my blood with heat, which only makes me more nervous.

That nagging feeling of something being off still hasn't dissipated. In fact, it's grown since all those weeks ago when I found that report. And if all goes well, Char and I will get our hands on it today. I didn't bother asking him about his trip when he didn't bring it up. I don't want to give him any reason to suspect that I've been wondering about him.

We're on the way back to my house for him to drop me off when my phone rings. Mom flashes across the screen and I debate answering it before sliding it back into my pocket. I'll call her when I get home. I glance into the back of the car to admire how clean it is. There's only one pack of empty smokes on the floorboard. I could be wrong, but I get the feeling he cleaned it for me because I'd always make a face anytime I caught sight of the mess.

"Is Char still coming today?" Lorenzo asks as I turn back to face the road. He's got one hand on the steering wheel while his other arm is bent on the open window, his elbow protruding from the car.

"Yes, she is!" I reply enthusiastically. I've grown more comfortable with the friendship part of our relationship. Or situationship, as the case may be. I don't feel the need to hide my true self at all.

"Thank fuck," Lorenzo mutters, his hair ruffling with the wind. I start to lift my hand so I can run my fingers through it, but I let it fall back into my lap. "Santi kept asking. Seems like she really had an impact on him when he ran into you guys at that store."

I didn't realize Lorenzo was aware of that. I hadn't mentioned it because of my paranoia surrounding the whole snooping incident. I'm surprised, really, that Santi would want to see me or Char again. He probably still doesn't want to see me, but we're a package deal, so he has no choice.

"I'm excited for you guys to meet," I say. Before, I'd probably be embarrassed to admit that, based on our casual relationship. Now, I'm not afraid to show how I truly feel. There's power in owning your choices and I chose this. I choose it everyday. And his phone call last week certainly helped.

I couldn't stop replaying our conversation in my mind as I was falling asleep that night. Of course I told Char about it once all the guests left. She was equally surprised and it convinced her that I mean more to him than he lets on. While there is evidence to support that, I'm still wary.

That's why our secret agenda for today—getting our hands on that police report by any means necessary—feels more important than ever. Char and I discussed our action plan and today's finally the day to execute. My stomach rolls over with nerves but I ignore it. Then another pending question pops into my mind.

"Hey, I never got to ask—why did you get a new number?" I slowly turn my head, leaving it at an angle to side eye him. His expression remains neutral when he responds.

"My other phone fell in the pool."

"Oh." I glance out the window before thinking of something else. "They couldn't transfer your number?"

I turn my head fully this time, catching his grip tightening on the steering wheel. "I don't like smartphones. It's easier to get a new phone with a new number, so that's what I did."

"Why don't you like smartphones?" I ask out of genuine curiosity. They feel like a borderline necessity in today's world.

"The phone doesn't need to be smart when the man is," Lorenzo says. I roll my eyes but feel a strange pit in my stomach. It feels like he's hiding something. I'm about to push further but we're rolling up to my building, so I table it.

"Okay, so 1 pm?" I ask, glancing at the time on the dash. It's 11:37 now, so that gives me enough time to shower and get ready.

"*Ish*. No need to be right on time, babe," he replies with a grin. It doesn't feel as condescending as it used to. If I didn't know any better, I'd think he kinda likes my time quirk.

"Lucky for you, I'm on Char's schedule today. She's picking me up on the way so I don't have to Uber."

"Just think—one day, you'll be driving yourself." The thought alone lodges my breath in my throat and he doesn't miss it. "One step at a time, princess."

He gives me an encouraging smile and I smile back, then pop the door open. "See you soon."

)))●(((

An hour and a half later, I'm dressed and packed. My bathing suit and towel are in a tote, along with sunscreen, a sunhat, sunglasses, and a protective UV shirt. I'll do anything I can to prevent getting skin cancer.

As would be expected, Char insisted we go shopping for cute St. Patrick's Day outfits after brunch last Sunday. While I normally have no problem shopping, we were tired and a bit hungover from the house-warming party, so I wasn't keen on the idea.

When she found white crop tops that had bright green sparkling clovers over each breast area, she *insisted* we match. Reluctantly, I agreed, and we found cute denim shorts that are high waisted and cuffed on the legs. The fold sits right under my butt cheeks and unless the mirror's lying, my ass looks damn good. The outfit is solidified with a jean hat that has a green clover stitched into it.

I have never felt so extra in my entire life.

Char wanted to wear her white converse and knee high socks with it, so I bought myself a pair of matching shoes and socks. This entire outfit cost over two hundred dollars but I have to admit, it's damn festive and fun. Plus, Rowan called me yesterday and said I was getting a raise for all the hard work I'd done on the increase in loans we've been getting.

I front face the mirror and raise my hands, watching the crop top slide up but not to the point that it reveals my boobs. I decided not to wear a bra because this shirt is tight enough. I let my hands fall limply at my side and the shirt settles back into place, stopping at my ribs.

My phone buzzes with Char's message that she's on her way. I call my mom real quick in the interim, telling her this weekend's plans. I leave out that Lorenzo is basically my fuck buddy, only saying that he's a coworker. I end the call when Char texts me that she's outside, promising Mom that I'll give Char a kiss for her.

"I'm so excited!" Char screeches the moment I open her door. I plop down in the seat and she peels off the moment I shut the door. "We look so freaking cute! But excuse me, where are your pig tails?"

"I'm not doing pig tails," I state, pulling on the end of hers after buckling my seatbelt. I left my hair down, feeling like a bun in this cap would throw it all off.

"Party pooper," she huffs.

"I'm excited, but I'm nervous, too. Maybe we should call this off," I suggest.

"Call *what* off?"

"The investigation."

"Phew. I thought you were gonna say going to the party. I did not spend fifteen minutes putting green glitter eye shadow on to not go."

"No, of course we're going. But it's wrong to be snooping into his stuff like that. He has a right to privacy."

"His right to privacy ended when he dug into your life."

"Good point. But what if the door's locked?"

"Kate! We've been over this, like, a million times. We'll try. If we can't get it, we can't get it. But this is our opportunity to try. Do you want answers or not?"

She pegs me with a quick stern look before putting her eyes back on the road. She's always been very understanding of my driving fear, but she's *extremely* supportive of Lorenzo teaching me to drive.

"I want answers. Of course I do."

"Okay. Then we do what we gotta do to get them," she states matter-of-factly. She follows the GPS instruction to turn left and I recognize Lorenzo's neighborhood. My belly flutters with anticipation of how today will go. Will him and Char get along? Will we get caught snooping or sneaking around? What if we can't get our hands on that report? Does it even really matter?

"Let's go, toots," Char says. I pull the visor down and slide the mirror open, checking my reflection one last time. I left my glasses behind, feeling it was too much with the hat. I didn't use green glitter eye shadow like Char, instead simply applying waterproof liner and mascara.

"Let's go," I say with a grimace. Char beams at me and we exit the car to head up the walkway. Char wastes no time in pounding on the door, and surprisingly, it swings open within seconds.

Santi's broad body fills the doorway so that I can barely see into the house. Music bumps faintly from the speakers, and I can smell the beer from his cup. He's in green bathing suit shorts with clovers all over them. My eyes skim over his chest and double take when I catch sight of the tattoo on it. It's identical to the one Lorenzo has.

"All right, you made it," Santi says, but his eyes are pinned on Char. This is the friendliest he's ever been around me.

"Hell yeah, we did!" she exclaims. Santi hugs the door with his back so we can walk past him, forcing my eyes off the tattoo. *Why do they have the same tat?* Char isn't shy about glancing around the room, and I can feel the disgust oozing off of her from the lack of decor.

"What is this, a prison?" Char says, looking down the hall with an expression of hope that there will be some redeeming quality down it. When she turns back, it's evident there isn't one.

"You guys want a drink?" I can't tell if Santi is purposely ignoring her question or if he didn't hear her. I'm still just as shocked as I was moments before that he's speaking and not just grunting and giving me weird looks.

"Duh. It better be green or I don't want it," Char replies, walking towards the patio as if she owns the place. It doesn't take anything for her to feel comfortable in any scenario.

"I fuck hard with a themed party," Santi says with a shit eating grin. Either he's already drunk, or he really fucking hates me. I feel like I'm meeting a different person.

Him and I follow Char to the back patio, the music bleeding into my ears. Char halts to take in the scene and I stop next to her. There has to be at least thirty people here already, and they're all holding green solo cups.

Santi sidles up to her other side. "The drinks aren't green, but the cups are." He points to the table behind the propped door.

Char glances at it and says, "It'll do."

I feel a brush on my arm and turn to find Lorenzo standing next to me. He's also shirtless, a dark green tie resting on his toned chest and black swimming trunks sitting low on his hips so I get a perfect view of his sculpted figure.

"Look who showed up at the *appropriate* time for once," he murmurs for only me to hear.

I nudge him with my shoulder, my skin sparking alive from the contact. "Don't be a dick. And don't set a time if you don't want people adhering to it."

"That's fair," he says. His eyes travel down my body and back up, and the timidness it once made me feel is no longer present. "What's not fair is how fuckin' sexy you look right now."

Flames. I'm bursting into flames.

"Isn't she so hot?" Char says from my left, startling me. I forgot where we were for a moment. The music thumps in my ears again, and I force myself to focus.

"Lorenzo, this is Char. Char, Lorenzo." I do a strange motion with my hand since I'm standing directly between them. Char smiles and puts her hand out, which Lorenzo takes into his instantly.

"Nice to finally meet you," Char says.

"I couldn't agree more. Any friend of Kate's is a friend of mine."

"Except Brad," Char says, still shaking Lorenzo's hand and smiling.

"Char!" I shout at the same time that Lorenzo echos, "Except Brad."

"I'm only teasing!" Char says, her eyes cutting to mine as she lets go of Lorenzo's hand. He puts his released hand onto my lower back, pressing gently. I can't explain why I know it, but I can tell he's trying to get across that he's completely unbothered.

"Let's get our drinks!" I shout with a little too much enthusiasm. I need to get her away from here immediately before she decides to blab about Gustav. Not that I'm necessarily hiding it from Lorenzo, but why light a match and throw it when it might set fire to a good thing?

"Grab them and meet me by the pong table," Lorenzo says before sliding his hand off me and walking across the pool deck. My body misses the feeling of him immediately, so I rush us over to the drink table. We fill our green cups with beer from the keg, then walk over to the table.

"Kate!" The squealing from my right has me whipping my head towards the sound just in time to see Larissa barreling towards me. I only just hand Char my cup before she leaps—literally leaps—onto me. I catch her and she wraps her hands around my shoulders as I hold her up by her thighs.

"I'm so happy you're here!" she squeals into my ear before pulling back to face me. I can smell the beer on her breath but I know she's not drunk. She's excitable like this.

"Me, too," I say with far less enthusiasm, but she doesn't seem hindered. I let go of her thighs as she unlatches her arms so she can slide off of me.

"Hi, I'm Larissa," she says to Char.

"I like you already. Char," she replies, handing me the cups and pulling Larissa into a hug. I knew they'd love each other.

"You do know this is a pool party, right?" Larissa says as Char releases her. She eyes our outfits skeptically.

"I brought my bathing suit," I say, wiggling the bag on my shoulder. Her and Char both laugh.

"Aye, Kate. You're so funny," Larissa says. I look between the two of them quizzically.

"Just wear your bra and underwear," Char explains.

"What? Why would I do that? Bathing suits were made for exactly this," I say indignantly.

"You can wear your bathing suit—"

"It's fun! We're only young once!" Larissa cuts Char off.

"I'm not even wearing a bra," I whisper loud enough so only they can hear.

"Even better," Larissa says with a grin.

I glance nervously at the pool. It was one thing to do it when there weren't many people here, and in the dark. It's another to intentionally not wear my bathing suit at a *pool party*.

"I... I'll think about it, okay?"

"Well think quick, I'm ready to go in, like, now," Larissa says, peeling her white shirt off to reveal her lacy green bra underneath. It's so sheer that I'm certain the second she gets into that pool we'll all be seeing her nipples through it.

"Let us finish our beers first, Larissa," Char says, clearly sensing my discomfort. "We'll join you soon."

"Fine. And call me Lari," she says before jogging to the poolside and peeling off her shorts. She was already barefoot, so she leaves the clothes in a pile and dives into the water. On the shallow side.

Mermaid.

"Come on, let's go play with Lorenzo," Char says, taking her beer and guiding me forward by the elbow.

"I just don't understand..."

Char laughs, carting us towards the pong table.

"Perfect timing," he says, giving me another once over before meeting my stare and biting his lower lip. "You guys are playing against me and Carter this round."

CHAPTER ELEVEN

March 17th

KATE

A couple rounds of some green liquor shot pong later, and I am drunk. Not in the bad way, when you're seeing double and ready to vomit. But in the good way, where you feel like there's nothing more important than what you're doing at this moment.

From the looks of it, Char is feeling just as good. Her and Lorenzo kept up a healthy dose of smack talking, which had me giggling throughout our games. Carter and Lorenzo kicked our asses the first time, but the second time we only lost by two cups. Which means Lorenzo must be feeling pretty good, himself.

He walks up to me and I start to giggle, giddy with the nice weather, drinks, and friends around me. He doesn't pull me in physically, but his eyes scream what he won't. They're full of dark promises and I want to hear every single one of them.

"Nice game," I say, poking him in the chest, right where his tattoo is. "Hey, why do you and Santi have matching tattoos?"

He shrugs and looks away. "College shit."

"Get a room, love birds," Char says obnoxiously. I glance around on instinct, used to our sneaky behavior. I still don't really want everyone knowing our business, but I do realize it must be obvious. Why would I be the only coworker he keeps inviting over?

"I've got a room, babe," Carter shouts from across the table with a wink. Char deadpans but I catch the teasing twinkle in her eye.

"Please. Don't flatter yourself."

Santi's voice floats over from across the lawn. "Yeah, fuck off, C." I squint against the sunlight to find him staring rather protectively at Char.

"Just sayin'." Carter winks again, which leads me to believe he's mostly joking. *Mostly.*

"A room does sound nice," Lorenzo whispers into my ear. He moved to stand at my back, his head leaned into the crook of my neck. Goosebumps erupt over my skin at his words. I turn around to face him, taking a step back so we're not right in each other's spaces. I can't help that I still want to keep a minimum of PDA. I'm not actually his, and he's not actually mine.

"I bet it does," I say with a coy smile. The drinks have me loose and silly, so I'm toying with him. Because a room really does sound nice. It's been a couple of weeks because each time we'd finish the driving lessons, he'd have somewhere to be. He did finger me again one time, but that's just an appetizer.

Right now, I'm craving a main course.

"You gonna tell me you don't need me as much as I need you right now?"

I make a show of checking him out as though I'm inspecting him, then I shrug. "I could take it or leave it."

He nods with a toothy grin. "Keep lyin' to yourself, princess. I bet your pussy's already wet for me."

I scan the area around us but no one is within earshot. Wondering where Char ran off to, I glance behind me and locate her near the pool, stripping her shirt off.

When I turn back, Lorenzo's heated gaze is sweeping over my body, finally landing on my lips. He hooks a finger through a loop on my jean shorts and pulls me to him, my hips resting against his thighs.

"Tell me. What would I find if I stuck my finger into these shorts?"

My clit throbs and desire trickles out of me, but I play nonchalant with a shrug. "Guess you'll have to take them off to find out."

He licks his lower lip and leans in by a fraction. I play with the end of the tie on his chest. "What's up with this, anyway?"

"Santi's idea."

"I'm surprised he was able to convince you."

"If you're a good girl, you'll learn exactly *why* I agreed to wear this silly tie." His smirk comes slow. "Either way, I'm gonna fuck that attitude right out of you."

I want to find out how this plays out. "I can do that."

His smile gets wider. He twirls a finger through a strand of hair on the side of my face. "Do what?" When I don't answer, his smile fades. "Say it, Kate."

"Be a good girl," I mumble incoherently, looking at the ground.

He lifts my chin up with his finger, his eyes boring into mine. "Louder," he whispers darkly.

"I'll be a good girl."

His chest rumbles. He takes my hat off and runs his hand through my hair, fisting it at the base on my neck. He starts to lean but suddenly stops and looks around as though he just remembered where we are.

He places the cap back on my head and tugs my hair. "Let's get out of here."

He reaches for my hand and tugs me through the house and to his room. He pauses, pulling out a key from his pocket and unlocking the door. I watch him drop the key back into his pocket as he pulls me into the room, making a mental note. Either I need to get a hold of that key or ensure he doesn't lock the door behind us.

The moment the door snaps shut behind me, Lorenzo grabs me by the hips, lifts me, and tosses me onto the bed. I quickly forget about the stupid lock and key when he starts to crawl on top of me, his bent knee between my legs. He presses it into my pussy, my shorts providing an extra layer of pressure. I sit up on my elbows to bring my lips to his. He wastes no time in gliding his tongue across my lips and into my mouth.

I moan audibly into him, letting cinnamon and smoke consume every part of my senses.

His hands roam over my thighs, grip my hips, massage my waist, then creep under my crop top. He pulls away from my lips and tilts his head back to look at my body.

"You're killing me in this outfit."

"I'll have Char dress me more often, then."

"Don't get me wrong, you're sexy in anything. But these shorts... I've wanted to rip them off since the moment I saw you."

I bite down on my lip, then answer seriously. "Please don't rip them."

He chuckles darkly. "I won't rip them. But I am going to take them off." His fingers trail down my stomach, which tightens in anticipation. He pops the button and pulls down the zipper before slipping a finger into the waistline of my shorts and pulling them off torturously slow. I raise my hips, and to my surprise, he speeds up the process.

Once they're forgotten in a heap on the floor, I kick off my shoes to let them join. He peels my socks and panties off, adding them to the pile. I meet his fiercely determined eyes as he brings his face towards my pussy. "I want to taste you," he growls.

I don't get a chance to respond. He grips my inner thighs and pushes them open, my legs splaying out and my hips stretching. My pussy throbs in anticipation, my clit aching to be touched. His hot breath teases me as he slowly brings his tongue to my entrance.

My muscles tense up, causing my hips to thrust forward and his upper lip to rub against my clit. It feels so good that I do it again intentionally. He lets me continue, bringing his tongue to swipe across my clit, replacing his lip. I'm aching when he finally slides his hands from my thighs and curls two fingers in my pussy.

I pant and moan, gripping the bed sheets. His free hand grabs one of mine, placing it on his hair. I grab a fist full and tug, releasing my building tension. He groans and rocks his hips against the bed where his dick is pressed thickly into it.

When I start to get close, I pull on his hair harder. Instead of increasing his speed, like I desperately need, he slows down. I whine and grind my hips into his face while pushing down on his head. His tongue does a final sweep down my slit before he crawls over me, his dick resting over my slick pussy. If I started thrusting I could get the perfect friction and would come immediately. He lowers his face to a mere inch from mine.

"Now I want you to taste you," he whispers before he brings his lips to mine in a featherlight touch. I indulge him as our lips move together sensually. I bring the tip of my tongue to run across his lips, inhaling and tasting my own scent at once. It's more intoxicating than I could have imagined, especially now that it's mingled with him.

He smirks against my lips. "I knew you'd like that."

I smirk back in confirmation. I rock my hips into him, satisfying my clit's throbbing, unignorable need. He leans back and pulls his shorts down, kicking them off. He throws his nightstand drawer open, taking out a condom and ripping it open with his teeth. I don't know what it is about him spitting the foil out, but it causes a surge of wetness to gush out of me.

He slides it on quickly before thrusting his cock into me with force. My head falls back with instant pleasure. He doesn't take his time, keeping a steady, quick pace that has both of us out of breath within minutes. My clit swells, rubbing on him and bringing me close to the brink.

"You're such a good girl, Kate. I love filling you up with my cock," he grunts between thrusts. "You take me so well."

The tie starts to flap with his exertion and he glances down at it, then looks back up to me with a devilish grin. "I almost forgot. You're too distracting." He slows down, to which I whimper, but he ignores me. He removes the tie and holds it taught before bringing it out around my head. A thrill shoots through my spine.

"As much as I'd like to hold this," he says, finishing the knot and holding the fabric out to me. "You're going to pull it."

"I..." I stare at the tie, suddenly nervous. "You want me to do it?"

"You'll know the right amount of pressure to use. And I'll get off on the fact that you're still at my mercy and happy to please me."

I start to pull on the tie, feeling it tighten around my esophagus. He resumes his pace from before, which brings me back to the pleasure of this moment. When my airway becomes a little restricted, I stop. Lorenzo's eyes are so hooded, they're almost closed. The only reason I know they're not is because they alternate watching my face, my neck, and his dick sliding in and out of my pussy.

As my moans become louder with the building climax, he lowers his body onto me and thrusts into me deeply. I'm just drunk enough that I don't care if anyone hears. Our bodies are slick with sweat, sliding against each other with his movements.

His lips cover mine, our tongues swiping each other in hazy lust. He puts his hand over my wrist and tugs slightly, causing the tie to tighten around my throat. I feel my vein thump into the fabric and my breathing gets shallower.

"That's it. Give yourself to me," he growls into my mouth between breaths. "Give. It. All. To. Me."

He pulses deep inside me and I explode, moaning into his mouth. He swallows my cries and bites down on my lip, which only causes my orgasm to intensify. As it peaks and settles, he slows down. It takes a moment for my alcohol and orgasm clouded mind to realize he hasn't come.

"What about you?" I mumble after releasing my grip on the tie.

"I'm gonna come for you, don't worry." His voice is still all sex while my entire body is limp and I'm ready for a nap.

I watch him intently as he pulls out and rips the condom off, tossing it on the nightstand. He steadies himself on one hand while tugging at my shirt with the other, pulling it off so I'm completely naked for him. With his knees on either side of me, he crawls up my body until his dick is right at my mouth.

"Please me, princess. Do what only you can do for me." I don't make him wait a second longer, because how the fuck do I say no to that? I strain my neck to take him into my mouth fully, the faint taste of latex coating my lips, mouth, and tongue. He's still rock hard from fucking me and I'm certain this won't take long.

I run my tongue down his shaft as I keep a tight suction with my lips. He groans and strokes my cheek. "Fuck, Kate, that feels so fucking good. Such a good fucking girl."

His moans and praises are totally doing it for me, reawakening the need in my pussy. My clit begins to throb, wanting to feel the same pleasure I'm providing him.

"Fuck, I'm so close," he says. Just as I'm certain he's about to come, he pulls out and throws his hand over his cock. A second later, he cums all over my chest. I watch it ooze out of him, my clit pulsing with his dick as though it's my own orgasm. I moan as he slows down and hollows out, his body releasing its tension.

Our eyes meet as he collects his breath. He collapses onto the bed next to me, never breaking eye contact. I get lost in his eyes, wanting more. I could go for round two after that blow job got me going again, but a glance at the nightstand reminds me that Char and I still have answers to get. I'm so close, yet so far. Another thought strikes me, my biggest fear with this plan. *What if the report's no longer in there?*

My stomach sinks but I renew my determination. It has to be in here, it just has to be.

"What's on your mind?" Lorenzo asks, his voice like molasses.

I'm about to say nothing, when I decide to go with a vague truth. "You."

He smiles, his eyes closed. I watch him as his chest resumes a normal breathing pattern. He looks so calm and peaceful, and I realize these are the only glimpses I get of this side of him. Something tells me they're reserved for me.

Sensing myself going into dangerous territory, I whisper, "Come on, let's get back to the party."

I loosen the tie and lift my head to remove it, tossing it onto his ribs. He pats it with his eyes sealed shut, then groans. "Fuck the party."

"Come on, it'll be fun. Isn't that what you're all about?"

He peeks at me and sighs. "Fine, let's go."

I sit up, prepared to leap off the bed, when I feel something trickle down my chest. I look down and see his cum leaking onto my stomach. Lorenzo must have been watching me because he swipes two fingers over it and rubs it into my skin. Then his fingers travel to the remains on my chest and rub those in, too.

"Marking your territory?" I tease.

"As much as I'd love for you to wear it the rest of the day, it is a pool party. Here." He leans over the bed and picks up a black tee that I didn't realize was down there. He hands it to me.

"Thanks," I say, wiping off the drying cum. His mention of the pool makes me wonder if he'd care about me only wearing my underwear in front of all these people.

I finish cleaning up and pass him the shirt back, which he barely grabs before tossing it back on the floor. When I shift to get off the bed and redress, he reaches for my wrist. "Kate."

"Yeah?" I turn and look down at him.

"Can you... um—" He looks so flustered, his eyes becoming more alert. "Will you stay with me tonight?"

"Oh." A blush creeps into my cheeks. "Um, yeah, of course."

I watch his eyes twinkle and I can feel that shift happening. The one where the blurred lines feel too blurred and everything that hasn't been said between us feels like a heavy weight I no longer want to carry. So I tear my eyes away and slide off the bed, putting my clothes and shoes back on.

CHAPTER TWELVE

March 17th

KATE

I have that just-fucked hair and pink-tinged cheeks, I can feel it. I run my hands through my hair meekly and search for my hat that Lorenzo tossed into the corner of the room. As I place it on my head, he puts his trunks back on and knots the tie around his neck.

I walk over to the door and pull it open as a sudden idea springs to mind. Lorenzo walks up and pauses next to me. "I'll lock it," I say with a small smile, trying to seem like I'm just being thoughtful. To my delight, it works. I twist the lock and instantly move it back so the click still sounds. I shut the door and follow Lorenzo back to the patio.

"Who are all these people?" I ask him.

"You met my friends from high school. Most of the rest are Santi's friends. We went to the same college, but he did a lot more socializing."

I nod, my eyes wandering across the different crowds of people. I spot Char and Larissa still in the pool, along with Maria and Melanie. I take a step forward then turn to check in with Lorenzo, who's watching me. "Go ahead. I'll catch up with you in a bit."

I nod, and our eyes linger for a moment before I head to the pool. All of them are in their bra and underwear, including Char. No one seems to care at all, though.

"Hey! Where the hell were you?" Larissa says as I kick my shoes off.

Crap. I didn't think this part through. "I—"

"Get your bathing suit and join us!" Char interjects. I meet her eyes and she winks. I look back to the pong table, finding my bag still tucked underneath. I jog over and grab it, then go inside to change. Once I've got my two-piece black bikini and sunscreen on, I stuff my clothes inside and wrap my towel around my body. I place my bag down on a patio chair and pull out my sun hat and glasses, then drop my towel on the deck near the stairs and wade into the pool.

"You came prepared," Maria says with no hidden sarcasm. I can't blame her for being bitter, so I don't feed into it.

"Yep. My dad had skin cancer and I don't need to follow in his footsteps."

Melanie and Larissa nod, and Char smiles proudly. "Good for you, toots."

While I have her attention, I give her the signal we discussed, rubbing my earlobe. I see in her eyes that my message registers, so I swim over to them grouped up in the water. We chit chat about random shit until Char says she needs to use the bathroom, which means she's going to do *it*. That sets all the butterflies in my stomach loose.

I watch her grab her towel and wrap it around her body before entering the house. Maria, Melanie, and Larissa keep talking, so I scan the party until my eyes land on Lorenzo. He's on the lawn, a cigarette hanging off his lips. I watch as he takes a drag but doesn't remove it, letting it dangle from the side of his mouth.

"Do you smoke?"

I turn to Larissa, embarrassed she caught me staring.

"Oh, no," I reply. Not that anyone in my family's had lung cancer, but it's a habit I have no intention of picking up. "You?"

"Nah, just the green stuff. Lorenzo won't smoke bud, though, just cigarettes."

"Oh," I say, unsure why she's telling me any of this. My buzz has mostly worn off post sex, but maybe she's drunk. I spot a group of cups by the poolside, remembering that while I was in Lorenzo's room, they were still partying. "Cigarettes are worse than weed, though, right?"

"As far as health goes, definitely. But my aunt, Zo's mom, died from a drug overdose. So he's pretty particular about what he'll use."

I peer at him again, my heart lurching for him. As though he can sense it, his gaze wanders to mine. The side where his cigarette is hanging tilts up, and he takes a pull. He turns back to Carter and D as he blows out the smoke. "Damn, I didn't know."

"Yeah, he doesn't talk about it. But I thought it was only fair that you know, seeing as you guys can't even keep it together at a party." My eyes widen but my shoulders relax when I realize she's teasing.

"He started smoking after she died."

"How old was he?"

"13."

13? That's a long time to be smoking.

Larissa must see the shock etched onto my face, because she adds, "He doesn't smoke too much, though. A few a day, max."

A few too many, in my opinion. I watch him again, and as he takes a pull, I find it hard to be upset. I have no idea what it's like to lose a parent, especially to something as terrible as drugs. Plus, he does look pretty sexy with it.

Larissa rejoins Maria and Melanie's conversation and I glance back at the house. Damn it, I got distracted with Larissa's information. How long has Char been in there? It should have only taken five minutes max. That was the agreed upon plan—get in there, snap a picture, get out. I drift over to the stairs and grab my towel, stepping up and wrapping it around myself. I pad over to my bag and pull out my phone but don't see anything from Char. I shoot off a message and nervously wait, rubbing my thumb for some sort of comfort.

When I don't receive a response after two minutes, I glance to where I last saw Lorenzo, finding him in the same spot. The cigarette is missing but he's still engrossed in conversation with the guys. I glance at the pool and around me, making sure no one's paying attention. I drop my phone into my purse and slip into the house.

When I reach the room, I open the door quietly and shut it behind me. Char's standing at Lorenzo's closet, a dresser drawer open. Her face is paler than I've ever seen it.

"What?" I whisper urgently, stalking over to her.

"Kate..."

"What?" I say a little louder. My nerves are shot with her behavior. Why is she at the dresser? The report was last in... I whip my head to the nightstand and see the drawer open. He must have moved it.

"This report was printed weeks before your date with Brad. Look." Her trembling fingers twist the page towards me. My stomach plummets when I see December 27th stamped on the top left.

"Okay... okay, but what can that mean?"

"Well, I read the report, and..." She points to the narrative and it takes me a moment to reread the line.

```
Victim advised he did not see the license plate
of V2 but described it as a black coupe.
```

I look up at her and her wide eyes meet mine. "Lorenzo's car..."

My brows furrow. "No... I..."

It can't be. I reread the line, my mind reeling. How did I never make that connection? And while my initial reaction was to deny it, the more I think about it... the more I *can't* deny it.

There are truths in life that are impossible to ignore once brought to light—that instinctual, inexplicable feeling in your gut. I know it in my heart of hearts—Lorenzo ran Brad off the road that night.

And didn't stop.

The same night he and I...

I throw a hand over my mouth.

Oh no. No, no, no, no, no.

My vision blurs and my heart thumps erratically.

"Kate, that's not all." She shifts the report in her hand to reveal a small bag. She grips it between her fingers.

"Is that—" I may have never done drugs, but I know what white powder is. "This doesn't..." My mind reels. Didn't Larissa just tell me mere minutes ago that his mom died from a drug overdose? I replay our conversation.

So he's pretty particular about what he'll use.

No, no, no. No! The room starts to spin before me and my hands feel shaky. I grab the report and reread that line. *A black coupe...*

The Audi. The car I've been learning to drive in. My hands have touched the steering wheel that ran Brad off the road. My fingers curl, feeling dirty from the sheer fact that they've been implicated in any way. Why wouldn't he have stopped?

My eyes shoot to the drugs in Char's hand, then to the open drawer. There are tons of bags, some fuller than others.

My head is shaking. I'm trying to speak but the words aren't forming. Char's hands grip my shoulders and I look at her face when she gives me a rough shake.

"Kate. Kate! We need to get out of here. Focus." I zero in on her eyes, her pupils reflecting the fear I feel. I nod slowly, trying to settle my pounding heart so it'll stop rushing blood through my veins.

Char gives my shoulders another shake but the room starts to spin faster. I lose my footing but her hands hold me up. "Kate! Let's go."

She grabs my hand and pulls me towards the door. I glance back and catch sight of the open nightstand drawer. "Wait," I mumble. "The... the drawer."

Char glances back, looks at me with concern, debating whether to just say fuck it or cover our tracks. She releases my hand and jogs over to the nightstand and dresser drawers, shutting them. My eyes linger on the used condom, still atop the nightstand. It's insane to think that not even thirty minutes ago, we were in here. Together. Him full of terrible secrets and me unable to imagine the severity of them.

Char replaces her hand in mine and we exit the room. "My bag," I whisper. The movement has my voice more sure, but it's a facade. I've moved into autopilot. Every atom in my body wants to move into a full blown panic attack, but Char's grip on my hand and our rush towards the front door grounds me enough that I don't succumb.

"Let's just leave it," she says in a rush.

"My phone's in there."

"Fuck. Fuck!" She glances around the living room, then towards the patio. "Okay. I'll go grab the bag real quick. Get outside and wait for me."

I nod. When she takes a step away, I say, "Our clothes."

She doesn't look back. "I'll try."

I watch her walk out, then beg my lead filled legs to move. I feel like there's extra gravity keeping me down, holding me hostage. My mind is going numb and I can't think. But I repeat two simple words.

Get out. Get out. Get out.

My legs finally cooperate. I focus on each step, slower than they should be. I pull the door knob and it feels like the door is made of stone. I don't realize I didn't shut the door until I'm down the walkway. By the time I turn around Char is rushing out of the house, shutting the door behind her with a slam.

"Come on, I'm ordering the Uber." Her phone is in her hand and she's typing away. My bag is slung on her shoulder but I don't see our clothes. "Thank god, there's someone three minutes away." She presses a few more buttons and then looks up at me.

"Our clothes," I say in monotone. I don't recognize my own voice. I'm like a zombie, focused on practical matters only, void of emotion.

He ran Brad off the road. He does drugs. He is a bad, bad man. I've been fucked by a bad, bad man.

"Kate!" Char's fingers are snapping in my face. "I know, toots, but I need you to hold it together until we're in the car."

She hoists the bag higher on her shoulder and grabs my hand, taking one glance behind her before dragging me to the road. An Uber pulls up after some amount of time, but how much it is, I have no idea. Time seems to have stopped existing for me.

She opens the passenger door and gives me a light push. I scoot into the car and she slides in after, slamming the door and patting the headrest in front of her. "Go, go," she tells the driver.

His eyebrows pinch together but he turns his head towards the road and accelerates. A tear is rolling down my cheek but I don't remember feeling like I needed to cry.

"Fuck," Char whispers. I turn right to find her looking out of the back window. I follow her line of sight, my eyes landing on Lorenzo. He's running down the driveway, coming to a sudden halt where the concrete meets the gravel road.

His desolate face fades from view as the car drives further away, then turns left.

The tears haven't stopped streaming.

CHAPTER THIRTEEN

March 17th

Zo

There are moments in life where you feel like you're in complete control. That's how I've always felt when I'm behind the wheel. The smooth leather under my assured fingers, the sound of the engine purring in my ears. The world's scenery blurred with my speed, my body alight with the adrenaline that courses through my veins.

It's one of the few times I feel alive.

Until I met her. Until I was buried deep in her pussy, when every inch of my bones sparked to life. I was more alive than I'd ever been. But I wasn't in control at all. Each time after, being near her was enough to feel that spark again, to feel just as alive and out of control.

That terrified me.

I knew the risks, but wanting her overshadowed them. My entire life has depended on my control. On my ability to limit what I say to who, what moves I make. To remain in a position of power in an utterly powerless situation. The resulting pain I've felt has never taken center stage, never held any ounce of importance. Because it doesn't matter. It doesn't change the fact that I'm here. That I have to do what I have to do.

But that pain has become a part of me. It's never what I focus on, but it's unignorable, nonetheless. Like a rotten apple, it eats at my core and reduces me to mere fragments of a man. It's a pain I'm accustomed to, but that doesn't change its potency.

And yet, that pain feels like a pinprick compared to what I feel now.

I'm running down the road, desperate to follow her, wishing for a way to turn back the clocks. To question Char when she was picking up her clothes from the pool deck and then stuffing them into her bag.

My own survival skills bit me in the ass. I didn't spring into action. I held back and watched, piecing together what she was doing before jumping to conclusions.

I knew she wasn't with her. I scanned the pool and lawn, confirming what my body already knew—she wasn't out here. I *always* feel her presence.

Once Char went into the house, I broke away from my friends and rushed inside. I still didn't feel her, but I refused to believe it. My trusted instincts had to be betraying me this time. There's no way this sense of doom could have validity.

I rushed to my room to find her, praying she was inside. The moment I put the key in and realized the door wasn't locked, every part of my body knew. My bones sparked but it wasn't from the current of feeling alive—it was the all-consuming fear I'd been trying to prevent from morphing into reality. I threw my door open, my eyes quickly scanning the room. Nothing seemed out of place, but I rushed to the closet. I threw the two drawers open, but only one was in disarray.

The one with the report.

"Fuck!" I yelled into the abyss.

I ran out of my room and out the front door, banging it into the wall in my haste. The car drove away in the next instant and I knew there was no way I'd catch her.

"Kate!" I shouted, knowing damn well the car wouldn't stop but unable to restrain myself. Char's head turned in my direction and her lips turned down, but the car kept moving and I couldn't see anything anymore.

My legs suddenly stopped, though I never told them to. My chest shrunk, my heart pounded. I couldn't breathe. I bent over and put my hands on my knees, forcing oxygen into my lungs so I wouldn't lose my ability to think.

My face felt wet. I looked towards the sky as I reached a finger to my cheek, certain it had to be raining. But it wasn't. And then I realized it was from tears. I remembered the last time I cried—ten years ago. If it hadn't been for the moisture, I wouldn't have known I was crying at all. My heart is hollow, intentionally numbed so I don't have to acknowledge just how miserable this life really is for me.

I heard the sob erupt from my chest and I did the only thing I knew how to.

I ran.

I'm still running.

I run until my eyes can't see and my ears can't hear and my mouth can't breathe.

I run until all I can feel is the desperate need to stay alive.

I run until all I can feel is the *illusion* of control.

Chapter Fourteen

March 17th

Zo

Time has ceased to exist. I'm not sure how I ended up sprawled on the driveway, my hands and legs splayed out. My chest rises and falls in failed attempts to recover my breath. I alternate between staring directly into the sun until all I can see is black and squeezing my eyes shut until they're filled with bright dots.

I need to dry these signs of weakness. I need to remember why I do this.

She knows. She knows. She knows.

"Zo, the fuck, man?" Santi's voice is elusive and distant, and I can't be sure it's not a memory streaming from the depths of my mind. I'm certain I'm imagining the footsteps growing louder until there's a nudge in my ribs. I force my eyes open, Santi's tall and muscular frame blocking out the sky.

"What's wrong?" The alarm in his voice should ground me, but I'm still spiraling in this foreign abyss.

I reply with the only words loud enough to be heard. "She knows."

Santi and I are kindred spirits. While we may have different personalities, we understand certain things about this life that no one else ever will. That's why it takes him less than a second to comprehend my meaning. Understanding flashes through his eyes and then—panic.

"I fucking told you it was idiotic. You put us at risk!" he yells at me, and I know he's right, but I'm so numb I don't care. I say nothing.

"Get the fuck up! We need to run recon on this! We need to contact Ted—"

"Control yourself." My eyes cut to his. As frozen as I feel, I'm still acutely aware of what he just shouted in a somewhat public setting.

He lets out a maniacal laugh. "Me? Control myself? This wouldn't be happening if you could keep your dick in your pants. But nooo, Zo has to go and fuck the *only* woman that poses a threat—"

"Shut your *fucking* mouth!" My body lurches, forcing me upright. "You don't know what the fuck you're talking about!"

"You don't know what the fuck *you're* talking about!" Santi roars back, yanking me by the arm and forcing me to stand. "You think you feel something for this chick, but you can't even see through your own bullshit!" He points an accusing finger at my heaving chest. "This is an act of rebellion."

Bile threatens to rise in my throat. "Shut the fuck up."

"I get it, man. We're in shitty positions. But that's not an excuse to—"

My fist lands on his mouth and I can't even say I regret it. He's my brother in every sense of the word, but he's pissing me off and pretending to understand when he doesn't.

Santi smiles sickeningly, blood painting his pearly whites. "I'm going to let that one slide because you're obviously going through some shit. But"—he cracks his knuckles—"lay so much as a finger on me again, and you'll be seeing stars."

Stars.

My breathing is erratic, and my fists are itching—*begging*—to lay into him again. But I know he means what he says. It's not that I'm afraid; I know we can handle each other. But a brawl is the last thing we need.

Instead, I turn and grab the first thing my eyes land on—one of the two perfectly placed pots at the head of our driveway. They rest in front of the brick walls outlining the garage, manicured biweekly by the person hired to keep up our front. No one would ever guess that they have cameras built into them to protect us. To protect our mission.

The clay pot is heavy with dirt, but the anger fueling me makes it weigh as light as a feather. I slam it into the front bumper of my car, the resounding crack of shattered ceramic satisfying me, filling me with a sense of power.

Illusion.

The soil splatters everywhere. All over the hood of the car I used to love, the driveway filled with dirty secrets, and my chest housing a black pit for a heart. I drop the pieces and locate the microscopic piece of equipment that would stare through a hole in the pot. I pick it up and slam it into the brick wall of this brick house built on brick lies.

The camera falls to pieces on the ground that supports all our deceptions, so I dig my phone out of my pocket and keep slamming. Once it's shattered, I pull out my pack of smokes, a sick satisfaction filling me as the cigarettes disintegrate and join the debris of destruction.

With nothing left to break, I repeatedly slam my fist into the house because I don't know what else to do. There's nothing else I *can* do. I can't explain the truth to her. I can't leave this all behind.

She knows. She knows. She knows.

I'm not sure how much time passes before Santi's firm grip on my shoulder forces me to whip my head to him, my fist halting mid-air.

His eyes are filled with pity and sympathy, and that's what does it. That's what breaks me. It puts the last crack in whatever flimsy glue was holding me together.

I crumple to the ground with my face in my bloody, throbbing hands and those wretched sobs wreak my body once more, the sound mingling with the distant party as the world goes on.

Chapter Fifteen

March 21st

Kate

Lorenzo's foot won't come off the pedal, no matter how much I beg and plead. Why can't he just slow down? We could—

My heart races as the car veers off the road, jostling over the uneven ground. I scream and shout as though that will stop the inevitable. I brace myself for the impact, but the moment the car slams into the thick trunk, the scene transforms. It's no longer Lorenzo in the driver's seat. It's Brad.

A beeping starts in the distance, but I can't peel my eyes away from the blood oozing from Brad's forehead, his eyes rolling dangerously into his head.

I haven't stopped screaming.

The beeping has become incessant. Tremors of anxiety course through me as my nerves skyrocket. Why won't it stop? Just shut it off!

Shut. It. Off.

I shoot up in bed, sweat trickling down my face with my heart ready to beat out of my fragile chest. I'd hoped the recurring nightmare was a one-off the night after we left his house, but now I'm afraid they're here to stay.

I shut off the alarm on my phone and stare at the time: 7:00 a.m. It would be time to get ready for work, if I was going.

I'd never called out sick in the four plus years of working at Valeri Financials, but today will be my third day in a row.

But it's not a total lie, is it? Is there really such a difference between a fever and a burning heart? Both mean something is wrong. Both mean I'm not functioning at my full potential. Unlike a fever, which helps my body fight the illness, a burning heart is slowly turning me to ash.

I would trade this torment for a hospital stay any day of the year.

How could I have been so naïve? How did I not piece together that Lorenzo *ran Brad off the road?* How could I not know he was using drugs?

Char suggested I take it easy and spend some time at home before deciding how to handle this. Because I have to turn him in, right? I have to let someone know—*anyone* know—that it's *his* fault Brad was in the hospital with a concussion. It's *his* fault Brad didn't show up for our date on December 22nd.

It's *his* fault we ever met at all.

I fall back onto my pillow and squeeze my eyes shut, willing myself to wake up from whatever nightmare this information has made my life. I was never supposed to be responsible for the culprit in Brad's accident.

I was never supposed to be responsible for turning in the person I was falling for.

Tears stream down my face as my entire body tightens with the suppressed sobs and screams. None of this is right, none of this is fair.

It's agonizing to reconcile the idea that I'm even *willing* to let him get away with his crime so he doesn't have to face the consequences, all because of my inexplicably irrational feelings for him.

I have justifications, sure. Brad didn't die. He had insurance. For all I know, it was truly an accident and everyone makes mistakes.

It's still wrong.

There's no excuse for leaving someone after you caused them to crash into a tree. What if Brad had died? Or been gravely injured? Lorenzo was fine with whatever outcome because he didn't stop. He. Didn't. Stop.

Was he high? Was he laughing as he sped away? Was anyone with him?

And what does this make me? An accomplice? What about Char? She's implicated in this, too. She knows just like I do. Is she going to do something about it?

She had to go back to get her car at some point, and I have no idea when she did it or if she had to see Santi or Lorenzo. I haven't looked at any of the messages or missed calls on my phone since we left his house. I haven't even had the energy to turn off the recurring weekday alarm that's set. The only message I've sent was the one to Jasmine letting her know I'm sick and that I'll return when I'm feeling better.

But I can't avoid it forever. I pick up my phone and finally turn off the set alarm, then sift through the missed notifications from the past few days. When I see Lorenzo's messages from after we left his house, I don't hesitate to read them.

Lorenzo: please let me explain

Lorenzo: it looks bad but i swear i can explain

Lorenzo: kate

He can *explain*? It *looks* bad? I guess I shouldn't be so shocked that he reached out, but there's nothing he can say that will make this better. He ran a man off the road! With trembling fingers, I block his number and move on to my other messages.

Char: how are you feeling?

Char: just picked up my car. I had the driver slow down at the end of the street to make sure no one was outside.

Char: I'm getting worried. I'll give you until tomorrow before I break your door down.

Jasmine: Feel better soon!

Mom: hope you had a great weekend honey

I need to prioritize. First, I shoot off a text to Jasmine, explaining that I'm still not feeling well. *Fuck*. I don't know what I'm going to do about work. How am I ever supposed to face him again?

I shoot off a text to Char, letting her know I'm safe and just resting. She replies immediately, saying to call her if I need anything.

I need a way out of this. I need a way to reverse time so I can go back to never having this knowledge. To making the choice to fuck off with him and keeping myself clueless. Better yet, to never having met him at all. To walking out of that bar and ignoring Trent's attempts to make me feel even shittier than I already did.

But the truth never stays hidden, and while ignorance is an easier pill to swallow, it rots you from the inside.

I've hardly slept the last two nights, and the sleep I *did* get was restless and disturbed. I toss a pillow over my head and hope to drift into a peaceful sleep, knowing it's futile. I haven't slept right since the St. Patrick's Day party. The day everything changed because I was too nosy for my own damn good.

It's a good thing you were nosy. If you weren't, you wouldn't know.

And if I didn't know, maybe I would be cuddled up next to him right now. We never cuddled before, but he'd never asked me to stay the night, either.

My heart aches with the reminder, wishing more than anything that I could turn back the clock and return to the time when I was in the dark.

I sigh, shutting my eyes despite my alert mind. It starts to do what it's done on an endless loop these last few days—it cycles through all the memories of us. Meeting him at the bar, the shock of seeing him again at Rowan's party, all the stolen looks when his eyes said more than his words ever could.

His hand on my throat as he thrust into me in the broom closet, me completely at his mercy and him taking what was his.

Then, something happens that hasn't before. My clit responds to the thought. My eyes shoot open, staring into my poorly lit room.

An orgasm could help me sleep... and after everything, lord knows I could use some sort of release.

I reach into my nightstand drawer, pulling out my purple friend. Excitement and lust fill me, and I wonder why I haven't thought of this sooner.

I turn her on and push her into my underwear, suddenly desperate to feel *something* that isn't pain and confusion and guilt. The vibration on my clit is immediately effective, transporting me back to my recollections.

I replay us in that closet, him thrusting deep into me and squeezing my throat as he nuzzles into it. He breathes me in, and I meet his dilated eyes, thrilling me with the look of pure need.

I moan into the loneliness of my room as my body tenses, already too close for my liking. I want this elation to permanently take over every sense of my being.

And then it stops.

"Fuck!" I toss the dead vibrator on the bed and shove my hand into my panties. My middle finger takes over the job, dipping into my pussy and restoring the place of pure joy as it works my clit.

My imagination moves from the broom closet, to the car, to his room, to the guest bedroom, finally settling on a fabrication I didn't realize I yearned for: us here in my room.

He's never even been to my apartment.

That thought evaporates just as quickly as it arrived. His face is between my legs, and he's sucking and gripping and devouring. I increase the small movements of my finger, using my other hand to slip two fingers into my pussy. They slide right in.

I curl them and pulse as my middle finger moves faster still. His voice in my mind sends me over the edge.

Come for me, my good little princess.

I fall apart, moaning his name for no one to hear, my legs quivering as I do. I still, floating on a cloud where nothing can harm me, and no one can bring me down. As it fades away, like every good thing ever does, the ache returns to my chest.

What I wouldn't give to change all of this, to make it so he was just a regular guy so I could be his wholly and unequivocally.

But that will never be. My orgasm morphs into sleep, and I pray my dreams will at least let me pretend.

Because ignorance really is bliss.

))) ● (((

I'm back in the same nightmare, but instead of the beeping waking me up, it's the pounding on a door. I shoot up again, the pillow that was covering my face tumbling onto the floor as Felix dashes off in fear.

The very *real* knock at my front door has me shoving the covers off my legs and throwing on shorts under the long tee I slept in. When I look through the peephole, I'm shocked to find Larissa's face staring expectantly at the door.

I open it thoughtlessly and instantly regret it when she takes a look at my disoriented face. I pat a hand over my hair to control the frizzy bed-head. "Larissa, what—"

"Can I come in?" she says, pushing the door open and barreling past me before I can respond.

"Uh, sure, I—"

"Kate, are you okay?" she asks, plopping onto my couch and eyeing me warily.

"Um—" I don't know how to answer that question, so I go with the socially acceptable answer. "Yeah, I'm good."

I blink a few times and circle the coffee table to sit at the other end of the couch, becoming more alert.

What is she doing here? How did she even know where I live?

"Zo called me. He asked me to come check on you."

What? "Why?"

She shrugs. "I was hoping you could tell me."

My brows cinch together. "How should I know?"

She pins me with a disbelieving stare. "He seemed to be concerned that you haven't been at work. He wanted to make sure you were okay."

"Oh. Um, yeah, I... I'm not feeling well. I called out."

She eyes me warily before accepting my response with a nod.

"What time is it?" I ask.

"10:30. Sorry I woke you."

"No, it's fine," I reply, my brain still trying to catch up to what's happening. *He was worried about me?* "Why did he send you?"

"I guess he couldn't leave work."

"Oh." Of course. "How did you know where I live?"

"He texted me the address."

"But he's never..." He's been to my complex but I've never brought him upstairs. I never had a reason to give him my apartment number. "How did he have my apartment number?"

"I don't know, Kate. He seemed worried and asked me to check on you."

I'm dumbfounded, and it must show all over my face because Larissa's eyes fill with that dreaded look I hate—pity.

"Did something happen?" she asks, tentatively placing a hand on my knee.

"What? No, nothing happened. Everything's fine." My words come out rushed, and I want her to leave. Now.

"Are you sure? I—"

"I really appreciate you stopping by, but like I said, I'm not feeling well." I fake a cough for emphasis, and she slides her hand off my knee.

She eyes me dubiously, but what choice does she have other than to believe me? *Look into your cousin if you want to find lies. Unless... does she know, too?* "Sorry for waking you. I'll go."

She stands up and I rise with her, ready to lock the door the moment she steps out. As much as I love her, she's a tie to Lorenzo, and this puppet is cutting her strings.

"No problem!" I say a little too emphatically. The moment she walks out the door, I slam it shut and fall back against the cold metal. I close my eyes for a moment, then rush to my room and yank my phone off the charger, dialing Char's number.

"Kate?"

"I need to pack and get the fuck out of here!" I've become frantic, desperate to leave all of this behind.

"What's going on?" Char's worry forces me to take a deep breath and calm down for a moment. But *only* a moment.

"Larissa just showed up at my apartment."

"Lari?" Char asks, clearly bewildered. We haven't spoken in days, and I'm not making much sense right now. I fill her in on the brief interaction while I pull my suitcase out of my closet. I start ripping my clothes off their hangers and stuffing them inside.

"Okay, let's think about this rationally. Is there any access to your personal information at work?" Char asks.

"I don't know," I say, not having considered that possibility in my frenzy. But open access to my personal information has to be a breach of privacy. "Wait..."

The memory of him finding out about my job search rings a bell, forcing me to think more about it. Did he really just happen upon that information? What if he pulled it?

What if he has access to more at that company? After all, they do live in a house owned by Rowan Valeri himself.

"Kate. Kate! What?"

"My mind is racing right now. I can't think straight!" I drop the last articles of clothing into my luggage and rub the bridge of my nose. "Look, I can't stay here. I know this may seem dramatic, but I don't want him having any access to me."

"What about your job?"

I tear my glasses off my nightstand and shove them on my face with newfound resolve. "I guess I'm quitting."

CHAPTER SIXTEEN

March 22nd

Zo

"If she hasn't gone to the police and you haven't heard from the victim, the chances of her saying anything are minimal," Ted says calmly. I glance at Santi, who looks as unconvinced as I do.

"So, what, we're supposed to ride this out? Hope for the best?" I snarl, my fists balling at my sides.

"You two fucked up. I'm not sure when this became my problem, but there's nothing I can do. Only *if* she brings this to light is there a possibility of my involvement."

I grit my teeth with hatred at the fact that he's right. *We fucked up.* It haunts me, knowing Brad was hurt and there was nothing I could do about it once it was done. We couldn't stop. Taking the blame was a risk we couldn't afford. Santi knows this. I know this. Ted knows this.

We've made our peace with it.

"May I remind you, Ted, that her friend also knows," Santi says through clenched teeth.

"Yes, yes. But the fact remains. Unless they say something, there is nothing for us to do. Until then, keep your mouths shut, and stay away from them." He looks between us, and when I open my mouth to speak, he cuts me short. "Don't even think about asking for a tail. We can't afford to follow around a loosely potential woman when we're this close. All of our monies need to be reserved."

My jaw clamps shut because goddamn it, I know he's right, but I don't want to accept that. Accept a life where I get to know nothing about what she's doing? It's a special kind of hell.

I don't know if she replied to the messages I sent in my moment of desperation *before* my phone was smashed to pieces. If it weren't for the fact that I know the best thing to do is to stay away from her, I'd have shown up on her doorstep by now.

Sending Larissa was an impulsive move; I shouldn't be pulling her information at work. While I'm highly aware of the fragility of her and Char knowing about the accident, the priority is making sure she's safe. Facing the consequences is one thing, but knowing something's happened to her... I would never survive it.

Ted breaks me from my thoughts by opening the top drawer of his desk, pulling out a small black phone. He hands it to me with a stern glare. "Don't break it this time."

I nod and stuff the crappy burner into my pocket, my healing scabs rubbing against the black jeans.

"What's her friend's name?" Ted asks Santi.

Santi's jaw clenches. "Char, presumably Charlotte. We didn't get her last name."

Ted tsks. "You two have gotten sloppy. We've made a lot of progress, and I'd hate for it to go to waste."

Santi and I exchange a look before nodding and slowly rising out of our seats in front of Ted's desk. He returns his focus to his computer, quietly dismissing us.

Once we're outside of the office building, we do a quick sweep of the lot before getting into the car, removing our jackets and tossing them into the backseat.

"He's got a point, man," Santi says, staring out the window as I pull onto the road. "And Jesus Christ, would you slow the fuck down?"

"Not you, too," I tell him, pulling a smoke from the pack.

"Zo, we have a major problem here, no matter what Ted fucking says! We're in the clear for now, but we've got another vulnerability on us. Reckless driving's what got us into this goddamn position!"

"Us?" I scoff, taking a drag from my cigarette.

"Don't," Santi says venomously. My eyes freeze over as I clench the steering wheel, letting off the gas. "And since when do you smoke in the car?"

"Since I stopped giving a fuck about it," I reply, flicking the ash out of the half-cracked window. Lou owns a body shop and was able to repair the front bumper, making it as though nothing ever happened. As though the very *real* pain of this past Saturday was merely a figment of my imagination.

"You're sure she wasn't at work?" Santi asks as he rolls his own window down.

"Positive." I can always feel when she's around; a low thrum in my blood. Still, I walked past her desk every day. She wasn't in the break room, either. It's not like I can ask Rowan or Marco; that would bring too much attention to her. Us.

There is no us.

I was on the brink of sending Lari back to her apartment when I decided that we should talk to Ted. Maybe he'd know what to do, and we had to pick up my phone, anyway.

Useless prick.

"Maybe Ted was right," Santi repeats, toying with his steel lip ring. "Maybe... she won't say anything. *They* won't say anything."

"Let's fucking hope," I grit out. The part that Santi is failing to understand is that this isn't just about our safety. This is about the fact that I have to lose her. That there are bigger things to worry about.

"If what you say is true... if there really was more to it..."

My cheeks flare with heat. "You callin' me a liar?"

"'Course not. You feeling that strongly towards her means she probably felt the same way. And that... might be the only thing that saves our sorry asses."

CHAPTER SEVENTEEN

March 23rd

KATE

"Kate. Kate!" Char's urgent voice jolts me awake. My body is scorching, sticking to the sheets like I'm some sort of glue stick. She stops shaking me when my eyes fly open.

"What happened?" I mumble groggily.

"You were screaming and thrashing," she says hesitantly. As I sit up, she takes a step back from the bed while studying me closely.

The memory of the nightmare washes over me: Lorenzo snorting a line of cocaine while Santi laughed at Brad's body lying in a heap in the black sedan that was crumpled against a tree.

"Nightmare," I whisper. She nods in understanding, her forehead creased with concern.

"Can I get you anything?"

"Water," I croak. She rushes out of the room and returns a minute later with a clear glass of ice water. I take a large gulp, allowing the liquid to cool me down.

Moving on, as it turns out, is a lot easier said than done. It's easy enough to distract myself during the day. But at night, when I'm unconscious, these demons feast on my vulnerability. The raw guilt, the longing for him—it's far too consuming.

It's been nearly a week, but the permanence of his absence shatters my heart into a million irreparable pieces. Not in the way glass shatters. In the way that something gets so hot it has no choice but to burn, eventually resorting to destroyed ruins of powdery residue. Even though I knew it was always just for then, I wanted it to be for always. And the fact that *this* was the reason for our end is the part that hurts the most.

But I can't look past a literal crime in which he didn't care about another person's injuries.

"When do you start at the new branch?"

"I don't know. Jasmine said it shouldn't be a problem, but I'm waiting to hear back."

When I got to Char's Wednesday night, she suggested switching branches rather than quitting. I've always loved my job, and this way, I wouldn't have the added stress of job hunting.

I came up with the excuse that my apartment had a pipe burst, which made it uninhabitable. That's the kind of thing that happens when you get involved with liars. You're spun into their web and the only way out is to resort to dishonesty yourself.

I told Jasmine I'd have to move back in with my parents, and the commute would be lengthy. She agreed and said she'd talk to Rowan, but seeing as it's already 11 am on a Friday, I doubt I'll hear anything before Monday.

While Char's place is a *hair* closer to Grove Shores, I'll still be tacking on time to my commute. Not to mention, I don't own a car and barely know how to drive, so getting to and from work will be a pain in the ass.

My chest caves in when I get a flashback of Lorenzo's driving lessons.

"Hey," Char says softly. "Everything's going to be okay."

I nod once and then shake my head, breaking down again. My forehead aches from the pressure in my face. She sits on the bed and hugs me while I sob.

I wish I had never met him. I wish he'd never run Brad off the road, so we would have had our first date. Maybe I could have liked Brad if I hadn't met Lorenzo.

But I *did* meet him.

It all happened, and the only thing left to do is accept it and move on.

"There are just so many unanswered questions," Char muses, wiping the last tear running down my cheek.

"I know," I say, wiping the snot dripping out of my nose with the back of my hand. "But I don't care to learn anymore. I'm done. I should have listened to you before, I should have..." We've talked this whole thing in circles, like a song stuck on repeat.

"I know, but it's okay. Shit happens," Char says.

"Are you sure you're okay with this?" I ask.

"Of course, you and Felix can stay as long as you need."

"Thank you. But I was referring to... not saying anything." I can't voice the truth out loud. I can't utter the cold facts of what he did.

"Look. We don't know with one hundred percent certainty."

I peg her with a cynical look. "It's pretty clear, Char."

"I'm not saying I don't *believe* it's true, but we're still just putting the pieces together. It's not like we saw it happen."

"That doesn't make me feel any better."

"My point," she continues as though I hadn't spoken, "is that I'm okay with it because I don't know for a fact that it's true. If you don't want to report it, I don't either. I'm on your team, toots."

I stare at my lap, searching for answers or guidance that might be hiding between my fingertips.

"Don't beat yourself up," Char says sympathetically. "Brad was okay, and it probably *was* just an accident."

Probably. The word that's not enough, and leaves the door open for all other doubt. *What else is he hiding?*

"He's obviously bad news, anyway. I mean, damn, cocaine? I dabbled with it in college, but that's never something I'd, like, keep in my bedroom drawer."

In my book, cocaine doesn't hold a candle to having run someone off the road and not caring to make sure they're okay. "I don't want to sink back into this hellhole of emotions. I've ruminated long enough, and it's time to move on."

"I think it will get a lot easier once you've moved branches. And who knows, maybe in a week or two, you'll feel safe enough to return home."

Safe. Because I have no real idea who he is anymore. I never did. He ran Brad off that road, and he didn't give a shit about it. He was able to give Larissa the address to my apartment. He denied stalking me before, and I was a fool to believe his excuses.

"Oh my god!" I shout suddenly.

"What?" Char replies with alarm.

"Promise me something, though."

"What?"

"If you actually do decide to date Brad, tell me."

"Do you think..." It's the only real explanation. That's why he kept insisting he wasn't jealous. *"That's* why he cared about my date with Brad."

It only takes a second for the understanding to dawn on Char. "Fuck. That's insidious."

My stomach rolls as a new sense of determination fills me: these are the last tears I will weep over this walking red flag of a man. "I'm done with him."

"Good riddance," Char agrees, standing up and clapping her hands. "I have to get some work done, but why don't we do a self-care day when I finish? Mani-pedi's, shopping, dinner... the whole shebang," Char offers.

"That sounds perfect," I say, my voice sounding more assured.

Char picks up on it and beams at me. "Great! Give me a few hours."

Once she leaves the room, I get up and make her bed. I focus on the soft, rose-colored linens and matching fluffy pillows as I sniff the remaining clogs out of my nose. The nicely made bed instantly lifts my spirits, making me feel a little more capable and put-together.

I head to the bathroom to shower and brush my teeth, realizing I have nothing else to keep busy with. I'm not used to being unemployed. What if Jasmine tells me that they won't let me relocate?

That fear drives me to spend the next few hours working on my resumé and searching for open positions on various websites. I don't apply to any of the postings yet, though I most definitely won't be applying for the accountant position at the company Brad works for. There's no way I can stomach keeping this secret in his presence.

The guilt gnaws at me already.

My preferred option is to remain with Valeri Financials. The pay is good, and I like what I do there; I just don't want to have to see Lorenzo.

"You think I want to think about you constantly?"

"To feel like I need you?"

"Please know that I do care about you, Kate."

His words have started to haunt me. Shaking my head, I close my laptop, feeling productive if nothing else. Just as I've stowed it in my bag, Char bursts into the room and claps her hands together.

"Okay, I cleared the pertinent things I had to handle. Time for some self-love!"

"Are you sure? I don't want you to fall behind because of me."

"Kate, stop. These are the perks of running your own business," she says with a flippant wave. Char has such a flair about her. I can't help but envy how she can effortlessly go with the flow, unconsumed by the chaos. Even the outfit she wears—tight ripped jeans, a flowy pink and light green striped blouse, and beige wedges—exudes her laid-back energy.

"Let's grab a late lunch, too. I'm starving," she adds, digging through her makeup box and pulling out mascara and eyeliner. I gaze at my reflection in her floor-length mirror, contemplating the message my simple black linen dress conveys. Perhaps the spaghetti straps and three brown buttons speak to my desire to break free from my constraints.

Shaking off the thoughts, I pull my phone off the charger, causing the screen to illuminate. I scroll through my notifications, tapping on a message from an unsaved contact.

Unknown number: a week out of work is unlike you and I
just need to know youre ok

It can't be...

"Char!" I exclaim, shoving the phone in her face. A moment later, her eyes search mine quizzically.

"Is it...?"

I nod, glancing back down at the message. "I can't... I can't respond." Thank the heavens for dresses with pockets; I shove the phone in.

"Is he seriously going to act like we didn't go through his drawer? I mean, he has to know... right?" Char muses.

"It doesn't matter. We did. That's all that matters."

Char nods affirmatively and I brush past her to wait in the living room. I don't want to keep going back down this path. I hate the pull he has on me, and the only way to sever the tie is to cut it altogether.

CHAPTER EIGHTEEN

March 24th

Zo

"Come in," I shout in reply to the knock at my door. Santi slides in and gives my messy room a once over before his eyes land on mine.

"I'm inviting the crew over," he informs me.

"Cool."

"You gonna join us?"

"Nah."

He stares at me intently. While I hate the way he's scrutinizing me, I can't say I blame him. I'd do the same if the roles were reversed.

His concern for me is not unfounded. I've resorted to doing the bare minimum. I go to work, I go to the gym, I come home. I've hardly spoken to him or anyone else.

I was always a shell of a man, but now I have no form. I'm lifeless. Even our mission has lost its appeal to keep me driven, to keep me going. I didn't ever think I could feel worse than I used to.

How wrong I was.

It's all because of *her*. She never responded to my message. But how can I hold that against her? She's protecting herself, and that is the one thing that keeps me hanging on. I never should have gotten as close to her as I did. It was always too risky—for both of us. I knew that, even if she didn't.

If I ever get caught, if Santi ever gets caught, we'd have wasted our time with nothing to show for it. We'd be up shit's creek without a paddle. Very likely without a goddamn boat, left to sink into the middle of whatever ocean our fathers threw us in.

"You can't lock yourself away forever."

"I know," I respond dryly. *It's hardly been a week, asshole.*

"Well, if you change your mind, we'll be out back."

"Got it." He eyes me one more time before turning on his heel. As he reaches the door, I ask him to bring me a beer. He nods without looking back. He returns a moment later with a glass of Fireball on ice, unlike I asked. But he had the right idea, bringing me my favorite drink.

He leaves it on my nightstand, and I wait 'til the door snaps shut behind him to sip on it.

Is this who I've become? Some lovesick sap who's nursing a broken heart?

Nah. It runs deeper than that, and I know it. Yes, I'm broken because I'm missing Kate. Just *thinking* her name causes my body to shudder. But it's the fact that I *have* to miss her. None of this would be happening if it weren't for the fact that Santi and I were thrown into matters we never should have been in.

I wish I had something to remember her by. Fuck, even a used condom just to have *some* physical representation of her. To know it was real—her, my feelings, all of it.

I down my drink quickly, the sudden impulse to lose myself to lady alcohol taking priority. I shuffle to the kitchen in my black basketball shorts and take the bottle from the counter, returning to my room with every intention of downing the entire thing.

Half an hour and two-thirds of a bottle of Fireball later, and I'm sliding my hand into my shorts. My dick is throbbing because I can't get her out of my head. I haven't been able to this entire week. She always made me feel such peace whenever I was around her, and this week has been anything but.

Now that the liquor is flowing through my system, the thoughts have morphed from missing her essence to memories of being inside her. In the guest bedroom, in the car, in the office... in this very room. I fist my cock, needing the release from these thoughts of her.

It quickly feels like not enough.

I wish I had her in this bed with me, right now, so I could thrust my dick deep inside her while she whimpers and moans. She could tell me how much she likes it while I force her to stop talking by wrapping my hand around her throat.

I'd never truly want to control her; on the contrary, I want to help her release her inhibitions.

But there's something so goddamn sexy about my hand wrapped around one of her most vulnerable areas...

I groan and leap up, hovering over my empty bed. I stop moving my hand and instead thrust my cock into it, steadily increasing the motion of my hips. Closing my eyes, I imagine her squirming under me as my thrusts get rougher and harder.

Zo, you feel so good. Please, don't stop.

Her voice in my head is the soundtrack to this unfiltered desire coursing through me, demanding its release. She's never once called me Zo, but I secretly wish she would. Only those closest to me do.

I shift the hand propping me up to press into the mattress as though it was wrapped around her neck. Her breathy moans fade in my mind because she can no longer breathe properly. My hips move at a chaotic speed, the bed frame banging into the wall. I can't bring myself to give a damn about anyone hearing me.

My breaths become ragged with my exertion, but I don't smell the air within my walls. It's her strawberry scent that fills my mind, regardless of being imagined. I would do absolutely anything to be filled with it again, to have it bottled so I could have it with me at all times.

I cum all over the crumpled sheets, collapsing into the hand that was holding me up. The moment the euphoria passes, her voice whispers one more thing.

I need you.

Fuck. I tumble into the bed, avoiding my cum, and force my breathing to return to normal. Tears prick my eyes. I'm so *fucking* angry. This isn't fair. And while the orgasm was fulfilling in the moment, it's proving to do the exact opposite of what I needed it to.

I crave her even more now.

Fixing my shorts, I hop out of bed, tearing the bed sheet off the mattress and tossing it into the corner of my room before grabbing a shirt from my dresser drawer. I take a swig from the bottle and wander into the front yard as I order an Uber that will take me to her. With what intention, I have no clue. I just need to see her. I need to explain all of this to her.

Consequences be *fucking* damned.

When I arrive at her complex, I race up the stairs and pound on her door. I never should have pulled her address from the database at work, but I won't regret it when I see her face in a moment. Leaning my forehead on the cool metal, the booze swims through my head, and the effects become more pronounced with every passing second. After what seems to be hours, I pound on the door again.

When the door doesn't open, I pound on it a third time. Then a fourth time. Then a fifth.

Mid-sixth-pounding, a door opens, but it's not the one under my fist. I groggily turn my head right, then left, my eyes landing on a brunette woman in the neighboring unit. There's a child cowering behind her legs, and I instantly think of Santi's little brother.

"Do you need help?" the woman asks.

"I..." Words are a lot harder to process when you're drowning in liquor and your own misery. "I'm looking for someone."

The woman's eyes linger on Kate's door before landing on me. "I don't think she lives there anymore."

My heart sinks, plummeting to the depths of my own miserable, disgusting body. "Wha..."

I have no words. I slump against the door and sink to the floor, though that may be a result of the drunkenness I've now reached. Normally, I would have noticed that I don't feel her on the other side. *Goddamn Fireball.*

The lady glances down both sides of the hallway before looking at me again. "Are you sure you don't need help?"

Her tone seems worried, but what is there to worry about? Everything's peachy keen. Great. Fucking fantastic.

"I'm good, ma'am. Give me a moment and I'll get out of your hair."

I stare at her until she comes into focus, realizing she looks a little frightened. Is that because of me?

She pushes her kid back into her apartment and follows him, shutting the door. I dig my phone out of my pocket and dial Santi's number.

"What's up, Zo?" he answers.

"How's Ryan?" I slur. I shove my palm into the ground and force myself to sit upright.

"Ryan? Hold on, I'm coming," he says.

"Don't bother, she's not home."

"Who's not home? Zo, where the *fuck* are you?"

"I had to try... And see her... I had to..." I start sliding against the door again, but I force myself back up. I shake my head, willing my bloodshot eyes to focus on the wall in front of me.

"Bro, what the fuck are you doing?" He doesn't sound angry anymore. More like he's at a loss. "I'll come get you."

"Nah, nah, I'm good. I'm coming back."

"Now." It's not a question.

"Now."

"Dude, what the fuck?" Santi rushes me the moment I walk up the driveway.

"Quit overreacting. I'm fine."

"You've gotta cut this out, Zo. She's..." He continues talking, but his voice is blocked out by the darkness of my mind. I don't realize I'm falling until Santi catches me.

"I'm good, I'm good!" I shout, forcing my eyes open. His wide stature blurs into focus, and I give him a cheeky grin.

"Come sit out back with us," Santi demands.

"Oh, everyone's here?" I grin, barreling past him. I'm ready for a distraction. I stumble over the step down to the patio, finding six familiar faces staring at me wide-eyed as I right myself.

"What's wrong, Zo?" Lari says, rushing out of her seat and over to me.

"Wrong? Nothing's wrong!" But she has to steady me by the shoulders when I start swaying.

"Come sit," she says, guiding me to the patio sofa and nudging me into the right seat before taking the left.

"He's a little drunk, if you can't tell," Santi says, taking a seat next to Carter.

"Fucking hell, bro," D says from my right.

"How are you, D?" I ask, patting him on the back with so much force, he lurches forward in his seat. He confuses me by frowning. Isn't he happy to see me?

"I'm good, man. You good?" he asks, arching an eyebrow.

"Great! Fantastic! Never fucking better." Maybe if I say it enough, it'll be true.

"Christ, Mancini. Get your shit together." I know that voice. I turn, my eyes falling on Maria. She's looking at me with venom in her eyes, but I'm not stupid. I know she'd take my cock any day of the goddamn week if I so much as winked at her.

"Maria, baby," I say, and I'm surprised how easily the words slip out. But *she* fucking left me. *She's* gone, and I'll never see her again.

Maria rolls her eyes, but I don't miss the tilt of her lips. I'm about to pull out my pack of smokes when Larissa speaks from my left.

"Lorenzo, can I talk to you for a moment?" Her use of my full name alerts me. I nod and follow her into the house.

As we walk away, I hear someone mumble behind me, "The fuck happened to him?"

"Mind your fucking business," I say in unrequested response, and I hear a chuckle. I start to chuckle, myself.

Once we're inside, Larissa closes the patio door and pulls me by the arm into the kitchen. She faces me and crosses her arms against her chest.

"What the fuck happened, Zo?"

"Everything's—"

"Shut the fuck up and spill it. I'm not an idiot. You asked me to go to her apartment and now you're acting like a drunken fool. Something happened."

I brace myself on the counter and stare at her. "She's gone."

She quirks a brow. "Kate is gone?"

I nod.

"What did you do?" She stares at me through narrowed eyes and pops her hip to the side. *Just like Ma used to do.*

"Guess I'm just a fuck up, *Larissa*. What can I say?" I know that's what she expects to hear. The truth is so far beneath us that it's easy to keep buried.

She sighs and looks down. "You're not a fuck up, Zo. This is your life. It's not your fault."

She only knows a part of my reality. The crew doesn't know what's happened in the past few months, and it's best we keep it that way. If we ever get caught, they'd go down with us, and we can't have that. Other people knowing allows too many vulnerabilities.

"Exactly," I finally say. "This is my life and I refuse to bring her down with me."

Lari's sad little eyes tell me she understands, and though she doesn't want to, she agrees.

"So let's get back out there and just fuck off with feelings and la-la land, where we pretend like this is okay. Like there was ever a choice in any of this."

She nods. "I get it."

You really don't.

She walks back to the patio, and I follow her after grabbing the bottle of Fireball from my room. I try to absorb myself in the conversation, to forget about the perfectionist, meticulous, beautiful girl that's stolen my heart and doesn't even know it.

I take chugs straight from the bottle, forgoing a cup simply because the effort is a waste. I offer it to the circle but everyone declines, sticking to their beers instead. Maria lights up a joint at some point, and though I normally decline, tonight I take a puff.

Drunk, high, and miserable is a dangerous combination.

I'm not sure what time it is when my friends start leaving. I'm close to nodding off in my seat when Maria says, "Zo, why don't you walk me out?"

"I can walk you out," Lari offers.

"I got it," I say, nodding at Maria and rising from my seat while taking a swig of the already empty bottle of Fireball. Tiny droplets land on my tongue and I swallow them back before following her through the house, leaving the empty bottle on the kitchen counter. Larissa and Santi remain outside, everyone else gone.

When we're passing the hallway, she halts suddenly and turns to me. "Seriously, Zo, you okay?"

Damn, I really must be a mess. Maria is as cold as they come, and she actually looks concerned.

"Yeah, I'm good," I reply, but the lie causes my heart to lurch in my chest.

"Anything I can do to help?" she says, taking a small step closer. It's subtle, but I know what she's implying. And fuck, I want it to help.

So fucking badly.

What's the harm in trying?

I take a step towards her. "What did you have in mind?"

CHAPTER NINETEEN

April 2nd

KATE

I walk up to the foreign building with the familiar company logo on the door. Drawing in a breath, I pull the handle to my new office. There's something about a fresh start that feels rejuvenating. Once you get past the fear of change, of course.

Jasmine finally called me last Monday to say that Rowan would be in contact. I was a little nervous, but when we spoke, he said he understood and that it wouldn't be a problem to relocate me. "We love having you on our team," he'd said. He told me to take the week to move my things, and although I wanted to get back to work, I didn't want to argue with him when I was lying.

Every fiber of my being wanted to ask him about being related to Santi, but I refrained. It's not my business, and as I've quickly learned, the less I know, the better. As much as I'd love to know *why* they live in Rowan's house, I need to leave it all behind me.

I walk down the hall and towards the back office. The space here at the Grove Shores branch is smaller than Azalea Pines, and I was told that all the workers are in one large cubicle space. I head inside and look towards the back for the new lead underwriter I'll be working under, Garrett Janson.

Locating him, I tug on the hem of my blouse and walk to his desk. When I arrive, he greets me cheerfully, pushing away from his desk to rise from his seat and shake my hand.

"It's a pleasure to meet you, Kate. I've heard wonderful things about you from Rowan and Jasmine."

"Oh, thank you. Nice to meet you," I respond with a blush. As ready as I am to move on with my life, I can't help but feel nervous. What if working here doesn't pan out? What if I hate my new coworkers?

"Come on, I'll show you to your desk and introduce you to the other underwriters here."

My role here will be identical to what I did at the Azalea Pines branch. The only difference is servicing the borrowers in this area. Once Garrett introduces me to some of my new coworkers and shows me where everything's located, he directs me to my new desk.

"Don't get too comfortable just yet," Garrett says as I place my bag in the desk drawer. "You're in luck. The boss is here today, so let's go meet him before you get started."

"Oh, great," I say, standing up. I'm pretty sure the boss here is the other co-owner of Valeri Financials. I've seen photos in random newsletters sent out to us with updates about the business, but I've never had a reason to know his name. The third branch, Westland, is operated by a hired manager. I don't know his name, either.

We reach the back of the office space where the wall is lined with two doors. One is next to a window, the table inside indicating that it's the conference room. Garrett knocks on the other door and a moment later, a voice says, "Come on in."

Garrett tugs on the doorknob and holds the door open for me. The man behind the desk looks up from his computer and a smile overtakes his face. His dark hair is peppered with gray and his energy reminds me of Rowan—inviting and warm.

"Ah, is this the transfer?" His eyes roam from Garrett to mine. They look so familiar. Almost like...

You're seeing things.

"Morning, Mr. Mancini," Garrett says. "This is Kate Appleton."

Mancini? No...

"Hello, there," Mr. Mancini says, circling his desk with his hand extended. I can't help but notice the same swagger that Lorenzo carries himself with.

I snap my jaw shut and clear my throat. "H—Hello, sir," I reply, shaking his hand. How did I never know this? I wrack my brain for any memory of seeing his name on an email or document. Maybe I did at some point. But until I met Lorenzo, there was no reason for their shared last name to carry any meaning.

"Please, call me Marco," he says, resting his hip on his desk. "I've heard wonderful things about you from Rowan! I'm very excited to have you on our team, even if Rowan was envious to lose you. I'm sorry to hear about the flood in your apartment."

Flood? Oh, right!

"Yes, unfortunately, the damage was extensive enough that it required me to relocate. Thank you for accommodating me on such short notice. I love working for Valeri Financials." My professionalism shines through, masking the gears turning in my brain.

Why is this company brimming with Lorenzo's people?

"Rowan is my partner. If he loves you, I love you." While Lorenzo and this man—his father?—share a similar suave demeanor, Marco's professionalism contrasts Lorenzo's rebellious nature.

Does he know about Lorenzo's drug abuse? That he doesn't care about other people?

I remember to smile in response to his statement. "Thank you."

"Well, let me know if there's anything you need to get situated." He taps on his desk before returning to his chair.

"Do you have a moment to review the docs I sent you last week?" Garrett asks. Marco agrees, and I seize the opportunity to make a hasty exit as inconspicuously as humanly possible. Once I'm back at my desk, I let out a bated breath.

What in the fuck is going on? This move was supposed to help me forget about Lorenzo, not create more intrigue.

Guess that's why they say you can run but you can't hide.

$$ \text{〉〉〉●〈〈〈} $$

"How was your first day, toots?" Char asks when I drop my keys onto her dining table.

I let out a heavy sigh. While my new coworkers instantly made me feel comfortable—we even sat at lunch together—I can't shake the ominous feeling of Lorenzo's... *something* being co-owner. "That's a loaded question."

"What now?" she asks.

What now, indeed.

I spare no detail as I fill her in on today's revelations while goose-bumps coat my skin.

"How did you not know they shared a last name?"

"I didn't even *know* his name! Out of sight, out of mind, I guess? Why would I ever need to? He didn't work at my branch!"

"I guess. But I mean, if he's co-owner, I'd expect his name to be plastered *somewhere*."

"I'm sure it is! Maybe I had seen it before but didn't remember because it was insignificant. It *would* be insignificant if it weren't for Lo—"

A pang hits my chest, cutting my sentence short. I trusted that sketchy asshole, and I hate that he has any effect on me.

"Hey," Char says, rushing to my side and rubbing my back.

"I'm fine," I grit out. I straighten and shrug her hand off. "I just—this was supposed to help me, not make things worse!"

"Maybe it's not a big deal," Char suggests. "Maybe in a few weeks, you won't care about seeing him there."

"If he's anything like Rowan, he'll hardly be there."

"There you go! So what's the problem?"

"The problem? You want to know what the problem is, Char?" My resentment is taking over, causing my speech to be ruder than I intended. It's not fair to her because this isn't her fault in the slightest. But I'm pissed off and I'm done. "Why are all of them working for this company? Better yet, why does it seem like a damn secret?"

Char shakes her head slowly. "I don't know, toots."

"Why does it feel like the world fucking hates me?"

Char stares at me wide-eyed, and I can't say I blame her. She's as dumbfounded as I am, only she doesn't have the anger to accompany it.

"I'm starting to think this runs deeper. Something's not right," I add, shaking my head.

"It's not really uncommon for people who know each other to work together and all that, but the fact that it's like, not open knowledge? Like why wouldn't Lorenzo ever tell you his own family runs the company?"

"Exactly."

We stand for a moment, searching each other's eyes. "I should have just found another job."

"I'm sorry I suggested you move," Char replies apologetically.

"Yeah, well, how could we have known?"

"So, what are you going to do?"

Every analytical particle of my brain wants to learn more. I want the answers. But at what cost? "I've always liked my job at Valeri, but I guess I could still quit."

"Why don't you wait to see how it plays out? Maybe dig a little tomorrow at work. If things still feel off or weird, then you quit and don't look back."

I shake my head. "I'm done searching for answers. Look where that got us!"

Char hums her agreement. I shake my head again, my eyes glossing over with defiance. "I'll see how it plays out. If not, I *will* find another job."

Char's expression brightens with a clap of her hands. "Okay, problem solved!"

There's another decision I make, one I haven't wanted to think about because it brings back memories of the person I am trying to forget. But how do you forget someone that lit you up from the inside? That made you feel like you were capable and strong when they were working to tear you down all along?

"I think I'm going to start taking driving lessons," I tell Char.

"What?! That's so exciting, Kate! I love that for you."

I found a company that promises they can teach you to drive in under four weeks. If I hadn't had those lessons with Lorenzo—a shudder passes through me—I'd be certain that four weeks wasn't enough. He got me to a point where I wasn't paralyzed by fear anymore. But he replaced that fear with pain. Now, I'm ready to build *myself* up.

I smile sheepishly, forcing myself to be brave, which actually makes me feel a bit better about this whole situation. "It's time. I'm 25, and this commute is going to drain my bank account if I do stick it out at Grove Shores."

"What about your pilates class?" she asks, passing me my phone charger.

Char is going out of town for a few weeks to work on a huge project she was hired for through Gustav. Lorenzo hasn't reached out to me again, so we agreed that it was probably safe for me to return home. I can't be sure he didn't send anyone to my apartment, but it's a risk I'll have to take. Moving is a hassle, and I'm comfortable there for now. I haven't been sleeping well, so I'm hoping being back in my own home will do the trick.

"They have a later class, so I'll start attending that one." Char nods and I finish stuffing my suitcase, then zip it up. We both don't voice the final question, one that I *really* don't want to address.

When will I move to be closer to Grove Shores?

It's a twenty-five minute drive on a good day. There's nothing tying me to my current apartment, and the lease ends in June. Hopefully I'll have my license by then.

Half an hour later, I'm pulling my packed bag and Felix out of Char's car. She joins me on the sidewalk to say goodbye.

"I'm proud of you, toots," Char says, planting a kiss on my cheek.

"Thank you so much for letting me stay with you."

She waves her hand. "Please, you're welcome anytime. You're welcome to stay there while I'm gone, if you need to."

"When are you leaving, again?"

"Wednesday morning!"

"So exciting! Well, I'm sure we'll talk before then, but have a safe drive."

"Thanks. Let me know when you're settled back in."

She waits for me to enter the building before pulling away from the curb. My thoughts drift to the mysterious events of today as I wait for the elevator, but I force myself to stop. No matter how weird it is, no matter how much it hurts, it's not my business anymore.

I'm not sure it ever was.

Chapter Twenty

April 21st

Kate

My routine is back in full swing with Saturday morning pilates and cleaning. It's always been a cleansing act for me, and I'm hoping it scours my mind of all this filth it's accumulated. But I'm proud of myself for cutting ties with Lorenzo and doing what's best for me. It doesn't matter how much I miss him. It doesn't matter that I wish this weren't the reality. It is.

He's a liar, and he doesn't even care. All those things he ever said about needing me and wanting me—they were lies, too. He just wanted to fuck me and live his dishonest life. He literally ruined a date just to keep the tracks covered about what he did to poor Brad.

And you're just letting him get away with it.

The guilt in my gut is like a stone that sits on the edge of a lake, hell-bent on sinking into the ground. Maybe I should tell the police what we found. If it's not what we think, there's no harm, no foul.

But for some perplexing reason, I can't bring myself to do it. Part of it is that I don't want to reopen this wound I'm working hard to heal. But the other part is that my feelings for him have gotten in the way, and I don't want to be the cause of his arrest.

I'm pulled from my thoughts, which have become cyclical these days, when my phone rings.

"Hey, Mom," I answer. *Crap.* I haven't returned her last few calls.

"Hi, sweetie. How are you?"

"Good, in the middle of cleaning," I say, passing the rag over my kitchen counter.

"You sure? You sound a little off," she says.

A beat passes before I deny it. "Yeah, yeah. Char's been out of town, so I haven't gotten out much."

I'm so relieved I never told her about Lorenzo, or I know she'd ask. It doesn't hurt the way it did before when I think of him, but I don't know that I want to talk about it, either.

"Where'd she go?" I explain the project Char was hired for at the new hotel being built in Willowbrook, a town about an hour north from Azalea Pines.

"Willowbrook is beautiful! They have so many wonderful lakes. Why don't you pay her a visit?"

"That's not a bad idea, Mom," I say thoughtfully. Char has texted me photos of the hotel she's at, and she mentioned a lake nearby.

"Yeah! Go have fun, be young," she says. "Your father and I went on a lot of lake dates in Willowbrook. One time..."

I get lost in my mother's stories as I continue wiping down the kitchen. Once we hang up, I call Char.

"Hey, toots," she says.

"What are you doing?"

"I'm waiting on my marg at the poolside bar," she says. "This project has been amazing but exhausting. I'm ready to relax."

"Oh, nevermind, then," I say dejectedly.

"Nevermind, what?"

"My mom said the lakes are pretty awesome and suggested I come visit you. But I don't—"

"Are you kidding? Get your ass up here! Oh my god, I'm so excited! We went to the lake last weekend. It was gorgeous, there's—"

"Okay, okay! Let me finish cleaning and pack my bags. What should I bring?"

"Fuck cleaning. We need to soak up as much fun as we can!"

I laugh and store my cleaning supplies as we discuss what I should bring. It's already ten in the morning and I really *do* want to soak up the fun.

I need a change of pace. I thought cleaning would cleanse my mind, but maybe it needs a deep rinse in a body of water. This is the perfect way to solidify letting go.

Life goes on regardless of my broken heart.

$$))) \bullet ((($$

"I didn't know if you'd be up for it, or I would have invited you myself," Char says. We're on our way to the lake near the hotel she's working and staying at. I met her at the pool, where I awkwardly ran into Gustav. He's managing the construction of the hotel while Char works on the interior design. We ran to her room to put my overnight bag down and change into my bathing suit, then hit the road.

"I've been doing okay. I feel good about my decision, at the very least," I say. I'm still sleeping like shit, when all the thoughts I successfully keep at bay come out in these strange, frightening nightmares.

"As you should," Char says firmly. "How are the driving lessons?"

"Great! I can't believe how much progress I've made. It's like I was never even afraid," I say. I deliberately ignore the wish that it could have been Lorenzo who kept teaching me.

"I'm so fucking proud of you," Char says. The tires crunch over the pebbles of the makeshift parking lot, signaling our arrival. The afternoon sun glitters over the calm waters as tree branches sway gently in the breeze. Surprisingly, there aren't many people here.

Char answers my unspoken question, throwing the car into park and opening her door. "There was a festival in town today." We grab our bags and walk past a couple snoozing on a blanket, settling between their spot and a family about a hundred yards further.

We unpack our towels and lay them down while Char tells me about the design work she's done. As I lather sunscreen onto my exposed skin, I stare at my bikini in appreciation. I bought it a while ago and totally forgot until it caught my eye as I was searching for my usual black one. But that bathing suit is tainted with memories from St. Patrick's Day—memories I want to pretend don't exist.

That suit went down the garbage shoot as I was leaving my apartment building.

This one's a vibrant red with strings tying the top and bottom. The textured triangles provide enough coverage while the bottoms reveal a little more of my butt cheeks.

"I wish it was night time," Char whispers as we walk towards the water, even though there's no one within earshot.

"Why?" I ask.

"I haven't skinny dipped in a while," she says.

"Oh." I chuckle awkwardly, knowing I've never skinny-dipped a day in my life. The closest I've gotten was at Lorenzo's house, when I first met Larissa.

If it hadn't been for him, that never would have happened. Isn't that part of what drew me to him so intensely? His resolute belief in my ability to be free of inhibitions, to live in the moment, to be a badass?

I don't need him for that.

Impulsively, I pull the string at my back, the cups sagging at my breasts. Once I untie the knot at my neck, I'll be exposed.

Maybe I want to be.

I pull the second string, letting the top fall into the water. Char gapes at me when she realizes what I've done.

"Kate, what are you—"

"I'm tired of sinking. Of hiding myself. Of being afraid." I step out of my bottoms, gathering the floating top and tossing them in the direction of our things on the grass.

I extend my arms and feel the sun heat the parts of myself I've never liberated. And it feels fucking fantastic.

"Fuck. Yes!" Char exclaims, pumping a fist in the air before removing her own black bikini. My breasts have always been fuller than hers, but her perky nipples seem as happy as mine do to be released.

I resist the urge to look around and see who's watching us. We wade into the cool water, sinking into it at knee deep. Char can't erase the impressed look on her face, to which I splash water in her direction.

"Why are you staring at me like an animal in a zoo?" I tease.

"Because you are! I love every part of you, but I think this new wild side might be my favorite," she says.

"We should get drunk and streak the neighborhood," I joke.

"We can get drunk tonight, but I'm not streaking in any neighborhood where my employer might see me," she says.

I realize then that I wouldn't care if Rowan, or Marco, or anyone I've ever known saw me right now. Taking off that bathing suit removed a layer of myself, the one that bogged me down and kept me small.

But I am big. I deserve to take up space. I don't need anyone or anything.

I am free.

CHAPTER TWENTY-ONE

April 30th

KATE

The lake trip with Char was exactly what I needed. Once the high of skinny-dipping with my best friend wore off, we put our suits back on and laid out until the sun was setting. We didn't get drunk that night, but we did have some daiquiris at the pool bar while we talked. It felt good to get back to some type of normalcy as my new and improved self.

I finished my last driving class yesterday, and as the Uber pulls up to my office, I can't help but think how this will be one of the last times. Once I schedule and pass my test, I can buy a car and drive myself.

I've gotten comfortable at my new branch. The hallways no longer foreign. I toss my bag on my chair and head to the back table where I fill my mug with steaming coffee. I take a sip as I stroll back to my desk when the shock at the person I see nearly causes me to spill the hot liquid all over me.

Santi?

I rush to my seat and place the mug down so haphazardly that droplets splosh out, wetting my mouse and keyboard. I ignore the mess, focusing on Santi speaking with one of the workers from IT, who seems to be showing him to a desk. My heart races with the implication.

Does he work here now?

I feel like my eyes are deceiving me. I adjust my glasses just to make sure they are, in fact, on.

This can't be happening.

Why are all of Lorenzo's friends somehow employed with Valeri Financials? Why is the ghost of him following me around like I'm some sort of haunted house?

I suppose it makes some sense—Santi *is* related to Rowan, after all. Perhaps the better question is why he's not working at Rowan's branch, and why Lorenzo's not working here.

I need to tear my eyes away, but how do you stop watching the train that's about to run over your tied up body on the tracks? Where's my trolley dilemma button? Someone needs to press it.

But it's too late. The worst thing that could possibly happen, happens. Santi looks up. And his eyes lock with mine.

I watch the familiarity fill them when he recognizes me.

Does he know that I know?

I break eye contact, pulling out a napkin from my drawer to wipe up the coffee spill. I go through the motions while my heart thumps erratically in my chest.

This will be fine. It has to be fine. I haven't said a word about Lorenzo's... accident, if we can call it that. I've downright acted like I've never known him, locking all thought and feel and hope about him tightly in the trunk I've created in my brain.

But I'm afraid that Santi will be the key to open it right back up.

Just as I'm returning to my desk after lunch with solace that Santi and I can carry on a professional relationship in which we pretend we've never known each other outside of these walls, he appears at my desk.

"I need to talk to you," he says abruptly.

"Hello, Santi. Nice to see you, too," I bite out sarcastically. I'm sick of him treating me like some sort of villain. It's *his* friend that's the villain, which makes him a villain by association.

He stares at me unabashedly, crossing his arms over his chest. He doesn't say anything, which only fuels my repressed anger. My next words escape me before I can think them through.

"Why would I talk to a cokehead like you?" I hiss. It's rude and judgmental, but fuck him. Fuck *them*.

His brows shoot up. "Cokehead? What are you talking about?" His expression is surprised enough that I'm close to believing him. *Close*.

"Are you really going to play stupid with me?" I ask with narrowed eyes.

He studies me then, and my confidence wavers. Did Lorenzo not tell him what happened? What Char and I discovered?

When Santi speaks, his voice is lowered. "Kate, you have no idea what you're talking about. Let's talk in the hallway for—"

"No." My voice is full of icy fragments and I intend for them to cut deep. What I didn't expect was for it to work.

"Look, I"—he runs his hand through the back of his short hair—"Zo is like my brother. You need to understand—he's not who you think he is."

I gape at him. "What—"

"I was driving that night." It takes a moment for me to process what he's saying, but the implications cut through like the shards of ice I wielded a moment ago.

"You? How could you—"

He looks around quickly before leaning towards me and whispering, "You need to be careful."

My mouth dries out and I'm suddenly filled with the deep need to ask him all the unanswered questions I've ignored. "Careful about what?"

He gives me a wary look. "Just... if anything weird happens, please tell me."

My mouth hangs open, but I shut it quickly. "What are you—"

"I can't say more. Wish I could, truly." His eyes soften, and I actually believe him. "Just—look, don't go searching. You'll understand eventually."

I simply nod, because what the fuck else am I supposed to do? Santi starts to walk away, ending our little chat as abruptly as he started it, but he turns back and adds quietly, "Oh, and thank you."

My eyes blow out. Is he seriously thanking me for not ratting him out? *Them* out?

He walks back to his desk and doesn't spare me another glance. I force myself to tear my gaze from him and onto my computer, but my mind is reeling.

Santi was driving the car? What will I understand? Why did he warn me about not snooping around? Was I right? This place is riddled with secrets, too?

This is exactly why I wanted to escape Lorenzo—he's not good for me. All those weeks of shoving him into the recesses of my mind, and all it took was one conversation with Santi to reignite the curiosity in me. And it's burning so bright, I can't ignore it.

I need to know what's going on with this place—because I *know* something is going on—but I have no idea where to start.

I rack my brain, going over every single interaction between me and Lorenzo, recalling things I've heard at work, and analyzing Brad's story. Something is not adding up. Why would they all work here while maintaining an air of secrecy about it?

I can't stop thinking about Santi's words: *I was driving that night.* Well, it certainly confirms that he *does* know that I know. But why would he want to make that clear to me? Was Lorenzo in the car with him? I should have asked. Either way, does it make it any better? Any more forgivable?

I also can't shake the guilt of holding onto all of this knowledge and not reporting it. What's my alternative? Turn them in and pose a risk for myself by outing them? Turn Lorenzo in to potentially suffer consequences? Consequences he'd deserve, yes. But at my hand?

There's no right answer. It feels like this is an impossible situation.

I glance at Santi across the office. He's deep in his own work, clacking away on his keyboard. I consider asking him outright about all of this, but why would he tell me the truth? He and Lorenzo probably have the same bullshit explanation, and it can't be trusted.

No... something is definitely off, and I need to figure it out on my own. I pick at the skin around my nails as my eyes go out of focus. It makes sense that he works here, seeing as he's related to Rowan. But what about Carter and D? Why are they in—

Rentals!

Inspiration hits me so suddenly that I nearly fall off my chair from sitting up too fast. I can feel my surrounding coworkers' eyes on me, but I ignore them, taking a sip of coffee to play it off.

Rentals was dinged on that audit, and Rowan asked us to keep quiet about it. What if that's the key to all of this? It's known that they charge less for rentals, but I have no idea how much. I navigate to the company website and search the Rentals tab. A quick read through confirms it's five hundred dollars less than what I pay at my place. I always assumed the low rates meant they were quaint apartments. But these photos are showing some lavish looking homes.

How in the world do these cost so little? And it's the same rate in all three towns. According to the qualifications, you don't need much. And they give a twenty percent discount if you pay in cash.

I glance around me again, double-taking to Marco's office. The lights are off, visible through the floor to ceiling windows that serve as a wall next to the door. Should I...

No. It's too risky.

But...

I want to know.

I *need* to know.

The hasty decision is made for me. I turn back to my computer and shoot off a message to Garrett through Teams, asking if I can work overtime tonight. It's time to get some goddamn answers.

Chapter Twenty-Two

April 30th

Zo

Ten steps one way, ten steps back. Glancing through the window above the couch before pacing again. Taking in the bare walls of this house that's never been a home.

But it's never felt so claustrophobic before.

Every day, I checked to see if her name had disappeared from our system. Every day, I checked her status on Teams. I nearly asked Rowan where she was too many times. But it was too risky. Even asking her team lead, whatever her name is, could somehow get back to him or Marco.

I refuse for them to ever know we had a relationship.

That's what it was, right? Even though I insisted I wouldn't commit, my heart had other plans. But I couldn't tell her that. It was a risk any time I went near her as it was. Putting more solidarity into us would have increased that risk exponentially.

I checked every day until finally, her status was available. I rushed to her office, intentionally slowing my pace to a casual, brisk walk when I neared her area. But her desk was still empty.

Returning to my computer, I reviewed her file and found my answer—she relocated to Grove Shores.

My heart sunk. I'd never be able to protect her there if she needed it. But my next thought was a silver lining—Santi would be starting there soon. We agreed—or I forced him to agree, rather—that he would keep his eye on her.

Today was his first day, and he should be home any minute. I've been pacing since I arrived from work, but this house is much closer to Azalea Pines than Grove Shores.

Mid-step, a door slamming alerts me and my head snaps to the window. I dash to the front when I see Santi's truck parked in the driveway.

"How was she?" I demand the moment his feet land on the driveway.

"Give me a goddamn second, dude," he says, pulling his laptop bag from the passenger side and exiting the car. I slam his door shut and turn to him expectantly.

"Let's get the fuck inside," he says, glancing around. I, too, glance around. Then, squeezing my eyes shut, I force myself to regain some level of composure. Once we're back inside, Santi places his bag on the couch and I round on him.

"How did she look?"

"I had a great first day, thanks for asking." My glare causes him to sigh in defeat. "She looked alright. A little tired, I suppose."

I wait expectantly, but he doesn't elaborate. "That's it? That's all you have?"

"I talked to her for a moment. She said something interesting."

He pierces me with an accusing stare, one I don't understand. "Spit it out."

"She called me a cokehead."

The laughter rises despite my misery. Kate *would* say some shit straight out of a 'say no to drugs' commercial.

"What's fucking funny, bro? How does she know about the drugs?"

I sober in an instant. "I told you, she found out."

"Yeah, I thought you meant about the accident! Not about the drugs!"

I can see this is all he really cares about. He couldn't give two fucks if I know about Kate's whereabouts or not.

"There were bags in the drawer with the report. I thought you knew that."

Santi seethes. "This is worse than I thought. She's working *for* the company, Zo. Do you know what kind of trouble this could cause? For any of us, if we're not careful."

"Yeah, well, she refuses to speak to me, so don't worry about it," I spit out bitterly.

"You shouldn't be speaking to her, anyway!"

"Yeah, you've mentioned that about a dozen times," I reply icily.

His expression softens by a fraction. "Zo, you know I care but—"

"The fuck you do!" I shout. The anger coursing through my veins quickly reaches boiling point; I'm always close to the edge these days. I stomp to my room and rip open the door, wading through the dirty cups and clothes littering my bedroom. Santi hovers in the doorway as I drop to the edge of my bed, adjusting my black tee and wincing.

I breathe heavily, keeping the constant simmering rage at bay. Santi moves to stand in front of me, stepping on a red solo cup as I focus intently on the ground.

"I don't think she's going to do anything, Zo. She would have by—"

"You think I give a *fuck* about that at this point? I want to make sure she's safe. If my father—"

"We're *this* close, Zo. *This*"—he holds his pointer finger and thumb a half an inch apart—"close."

I avert my gaze, my jaw ticking. "Well, at least you can keep an eye on her."

"Exactly. She's safe, so quit moping around. I'll keep a watch on her, make sure she's not doing anything stupid."

"If my father ever finds out..."

"He doesn't know!" Santi roars. "We've gone over this already. There's no way for him to find out now. You're not hanging out with her. He can't know about the past because there are no cameras in the office."

Pinching the bridge of my nose, I'm grateful for the fact that our fathers are too paranoid for their own good. They're more concerned about footage being used against them than protecting them. "What if they already know? What if they're playing us?"

His pained expression matches my own. "We have no control over that now." He gingerly places a hand on my shoulder, as though I'm a ticking bomb. I can't deny that I've been explosive.

"You were right. I should have stayed the fuck away from her. At least 'til this was over."

"I fucking know I was right," Santi says, but it lacks the proper conviction. He's trying to humor me. Unfortunately for him, I've lost the ability to find amusement in such things. "Hold out a little longer. Sacrifice a little while longer. It's just for now. The stars await."

He pats my chest, right where the matching tattoo is etched into my skin. Bold stars amidst the spiral of chaos. I place my hand over his, and we eye each other for a moment before I release him.

"*In the darkness, seek the stars. You may not see them, but they are always there for you.*" I recite the words my mom would whisper to me while she held me close at night, though they fail to provide the optimism they used to hold.

What about you, Ma? Where were your stars?

"I'll keep an eye on her. You have my word," Santi promises.

"She has an allergy," I say lamely. "To nuts, I think."

Santi looks like he wants to laugh, but thankfully, he restrains himself. I'm not sure I could take the sound of joy. "Got it. Now come on, let's hit the weights."

CHAPTER TWENTY-THREE

April 30th

KATE

The last person starts packing up their bag at 7:30 pm, and my heart begins to race. I've been going back and forth in my mind all afternoon, debating whether I should go through with this or not. But I can't shake the feeling that something bigger is going on here, and I need to find out what. Too many of them work at this company for it to be coincidental.

As soon as my coworker's footsteps descend the hall, my eyes sweep the floor one last time as I stop pretending to type.

No one's here.

It's go time.

I tiptoe towards Marco's office, though why I'm tiptoeing, I don't know. It's not like anyone's here. But when you're doing sneaky shit, your body follows suit.

I get to his door and say a small prayer that it's unlocked. That prayer goes unanswered when I tug on the handle and it doesn't budge.

Like father, like son.

Expecting this, I dig out the paperclip I'd stuffed in my pocket. Following the instructions from the video I watched earlier, I carefully bend it in the proper direction and stick it into the keyhole. With gentle motions, I work it back and forth.

I've never done something like this before, so I have no way of knowing if it'll work. But I refuse to think deeply about what I'm doing, focusing on one thing and one thing only—answers.

I. Want. Answers.

Santi's cryptic warning only furthers my belief that there are concealed truths here, and Marco's office seems like the most likely place of uncovering them.

Sweat builds at my brow, not from exertion, but from anxiety. My heart is prepared to leap out of my tight chest so it can be free from this insanity. The only way out is through. Knowledge is power, and damn it, I'm tired of feeling powerless.

I wiggle and push, but the door won't budge. Becoming frantic, I pull out my phone and search the web for images, convinced I'm doing something wrong. I review the text and photos, then try again. I turn left and right... nothing.

"Fuck!" I shout in frustration. Looking around, I confirm what I already know—no one's here.

But that doesn't mean that someone won't come. I need to hurry.

Maybe there's a spare key hidden. I run my hand along the frame of the door.

Nothing.

I look down to see if there's a doormat. Plenty of people stuff extra keys under their doormats in case they lose their set. But there's no good reason for a doormat to be *inside* of an office, so I shouldn't be as peeved as I am when I don't find one.

Try one more time.

I take a cleansing breath to clear my mind and focus. I reinsert the bent paperclip and resume my task. When I hear the soft *click*, I nearly shout and dance in victory.

Pulling the handle, I enter the office quickly, closing the door quietly behind me.

Just in case.

I stuff the paperclip into my pocket and squint in the darkness. Circling the desk, my eyes roam the spotless surface. I'm sure the computer is a goldmine, but I know for a fact that it's password protected. And I can't learn password hacking in an afternoon on the internet.

I pull on the file cabinets, but of course, they're locked. I can try to pick them, but I'm nervous to use light in case someone does show up. The only possible way of keeping myself hidden is in darkness. Which makes me realize I should predetermine a hiding spot in case I need it.

I feel around the walls, starting with the one next to the office door. I move to the back wall, opposite the door and wall-to-wall window, checking for a possible exit. Sliding my hands across the wall, my fingers brush against a picture frame, causing it to swing before banging into my hand.

I yelp on reflex, shaking my hand out. Reaching out to grab the frame, I stop it from moving, or worse, falling off, when I see a reflection of light.

What the fuck was that?

Shifting the picture frame aside a few inches reveals a square of metal behind it. My heart races impossibly faster.

A hidden safe?

I push the frame a few more inches, but it's too far. It detaches from the wall and I throw my other hand out just in time to balance it. Gently placing it on the floor, I rise to face the small metal box that's in the wall.

There's no keypad, but there are hinges, so it has to open.

But how?

While the light from the office space reflects on the metal, it's not enough to see the box clearly. Leaning in closer, I meticulously scan every inch of the surface, tracing my fingers along it. My finger catches on a small hole close to the edge, but it's too dark to see inside.

Damn it, I'm going to need light.

Pulling out my phone, I access the flashlight, quickly putting it over the hole.

A keyhole. A *tiny* keyhole.

There's no way I can pick that lock. Maybe he has the key in this office?

I shut off the light and scurry back to the desk, careful not to move anything as I feel around. My eyes have adjusted to the dark, so I can tell my search will be fruitless. Plus, who the fuck would leave a key out for anyone to find?

Better yet, why would there be a goddamn safe in the wall?

Is that normal for CEOs?

If I'm going to find a key, it's going to be hidden. Could it be in the locked file cabinet? Crouching down, I confirm the keyhole on the cabinet yields the same issue as the safe—it's tiny. Do I risk leaving scratch marks on the metal if the paperclip misses the hole?

I need to know.

I move to pull the makeshift tool out of my pocket when a sudden thought crosses my mind. It can't be explained as anything other than a gut feeling.

Check under the desk.

I drop to the floor so suddenly that my knees scrape against the rough carpet. I'm definitely going to have a rug burn. Ignoring the pain, I crawl under the desk. Pulling my phone back out, I turn on the light. A quick scan of the underside confirms there's nothing.

Damn it!

I wipe sweat from my brow and prop myself up on a hand, beyond frustrated. This can't all be for nothing. I have to find *something*.

I start to crawl out from under the desk, the phone light shifting with my movements, when I catch a glimpse of something on the desk frame behind the built-in filing cabinet. I hover my light over it, revealing a button.

I don't even think about it. I slam my palm over it.

A *click* sounds behind me and I shove myself out from under the desk, my eyes darting to the safe. I see movement of light and I jump up, rushing over to the wall.

The safe is open.

Cracked, but open all the same. I pull on the metal door, excitedly peering in. My eyes land on a manilla folder and my heart deflates. That's not exciting. Although what I was hoping to see, I'm not sure.

I pull the folder out and open it, revealing a sheet of paper. When I move it straight to try and read it, something falls out. I bend to pick up the fallen object, my hands landing on a card.

A credit card?

I flash my phone over it. Nope, not a credit card.

A hotel room key.

What in the...

Standing back up, I return my focus to the paper inside. Shining my light over it reveals a hotel invoice. It was paid in full for a year, August to August. There's no other information besides the room number and a name: Lily Valeri.

Rowan's Wife.

A quick search of the folder confirms it only contained the two items. I feel around the safe to see if there's anything else.

Nothing.

Why is there a hotel key?

I don't know, but I'm going to find out.

CHAPTER TWENTY-FOUR

April 30th

KATE

Clutching the stolen key card, I hurriedly exit the building. Once my feet hit the sidewalk, I order an Uber, then dial Char's number.

"Hey, too—"

"Some weird shit is going on! I looked up Rentals, and I went into Marco's office, and—"

"Woah, Kate. Slow down. Start from the beginning. What's happening?"

I force myself to take a deep breath and fill her in on today's events. She's entirely silent as I speak; at one point, I said her name to make sure she was still listening. When I finish, I receive nothing but continued silence.

"Char?" I ask again.

"Kate, don't they have cameras in there?"

My face blanches, my heart popping like a balloon. "I... I didn't..."

"What if they decide to check?"

Dread fills me and my stomach rolls. "Fuck!"

"I mean, what you did was totally badass. But definitely a tad... reckless. You go skinny dipping *one* time—"

"I don't know what got into me," I say hysterically. "I just..."

"I know. You can't help yourself when it comes to answers."

A few tears roll down my cheeks. "So stupid."

"Hey! You are *not* stupid. I can only imagine how triggering it must have been to see Santi."

I let out a heavy sigh, trying to remain calm as I sift through the panic. "I've never seen cameras there before." But my argument is weak. I've never looked for cameras. *How could I not think about cameras?*

"There are cameras everywhere these days. I mean, they'd have to be watching, but—"

"Well, it's too late, Char. What's done is done." What other choice do I have but to move forward? I'm already in too deep.

"Do you want me to come over? We can—"

"I'm going to the hotel!"

"Are you crazy?" Char yells. If she's the level-headed one here, it's a clear sign I've lost my mind. Maybe I have. But now's not the time to find it.

"I'm *this* close, Char! I'm not going to let my break-in go to waste."

"Well, you're not going alone. I'm coming with you."

The Uber pulls up to the curb. "Fine, I'll text you the address."

Fifteen minutes later, I practically jump out of the Uber when we reach the hotel that was listed on the invoice. I start to anxiously pace the sidewalk after a quick glance around the lot confirms Char hasn't arrived.

I didn't expect the hotel to be in a run-down part of Azalea Pines. The paint is chipping, the concrete wall is littered with cracks, and the roofing is in obvious need of replacement. My nerves skyrocket, and I mentally berate myself for not even *thinking* about cameras in the office.

Should I call this off? Is going into this hotel room a bad idea? And what about the key card? How am I supposed to get it back into his office? This entire plan is sounding stupider and stupider the more I wait.

Being a badass is great. Revel in it, Kate.

Lorenzo's words strike out of nowhere, propelling me into motion. I text Char the room number and tell her to meet me up there, then stuff the phone into my pocket and take the stairs two at a time. When I reach the third floor, I check the placard on the wall and follow the arrow to the room at the end of the hall.

With trembling fingers, I slide the key into the door. A green light flashes, and I tug on the handle, hesitating. What if someone's in here?

When nothing but silence greets me, I step through the threshold. It's a standard room with two double beds. I doubt this hotel has any suites or the like. If the musty smell that permeates the entire building is any indication, this is a shit hole.

I locate the light switch on a wall in the narrow hallway and flip it on. Next to the switch is what has to be the bathroom door, which I confirm by opening it. When I get to the main part of the room just two steps further, I glance around.

Why in the world would they have a hotel room?

I start opening all the drawers, checking behind fixtures, looking under the bed, but there's nothing. Everything points to this being an ordinary room.

I'm about to plop myself on the bed but I think twice, not wanting to leave any evidence of my entry. I stare at the blank wall where a nicer hotel would probably have a sliding glass door for a balcony.

At least the walls are freshly painted.

Part of me wants to give up and leave, accepting that this was a dead end. But the stubborn, inquisitive side of me—the one that Lorenzo always seemed so annoyed by—wants to keep searching. Problem is, this is a tiny room and I've pretty much torn it apart without actually disheveling anything.

As much as I don't want to, I have no choice but to leave. And now, with this letdown, I'm hyper aware of the fact that I'll have to risk myself again to get this hotel key back into the safe in Marco's office.

My fingers graze the dresser, lost in thought, when I figure I should check behind it. The narrow space between the dresser and corner wall is tight, making it so I really have to squeeze in. Dropping to my knees, I check the floor behind it.

Just when I'm about to stand up, I hear the click of the door. I push off my hands but before I can turn around, a hand flies over my mouth.

I try to scream but the hand is pressed so tightly to my lips that the sound is muffled. I gag on my assailant's skin as an arm wraps around my chest, followed by a prick on my arm.

I can hardly breathe as the hand presses tighter still on my mouth. Panic floods every fiber of my being, and I can't think past that fact that something was injected into me.

It's not like in the movies; I don't feel an immediate sensation. I start to thrash, my foot easily sinking through the drywall in this cramped space. The assailant grips me tighter, my boobs squeezing together from his stronghold. Between his chunky fingers partially covering my nostrils and my panic, air is getting harder to properly breathe in.

But I'm distracted by what is now visible through the hole I kicked into the wall.

Cash.

Stacks and stacks of cash.

It must start at the floor because all I see is wads of it in chunks separated by sleeves. I try to make out the familiar smell of it.

Why would there be...

My thoughts grow hazy from the lack of oxygen, and that's when the drug hits. My legs stop moving, suddenly weak. There's a tiny voice in the back of my brain screaming at me to stay alert, but I can't. I should be fighting to keep my eyes open, but I can't muster the energy to put on my boxing gloves. It takes too long to register that I'm being dragged.

And then

CHAPTER TWENTY-FIVE

April 30th

Zo

I peel my sweaty shirt from my body and toss it to the side before plopping onto the patio sofa. Santi joins me a few minutes later, passing me a cold beer. We got into this nightly routine of sitting in companionable silence after our workouts when he insisted that I couldn't stay holed up in my room.

So, every night, I stare at the moon while he scrolls on his phone. My peculiar interest in the lunar body led me to learn the identification of all its phases. It's nearly full tonight—a waxing gibbous moon. Apparently, the moon is slowly moving away from Earth, its gravitational influence on us lessening with each centimeter it distances itself.

I suppose I'm not much different from our planet. Here I am, in the same position I've always been in. And the only person who ever made any of it worth it was never really mine, always slowly moving away.

I'm torn from my thoughts when one of my phones rings in my pocket. I pull it out, *Marco* flashing across the screen. Santi gives me a curious look as I answer it.

"Hello?"

"Son, how are you?"

Son.

That's all I've ever been. The means to an end. A pawn in his game. A tool he can use.

"Good," I reply curtly. I typically hold more tolerance for the old man, but I've been strangely on edge today. I've felt a sense of impending doom, chalking it up to the extended time without my princess.

My eyes lock with Santi and he gives me a silent warning, one only I could read. His expression is neutral and no one would ever know. But we're close enough to know what the other is thinking without ever really having to say it.

"Aren't you going to ask how I am?" Marco's words have me sitting a little straighter. He only ever says shit like that when he's got something he wants to share.

"How are you?" I force myself to sound interested.

"We got 'em."

"Who?" Santi pipes up from beside me.

"The rat, Santi," he replies jubilantly. Santi and I share a look.

"Oh, shit," I say, clearing my throat. "Who was it?"

"The recent transfer, Katherine Appleton."

No...

My wide eyes search for Santi's, hoping—*praying*—for this to be some horrific nightmare. But Santi's very somber eyes only serve to confirm the cold, hard fact.

No!

"With any luck, we'll know who she's reporting to before the night is over," Marco continues gleefully, but it sounds so far away because I'm no longer here.

They have Kate. How? Why?

"How'd you catch her?" Santi asks nonchalantly.

"You know we've been keeping tabs. But she couldn't have made it any easier for us."

He pauses for dramatic effect, which typically I'd ignore, but I need to know everything, now. "How so?"

"Imagine my surprise when I got a notification for activity detected from the camera in my office. She was snooping."

My jaw would hit the floor if it could. *Why in the fucking world would she do that?*

"Well?" Marco asks when Santi and I are dead silent. "I'd expect you to be excited. We're no longer under threat!"

"That's excellent news, Mr. Mancini," Santi offers. His expression matches my surprise.

"Seriously," I add, forcing life into my numb body so we can get the information we need. "Where is she at?"

"Ron is taking her to one of the warehouses as we speak. I've got to say, I was surprised. She doesn't look like she holds a bad bone in her body."

Oh, how wrong you are.

"But you never know. Appearances are just that. Isn't that right, boys?" We force out our laughs a moment too late, but he doesn't seem to notice.

"Anyway, I need a favor. We need to pull the money out of the hotel just in—"

"Hotel?" Santi says at the same time that I say, "Money?"

"Oh, right," Marco says with a chuckle. "Yes, we have a hotel room with hundreds of thousands crammed into the walls. Gotta keep it somewhere!"

"Wha—"

"Why didn't you tell us?" I demand, cutting Santi off. My tone stays neutral despite the rage begging to spill out.

"We didn't feel this was information you were privy to. Until now, at least." Santi's glare turns murderous, sharing my sentiment. "She found the safe in my office wall housing the hotel key. I assumed she'd report us, so I sent Ron to pull out the money. Ron had to handle the girl once he found her there, so I need you two to tear down the walls and get the money over to Rowan's immediately. She'll be disposed of before the end of the night, I'm sure, but how do we know she hasn't reported this to whoever she's working with? One can never be too careful."

So many thoughts fight for my attention.

What the fuck was Kate doing in that office? Why didn't our dads trust us with this hotel room? It would have made our lives a fuck ton easier! I need to ask which warehouse he took her to, but I have to play my cards right. I can't give away any inclination that I care.

And we need to call Ted, immediately.

"Give me the hotel info, we'll head over," Santi says, feigning obedience. It doesn't go over my head that Marco has no problem sending us into a dangerous situation; in his mind at least. If Kate were actually the rat, and *had* reported this, going there would risk us getting caught with the money. Luckily, she's not, and we know that.

But it only proves that Rowan and Marco don't give a *fuck* about us. We're pawns, just like the rest of the world.

Marco rattles off the location, explaining that we'll need to take a few suitcases for the cash. The moment I hang up, I lose it, chucking my half-empty beer bottle at the brick pillar holding up the awning. "Fuck!"

"Zo," Santi says cautiously, tensing beside me.

"What the fuck was she doing in Marco's office?" I glance at him as he shakes his head.

"I don't know, bro," Santi says quietly. He must be siphoning through the information since I'm unable to do anything but panic. Why did she do this? And why today? Was it Santi starting?

The seams containing my pent-up rage have burst. I glare at him accusingly. "What did you say to her?"

"Nothing, man! I told her to come to me if anything weird happened," Santi defends.

As much as I'd like to force him to regurgitate every word of their conversation, it's wasting precious time. "We have to find her. Now."

"Zo, we'd be—"

"NOW!" I roar. I leap up, scooping my shirt off the floor and tossing it back on.

"I'll drive, you call Ted and get this information to him. This should be enough to indict."

Santi is hot on my tail as I rush to the front door. "Zo, we should check with Ted first. What if—"

I stop dead in my tracks and turn around so suddenly, Santi walks into my torso. But I'm too pumped up on adrenaline to feel it. "*What if* she's being tortured? *What if* she's dead by the time we get this all figured out? We don't have—"

"Alright, alright, point taken," Santi says with his hands raised in defense. I'm sure he's never seen me this crazed. I've never *felt* this crazed.

I turn towards the front door and yank it open, but I'm abruptly halted by a woman's fist raised mid-air, prepared to knock.

"Char?" Santi exclaims from right behind me.

"Where is she?" she yells, shoving my chest. The unexpected impact catches me off guard, causing me to stumble back a step. Before she can strike again, Santi swiftly steps in, catching her wrists before they make contact.

"I know you have her! You won't be able to stop me!" Her voice echoes with desperation as she struggles against Santi's iron grip, but his hold remains unyielding.

I'm not sure how the fuck she could possibly know Kate's been taken, but there's no time to figure it out. "We don't have her!"

"Don't lie to—"

"We don't have time for this shit!" Santi shouts, effortlessly lifting her by the waist and throwing her over his shoulder. Her punches land uselessly on his back as he strides out the front door with me close behind.

Retrieving my keys from my pocket, I unlock the doors as Santi drops Char on the hood of her car before jogging to the passenger side of my vehicle.

"You're not leaving!" she shouts, leaping off her car and running to stand behind my trunk.

"We're going to get Kate, you idiot!" I bellow. I have no patience for this right now.

"We know everything!" Char's scream pierces the air. "You're criminals, and—"

"If you care about Kate, get out of the fucking way! Every second we waste here is a second closer to her death! I won't hesitate to run you over if I have to."

Char's expression wavers. "You're... you're going to save her?"

Santi and I nod in unison. She moves out of the way and we jump into the car. As I shift into reverse, she pounds on my window.

"Take me with you," she demands through the glass.

"Absolutely not," Santi says firmly.

I crack the window. "This isn't going to be safe. We'll be back."

As I roll the window back up, she shouts, "I will follow you in my car! I'll report you to the police! I'll—"

"Oh my fucking god," Santi sighs exasperatedly as he rips open his door, steps out, and opens the backseat door. "Get the fuck in, then. Hurry!"

The second she's in the backseat, Santi slams her door shut and jumps back into the front. I peel out of the driveway, my foot pressing hard on the pedal. The engine roars into the wind as the street lights become a blur.

"Yo, slow the fuck down. We need to get there in one piece, *unarrested,*" Santi mutters from beside me.

No part of me wants to do it, but I release the pedal. The car reacts instantly, decelerating. I wish someone could release the pedal on me, to slow down the racing thoughts in my mind. As the car gradually slows down, my entire body trembles with the surge of adrenaline.

"Where should we look first?" I bark.

"Donovans," Santi quickly responds. I navigate us to the location that's fifteen minutes out.

"Um, hi," Char says, causing me to jump in my seat. I forgot she was with us.

"Doll, why don't you let us drop you off somewhere? This can get dangerous *real* quick," Santi says.

"We don't have time for that," I interject.

"Let her out a few minutes before we get to Donovans. She can Uber. It's not worth—"

"Yeah, hi? I'm right here." I catch her waving in the rearview mirror. "You're not leaving me anywhere. I don't trust you two."

"You don't know shit about us," Santi retorts.

"I know everything I need to know, Santiago."

Santi rolls his eyes. "We—"

"We're working with the FBI."

My admission hovers in the air while Char gapes at me like a fish out of water. "The Federal Bureau of Investigation?"

"The one and only. Speaking of which, call Ted, Santi."

I toss him my second phone and he quickly dials, putting it on speaker.

"Lorenzo," Ted answers after two rings.

"And Santi," I add. "We've got news for you."

Santi swiftly brings Ted up to speed as Char listens with rapt attention. But all I can think about is Kate. Is she hurt? Fuck, is she alive? I have no idea how many warehouses we'll have to hit before we find her.

"I'll see if we can get a warrant issued immediately to search the hotel and rescue Kate. In the meantime—"

"If you think I'm going to wait for a warrant, you've lost your goddamn mind! I'm not leaving her—"

"It could be dangerous and—"

"I don't give a damn! If—"

"Zo." Santi's stern voice puts an end to our dispute. The silence that fills the car is so thick with tension, I could cut it with a knife.

Ted speaks first, conceding. "If you find Kate, make sure to get video footage. We—"

"What do you mean 'if'? We *will* find her!" I shout, refusing to accept any other reality. I press down on the gas, propelling the car forward at full speed again.

Ted waits a beat before speaking. "Good luck."

He disconnects the line, and I scream at the windshield, shaking the immovable steering wheel in my fists. We *can't* be too late.

"You're working with the FBI?" Char whispers from the back. I don't jump this time, but I had once again forgotten she was with us.

"Yes, doll," Santi replies a tad sardonically as he types the info to send to Ted.

"Excuse me, but how the fuck were we supposed to know? And don't call me that," she snaps.

"Maybe if Kate had *trusted* me today when I—"

"You ran a man off the road!" Char shouts.

"That was an accident! And we had no choice but to keep driving, or we could have been arrested, and Marco and Rowan would never be stopped!"

"Santi, chill the fuck out," I tell him quietly. Glancing back at Char through the rearview mirror, I say, "Look, I understand why you don't believe us. Yet you still got in the car with us. You trusted enough to believe that we were actually going to save Kate."

There's a palpable silence as my words take effect.

"Why couldn't you stop?" she finally asks.

"We had kilos of fent in the car," Santi admits. It's a bizarre feeling to hear him confess this to anyone other than me or Ted. We've kept so many secrets for so long... but it all ends tonight.

"Fent?"

"Fentanyl," I clarify.

"Wha—" I catch her staring at the road pensively, analyzing the limited information she has. "Your dads..."

"Yep," I say, popping the p. "Our dads lead the fentanyl distribution to tons of drug rings. They dabble in dealing other drugs as well, but their primary business is the creation and distribution of fentanyl to other dealers."

"The hotel is full of drugs?" she guesses.

"Cash. Which we only just found out tonight," I say bitterly. "Wait—how do you know about the hotel?"

Char tells us about her conversation with Kate after she went through Marco's office. "When I got to the hotel, her phone went straight to voicemail. I went to the room and knocked multiple times but I got no answer. That's when I concluded you guys took her. I don't have your numbers, so I did the only thing I could think to do—show up at your door, hoping you took her to your house."

"I know we look like the bad guys," Santi explains. "And it's not like we haven't done some fucked up shit. We've been waiting for a big deal in order for the FBI to have concrete evidence of their workings. The next one was set for August. Ted explained that the more they have on them, the stronger their case presents once it goes to court. Our testimonies, while significant, aren't strong enough to imprison for life. In order to do that, we needed proof of a deal going down."

"The cash isn't as strong as what we could have gotten in August," I chime in. "But I can't let Kate die for this cause, and Ted damn well knows that. So the cash is the best we've got.

"Hopefully, along with the video footage of Kate," Santi adds, unknowingly shooting an arrow through my chest. If I weren't driving, the pain would be too much to bear. What condition are we going to find her in?

"I have so many questions... how did you get involved with the FB-fucking-I? Oh my god, is this why you wouldn't commit to... oh my god so many things are clicking!"

"We're close," I murmur. As much as I want to *finally* have a chance to explain it all, we're turning down the street for the warehouse I pray Kate is at. "We'll have to explain everything later."

"Please just let us drop you off at the corner. Get in an Uber and go home. This isn't safe," Santi pleads.

"No! I care about Kate more than either of you. I'm not leaving my best friend!"

"That's not true—" I start to argue, but Santi cuts me off.

"You stay in the car and wait for us. Don't leave for any reason other than someone coming after you. Got it?"

Once Char nods, he faces forward. When we pull up to Donovans, Santi opens the glove compartment as I throw the car into park, handing me a pistol while handing Char the other.

"I've never used a gun before," she confesses, taking it with shaky hands.

"You shouldn't need it," he reassures her. "But I'm not about to leave you out here defenseless. No one is expecting us to show up, but I'd rather be cautious."

I ensure my gun is locked and loaded while Santi teaches Char to remove the safety and pull the trigger.

"Be careful," Char says once Santi returns the gun to her and opens his door.

"We'll be fine. You need to be careful. Please, just let us take you—"

"We don't have time!" I insist as I open my door.

Santi gives me a grim look before turning to Char. "Remember what I told you."

Char nods and we slam our doors shut, meeting at the trunk. Locking eyes, we share a nod of solidarity before sprinting toward the metal door. I fumble with my keys, but Santi yanks them from me, unlocking the building entrance.

We race up the stairs, and I waste no time in kicking down every door in the place. But with each empty room we encounter, hope slips through my fingers like sand. The walls of this desolate warehouse seem to close in on me as I desperately clutch at the fleeting possibility of finding Kate.

"FUCK!"

CHAPTER TWENTY-SIX

April 30th

KATE

"It was always you, princess." His voice is all silk, tickling my skin. My heart is a bird, it's so light and free. I don't bother replying, simply smiling at him with closed lips. He takes one step closer, and my heart takes flight.

He continues to move closer, one step at a time. My eyes flutter shut in preparation for the kiss I just know he's going to plant on my lips. I want his sinful lips to corrupt mine. He leans in, and just as he's about to give me what I need, my eyes fly open.

It's much too dark as I blink three times to try and unblur my vision. It takes me a moment to realize my head is hanging and there's drool dripping out of my mouth.

What happened?

My brain is mush, taking far too long for my memory to kick in.

Marco's office.

The hotel.

The prick on my arm.

The hand over my mouth.

I want to scream but I can't even lift a finger, let alone my head. My lungs won't cooperate when I try to take in a desperate breath.

Everything feels like it requires too much energy. Energy I don't have. My body feels like a burden, heavy and lifeless.

My thoughts are like molasses trying to flow uphill. I keep forcing my eyes to stay open. I'm not sure how long I sit here, fighting myself to stay conscious, before my thoughts start to filter through the haze.

I'm seated in a chair, still dressed in my work attire of slacks and a blouse.

The dream I was having rushes back to me, and I let out a weak breath as my heart quickens.

Lorenzo.

He's behind this, I know it. He's the only person I know, along with Santi, who could be involved in something like this. Unless...

Could Brad have found out about the report?

Maybe he found out what Lorenzo and Santi did. Maybe that accident was never an accident. But Brad doesn't strike me as the type to kidnap me. He'd probably call me and ask for an explanation. He'd actually listen to my response, too.

No... Lorenzo makes more sense. That's why I was having that dream. My brain was trying to tell me. But how would he know I was in the hotel?

"Kate, don't they have cameras in there?"

It's the only explanation. One of them must have seen me and come after me. I pushed it too far. I went straight into the fire without an air pack, not bothering to consider the effects of smoke inhalation.

Was Lorenzo the one who injected me?

I want to cry but it's like my brain can't signal my eyes to cooperate. I can't take a deep breath because my chest is too tight. Summoning what little energy I have, I try to move my arm, but it's immediately restricted by something around my bicep.

My head lolls as I strain to discern the restraints binding me. Through my blurred vision, I manage to make out a tight coil of rope wrapped around my body six times.

I close my eyes because it's the only thing that takes no effort. My brain begs and pleads for me to stay alert, but sleep sounds so much more appealing.

I let it take me.

There's an incessant tapping that I want to make stop. I expect to struggle to come to, but as I lift my head, my eyes open with renewed energy. It takes a moment to remember why.

Then, the panic floods in.

Where am I? Who did this? What is that tapping? What was I drugged with?

"Hello."

I shriek in surprise and seek the source of the voice, finding a man leaning against a bare concrete wall with his arms crossed over his chest and a foot propped against it.

He chuckles darkly. "Scream all you want. No one will hear you."

His face is cast in dim shadows due to the only source of light being a small lamp tucked into the corner of whatever room we're in.

"What—" My throat is so dry that my voice is raspy and low. I clear my throat and try again, able to get the words out, albeit more like a whisper. "What am I doing here?"

"Please, excuse my manners." The man steps into the light, but the only thing about him that's recognizable is his voice; I feel like I've heard it before. "I would normally introduce myself, but you already know who I am. Don't you, Katherine?"

I gape at the man who must be my abductor. *Do I* know him? What if the drug messed with my memory?

"I... I have no clue who you are," I say shakily. My body doesn't feel like a ton of lead anymore, but uttering those few words has me catching my breath.

"Is that how we're going to play this, sweetheart?"

Play? What in the world is he talking about?

"I... don't..." Before I can try to get the rest of the words out, he stalks over and slaps me across the face. My tongue swipes my stinging cheek as blood pools over my teeth. I let out what feels like a half-cough, half-sob, but it sounds like a cat heaving.

"Let's try this again." He drops the pleasantries, a sinister gleam in his eyes. "Who are you with?"

I force myself to take a gulp of air so I can get my words out coherently. My cheek is starting to throb and I'll do anything to not get hit again. "Do you mean like a boyfriend or something?" *Is he working with Lorenzo?*

"I really wanted to do this the easy way, Ms. Appleton. But you're proving to make that very difficult. I'm a busy man; I don't have time to entertain your games."

Games?

The man moves to the corner opposite the lamp, where he bends down and digs through a black bag I hadn't noticed before. It doesn't take me long to realize that he must be searching for something to use against me.

"Please! I don't know what you're talking about!" I wanted my plea to come out in a strong and convincing voice, but it's so weak and low that I'm not sure he heard me. He stands a moment later, gripping a knife.

I'm pretty sure my eyeballs are about to pop out of my skull when he speaks, prowling towards me. "This should get you talking."

"I *am* talking!" My tear ducts finally work, tears streaming down my face as my chest rattles with heaves. "I'll tell you anything!" A sob erupts from my throat. "Please."

"Tell me who you're working with."

Something that can't be described as anything more than a gut feeling tells me not to mention Lorenzo. "I work at Valeri Financials!"

He slaps my other cheek and the iron taste of fresh blood fills my mouth. "Next time, it's the knife."

"I don't know what you're asking," I choke out between sobs.

He laughs maniacally. "You don't know what I'm asking? Please. *You* went into Marco's office. *You* were inside of that hotel. Are you *really* going to tell me you know nothing? I am not easily fooled by horseshit."

I'm at a loss for words. I need to explain myself. I need to tell him that Lorenzo was a liar and that's the only reason I cared, but everything in my gut begs me not to say that. I decide to give him a half-truth.

"I noticed weird things at the office," I say lamely.

The man swipes the knife across my cheek so quickly, I didn't see it coming. It burns as the blood runs down my cheek, drips off my chin, and splatters on my thigh.

He crouches down and puts his face mere inches from mine. Squeezing my knees with bruising force, his face inches so close that his hot breath fans across my perspiring skin. He still looks unfamiliar to me, and yet, I can't help but feel a familiarity in his voice. "You're obviously a novice. But you're going to tell me who you're working for, and then I'll dispose of you."

He stands suddenly, and I let out a mangled sob. How could I have been so stupid?

"Let's try this again." He digs in his pocket and pulls out a pen. "Why did you plant this in Rowan's house?"

"A pen?" I say, my lip trembling.

"We found this in the guest bedroom a few days after the holiday party. A party *you* attended."

The guest bedroom? That was... that was months ago, when Lorenzo and I...

I squint at the pen, trying to understanding why it would matter if it was left in the room. How does he even know I was in that room? Does that mean he knows *we* were in that room?

"That's not mine," I finally say with a little more bravado. If this man is going to attack me while I'm obviously clueless and afraid, I might as well try to be courageous. "I have no idea what you're talking about."

"You know, Katherine," he says, wiping the knife clean with a rag he pulls from his other pocket. He tosses the rag onto the floor before looking at me with an evil gleam in his eye. "If you would just confess, this would all be over a lot quicker."

"I have nothing to confess to!" I shout. My voice is getting stronger even though my throat is drier than ever. "I was noticing weird things around the office, so I decided to investigate. I had no idea what was in that hotel roo—"

A sharp, agonizing pain rips through my thigh when he slices the knife across it. I let out a piercing scream as my eyes fixate on the deep gash, blood seeping into the torn fabric.

"I'm a busy man, Ms. Appleton, but my schedule is cleared for this. I can guarantee that I've got a lot more stamina than you."

"Sir," I say, my voice shaking. The bravado lasted point-five seconds. "I wish I could help you. But I don't know anything. I went to the hotel to try and find out."

"Who is it? Another runner? The Feds?"

My thoughts are going a mile a minute, desperately trying to piece together what's going on.

Lorenzo.

His friends. One of them is *related* to Rowan, while Lorenzo himself is related to Marco.

The drugs.

The cash.

Rowan and Marco's lack of involvement.

Their trust in their employees.

The cheap housing.

The cash discount.

The audit ding.

The pieces of the puzzle snap together all at once.

It's a front.

It's a drug front.

And this psycho in front of me thinks I was working against them.

The epiphany sinks a rock in my gut as the man touches the tip of the knife to my stomach, and I know he's only a moment away from twisting it through my insides. I rack my brain for something—*anything*—to say to make him stop. Fuck Lorenzo and fuck my gut feeling. I open my mouth to tell him the truth, but he speaks first.

"If I wanted your silence, I'd have cut out your tongue. Tell me who you're with or I will make your last minutes on this earth long and tortur—"

His words are abruptly silenced by a resounding slam from behind me. His eyes dart towards the source of the noise, but before I can turn my head, the sharp echo of a gunshot reverberates off the walls.

CHAPTER TWENTY-SEVEN

April 30th

Zo

The bullet sinks right through Ron's forehead as I release the trigger. Kate's assailant drops to the floor, the knife clattering on the concrete. I rush to her as she screams and kicks the floor, trying to back away from his crumpled body with blood leaking out of the hole in his head. But the chair hardly moves because she can't get enough force into her legs with the ropes around her body.

"Untie her," I demand of Santi as I drop to my knees in front of her. Fury consumes me at the sight of her condition, but I force myself to stay focused. Fresh blood splattered across her face, but I'm relieved to find the cut in her cheek isn't too deep. That relief evaporates in an instant when my eyes land on the gash in her leg, blood oozing from the wound.

Her eyes catch with mine as they roam over her face again, and I feel like I can breathe properly for the first time in weeks. It's short-lived, however, because I note the fear in her wide eyes. Her lips move, but no sound escapes.

"Kate, I'm so sorry." My words are rushed and laced with pure agony. She blinks hard as Santi works on the knots at her back. I gingerly place my hands on her shoulders, but she flinches, shattering my heart. Then

I remember I'm still holding the gun. I give her a light shake and repeat her name, to which she lets out another blood-curdling scream.

Santi's hand flies over her mouth, but he releases it just as quickly when she bites him.

"Fuck!" Santi shouts, shaking his hand out.

"She's gone through a lot, man, leave it," I snap.

"The door is still open!"

"Go close it!"

Santi jogs to the door as I inspect her for the third time. "It's going to be okay, we're getting you out of here." She doesn't look soothed by these words. Like Char, she has zero trust in me, and I can't fault her for that.

Santi jogs back over and continues to work the knots. "This shit is on here *tight*."

I release her shoulders to collect the knife, passing it to him.

"Thanks," Santi says. The ropes pull as he works them, but my eyes find hers again.

"Did you get the footage?" I ask without breaking eye contact. I see Santi nod from my peripherals.

"What is happening?" she whispers.

"Don't worry, we're getting you out of here."

"Why should I trust you?"

I let out a dark huff just as Santi finishes sawing the rope. The only solace I find in this shit situation is that I can finally come clean with her. But first, we need to get the hell out of here. When the rope sags and Santi unwraps her, I scoop her into my arms. She attempts to squirm in my embrace, but she's obviously depleted of energy.

"Don't worry, I've got you," I tell her, then I address Santi. "Let's go."

Santi tosses the knife and joins my side as it clatters on the ground.

"I'll run a check, if I'm not back in thirty seconds..."

He gives me a meaningful look before he dashes to the door and out into the hallway. I look down at Kate, whose eyes have closed. Her body moves up and down with my silent breath. There's so much I want to say, but I don't know where to begin or how to say it.

Time has ceased to properly exist for me, so I'm not sure how long it takes Santi to reappear in the doorway. He nods, and I tighten my grip on her body as I hoist her up, exiting this godforsaken building. I steal glances at her as we move quickly through the long hallway towards the exit. Santi presses on the bar and holds open the metal door as I duck my head over Kate. Her faint strawberry scent is exactly as I remember, and it renews life in me. Rain patters over us, but I keep Kate tucked into my chest, my head acting as a makeshift umbrella.

We cut through the dark alley and rush back to the car. Char throws the back door open and I rush inside with Kate on my lap.

"Go to the front," I bark at Char. She doesn't hesitate, clambering through the center console and dropping into the passenger seat. Santi's in the driver's side a moment later, and I toss him the keys from my pocket.

The wind whips through the rain, causing Kate to shiver in my arms. I quickly close my door and shift her onto the seat beside me, cradling her head on my thigh. Santi peels away from the rows of warehouses as I hastily tear off my shirt.

I dry her body with my shirt, then delicately dab at the drying blood on her face. While her eyes remain closed, the comforting sensation of her nuzzling into my lap boosts my composure. I can't afford to lose control when she needs me most, no matter how much I want to.

Simply killing Ron wasn't nearly what he deserved, but time wasn't on our side.

"Where are we going?" Char asks from the front.

"The Getaway," Santi says.

"What's The Getaway?" she asks.

Kate stirs in my lap as Santi's response fades into the background, my attention focused on gently stroking her wet hair. "Go to sleep, princess. You're safe now," I whisper softly.

Her breaths become deeper, and I'm certain she's fallen asleep. I proceed with my careful cleaning of her face, unsurprised that she doesn't wake up. There's no doubt in my mind she was drugged. Once the cut is clean, I start to reach for her thigh, but halt mid-motion when the movement jostles her.

"Let me," Char says quietly, taking the now damp and dirty shirt from my hand. She leans over the console and mimics my gentle dabbing. Char meets my eyes, and a new understanding passes between us.

"Thank you," Char whispers.

"For what?" I whisper back.

"Saving her."

"I wouldn't have needed to save her if I'd just stayed away in the first place," I confess, peeling my eyes away to stare at the rainy night outside the window as a new wave of guilt washes over me.

"Don't," Char and Santi say in unison, forcing my head to snap to them.

"You obviously care about her," Santi adds.

"Care? Psh. He's *in love* with her," Char argues. They continue to bicker but my mind focuses on two words.

In love.

That's exactly what I am.

A groan escapes Kate's lips, and they immediately cease their conversation. I sit a little straighter, caressing her head again. Her breathing returns to the deep, melodic pace it was at seconds before, and I slump back into my seat.

"How far is this place?" Char asks.

"'Bout an hour," Santi replies.

"Well that's plenty of time for more explaining," Char says, dropping my shirt onto the floorboard and settling into her seat.

Santi opens his mouth but I cut in. "First, we need to call Ted. And Marco. This isn't over yet."

"Fuck," Santi mutters. He passes me my phone from the cup holder and I dial Ted.

"We got it," he says immediately.

"The warrant or the money?" I ask impatiently.

"The warrant. I've got two agents on their way to the hotel, and I'm prepping a team to meet tonight. Did you find her?"

I stare at Kate as I respond. "We did. We're dropping her at The Getaway, and then we'll come meet you."

"We'll go over the plan when you arrive."

"There's going to be some... clean up," Santi says warily. *Ron.*

Ted sighs. "I figured as much. I can't say it's undeserved."

Santi and I share a dark look through the rearview mirror.

"I'll take whatever charges are necessary," I say through gritted teeth.

"We'll get it cleared. I assume you got the footage?" Santi grunts in response. "Very well. I'll let you know once we're ready."

We hang up, and I consider what to tell Marco. He really had no problem assigning some shit like this to us. It would probably take hours to tear down those hotel room walls. And what if a neighbor heard and reported us?

I dial his number. "Son."

"We're here, but it's taking some time. We're doing this quietly so as not to call any attention to ourselves."

"Excellent. Great work, both of you. Let me know when you've got it, and we'll meet at Rowan's."

"You got it."

"What's the update on the rat?" Santi pipes in. *Smart thinking.*

"I haven't heard from Ron yet, but I'm sure he's working her. She's holding up longer than I expected. Or she hasn't come out of her drug stupor." His laugh infuriates me, uncapping the lid on the always-simmering rage.

"We'll let you know once we've gotten everything," Santi says. I disconnect the call, resisting the urge to yell into the car.

"This is really some crazy shit," Char mutters. "How did you guys get involved with the fucking FBI?"

"It's a long story," I say, but the truth of it is I don't feel like getting into it right now. Not knowing if Kate was alive or okay, then seeing her like this... it's completely shattered me. And I don't care what Santi and Char say, it's my fucking fault. Santi said it himself—I should have stayed the fuck away.

"Zo and I go way back," Santi starts. "Since we were kids. Shit, toddlers, really. And there's one reason for that—our fathers.

"They started selling weed and coke back in high school. As they got older, they got greedier. Hungrier for money, and the power it brings. They got into prescription drugs, heroin, the whole deal. Once they learned about fentanyl, they went hard. They got in when it was up and coming, so now they're one of the largest distributors of that shit."

"Isn't fentanyl the stuff that gets laced into drugs?"

"Correct. Kills people too often," Santi says with disdain. "It's the exact reason we wanted to bring them down."

"Long story short," I jump in, wanting this story time to end. There's already too much shit going on, and when Kate hears about this, I want it to be from my own mouth. "We contacted the FBI and requested to become informants so we could take them down. Turns out, they were already in the works of sending someone undercover. So it was a mutually beneficial agreement."

"How long have you been working with them?" Char asks.

"Since December. Right before Zo met Kate, actually," Santi says.

Char mulls that over. "So, all this time... that's why you wouldn't commit to her?"

"I told him from the jump not to get involved with Kate," Santi says. "It wasn't personal, we just didn't need any liabilities. What if Marco and Rowan found out about what we were doing? I didn't want blood on our hands."

"Marco and Rowan have no problem putting someone in the grave, and they have the means to ensure it goes undetected," I add, goosebumps coating my skin.

"Then we find out she knows the guy we ran off the road?" Santi shakes his head. "I mean, fuck, what are the goddamn chances of that?"

"She was supposed to meet him for a date that night, you know," Char says quietly. When Santi's brows furrow, she adds, "Brad."

Santi blows out a breath, and I stare at Kate's limp form. The entire reason we met is the result of one of one of my biggest regrets?

Life is fucked up.

When our silence extends into more silence, I resume stroking Kate's hair and rest my head against the seat. None of us speaks for the rest of the car ride, lost to our own thoughts.

I want to explain everything to her, now that I'll be a free man. Free from my father's restraints. Free from the fear of being caught. Free from the guilt of what we've done.

All because he'll be behind bars, and his distribution will no longer continue. I'm not naive; I'm sure other people will continue to sell this devil's poison. But I will no longer play a part in it.

Will she understand, though? Char seems to. But is it forgivable? Understanding something doesn't mean you allow it into your life.

I'll remain a broken man, but whatever makes her happy is all that matters. I need her to have all the knowledge so she can make an informed decision, and I'll accept whatever it is. Even if it destroys me in the process.

CHAPTER TWENTY-EIGHT

April 30th

KATE

I'm so warm. *Too* warm. Hot, stifled. But my body doesn't want to move, and my eyes don't want to open. I become aware of my breathing, my belly rising and falling with each peaceful sounding inhalation and exhalation.

Man, that was a crazy dream I had. The knife in my skin felt so real. The heat radiating from Lorenzo as we sped away in that car... It's insane how much I crave it. It's crazy to wish it were true, just so I could be near him again.

A body shifts under me and I startle, my eyes flying open when my head drops onto a firm cushion. I sit up, my head pounding with a headache I didn't know was there. I search around me, quickly piecing together that I'm in a car.

Lorenzo's car.

Is that—

"Char?" I croak.

"Shit, I didn't mean to wake you." *His voice.* It sends electricity coursing through me, every nerve-ending on alert.

It was real.

And suddenly, my ears are ringing with the reverberating gunshot. My head throbs as hands gently touch my arm, but I instinctively yank it away. It's all too overwhelming.

"Let's get her inside," Char says. A door opens from the left and Santi steps out of the car.

"This shit is on here tight."

Hands are on me again, but when I flinch, Lorenzo's face lowers to mine through the door frame.

"Hey, I'm going to take you in now. I'm not going to hurt you," he says softly. For some reason, I don't think he's going to hurt me, but I still don't feel safe. Remembering that Char is with him, I nod, letting him pull me out.

"I can walk," I manage, but my legs feel weak the moment they touch the ground. He scoops me into his arms, carrying me towards a pristine white residence with a spacious front porch and a navy blue door.

Where the hell are we?

He tows me across the threshold and despite how shitty I feel, my breath hitches. Before us is an open layout with a kitchen overlooking the living room. The white walls and white furniture, complemented by cabinets painted in the same serene blue as the front door, exude an atmosphere of charm. The back wall adds to the tranquility with floor-to-ceiling windows overlooking a bay with gentle waves lapping against the shore.

This has to be the most beautiful home I've ever been in.

"I'm taking her to my room," Lorenzo says.

This place is his?

He breaks left and climbs the spiral staircase I missed before. When we reach the landing, he walks down a hallway, passing two closed doors and entering the final one at the end.

The room is just as spacious and open as the living room, with identical white walls and a sliding glass door leading to a balcony. It's quaint and cozy, an obvious sanctuary.

Lorenzo deposits me into a massive bed, larger than any king size bed I've ever seen. There's a bamboo headboard behind us with cubbies and drawers. Matching white and bamboo nightstands adorn each side. He tucks me under a thick, white comforter, my head resting on a feathery pillow.

"I'll be right back," he says, placing an airy kiss on my forehead before hurrying out of the room, shutting the also blue door.

My senses are sharpening, and the events of the past—*fuck*, how many hours, days, or even weeks has it been? What day is it? Where's my phone? Oh my god, is Felix okay?

My brain turns on like a motor that hasn't run in years, sputtering and whirring until it finally gets enough gas to thrum properly. I flex my thighs and the gash burns with the effort. All of it rushes back to me as I lift my hand to graze the stinging cut in my cheek.

The injection, the grogginess, the man with the knife. The blood. The gunshot.

Santi and Lorenzo.

My body stiffens. They may have taken me out of there, but I have no idea why. Are they prepared to do worse things to me? Why should I lay here, trusting him, after everything he's lied about?

Char.

Why was she with them?

Lorenzo returns with a glass of water, quietly shutting the door. He places the glass atop the nightstand and walks over to the closet, throwing a shirt on. I stare at him for the first time since... St. Patrick's Day.

My body doesn't feel heavy anymore, like it did when I was strapped to that chair. But I'm definitely weak and tired. The dryness in my throat hasn't gone away. I take the glass of water and the moment it touches my lips, I down it like I haven't had water in days. Maybe it *has* been days.

I have no idea where I am, but the urge to go home is suddenly so overwhelming that I shove the blanket down as Lorenzo climbs into the bed from the other side. Misreading my action as an invitation, he slides his legs under the covers.

The expression on his face stops me from leaving. He looks... more peaceful than I've ever seen him.

I'm so accustomed to seeing him in black that the white backdrop of the sheets and pillow make me feel like I'm drinking in a different person. His hair is more disheveled than usual. His features are relaxed. It's never occurred to me until now just how much pressure he seemed to be under.

What pressures, exactly? What secrets is he carrying? How did he know where to find me?

Our gazes lock and my body stills when his lips tug into a faint smile. All the lies, all this time apart, and he still holds the same power over me. Every fiber of my being wants to be enveloped in his arms again. To feel his heartbeat sync with mine.

"How are you feeling?" he asks throatily. His voice, his gaze, everything about him is softer than I ever remember seeing. It does stupid things to my heart.

"I'm..." My voice is croaky, the dryness worse than I thought. Lorenzo glances at the empty cup and hops out of bed, grabbing it. He exits the room, leaving me dumbfounded. Partially because I'm not used to this attentiveness, but mostly because the feeling to escape has evaporated into nothingness.

When he returns and hands me the glass, I down it just as quickly as before while Lorenzo crawls back into bed.

"I was so afraid I'd lost you for good," he whispers. "I'm so sorry this happened to you." The agony in his voice feels imagined. I'm so lost, and I'm not sure I'm prepared to go down this road, so I pivot.

"Where"—I pause to clear my throat—"Where are we?"

"This is a place Santi and I rented in Willowbrook."

"But..."

"Yeah, that house was our primary location. In fact, I've only ever been here once before. But Santi and I always wanted a place we could escape to, if the time came."

Escape to?

He responds to the quizzical look on my face. "There is... so much I need to explain to you."

The foreign peace that was there moments ago is gone, replaced by pain and exhaustion. I simply nod, the inexplicable pull to him keeping me rooted to the spot, desperate to hear what he has to say. Although the knowledge that Char is here, and she didn't seem scared, provides a sense of security.

He lets out a mangled sigh. "I..."

What's he about to say? Will this change everything? Is it just another lie? How will I ever know?

I decide to start small. "What day is it?"

"It's still Monday."

My face falls. How can all of this have happened in a matter of hours? "Oh."

"Hey, hey," he says so soothingly, it has me second guessing he said it all. "Take it easy. You've been through a lot."

"I'm fine, I'm... I'm so confused. You—you rescued me?" He nods. "How did you know where I was?"

He laughs humorlessly. "My father."

"Marco?" I ask. He nods in confirmation as I remember what I deduced when I was being... I can't think of it without shuddering. "Why would he tell you? I know you sell drugs together."

Lorenzo snorts. "By force, more than anything. Santi and I, at least. Our dads... well, I need to start from the beginning. We—"

"Why didn't you tell me your dad runs the Groves Shores branch?" I interrupt accusingly.

"I told you as little as possible for a reason. I shouldn't have gotten close to you at all, but secrecy was *some* form of protection."

"Well, look where that landed us," I snap spitefully.

His expression turns solemn and he picks at the bed sheets. So many questions go through my mind but I focus on the pertinent ones. "How did you know where I was? Why would Marco tell you?"

"Our fathers—Rowan and Marco—have suspected that we've been under watch for a long time. They suspected inside work."

"We? So you are with them? Running drugs? What—"

He places a hand on my arm and squeezes, quieting me with his touch. This is nothing like the peace I felt when he carried me. It's scary because I don't know if he should be trusted, but I also love the feeling of it.

"Please just let me explain," he says, his eyes pleading with mine. I nod, despite myself. He catches me up on what he and Santi explained to Char regarding Marco and Rowan's roots and how they ended up in business for fentanyl distribution.

"That's why it's a front!" I exclaim.

"How do you know about that?" Lorenzo's eyes pierce mine.

I don't trust his level of involvement, so I fish instead of admitting what I know. "It's Rentals, isn't it?"

Lorenzo's brows shoot up, but he nods. "Yeah. Why do you think they give a twenty percent discount on cash transactions?"

"That's what I pieced together."

"They try to keep that department under wraps. But they provide housing for a supposedly low price. They're only charging the renters half of what it's actually worth. Then, they change the paperwork and put in their own cash to cover the rest. They pocket the profits, anyway. No harm, no foul."

The audit ding...

"That's why Rowan was so pissed about the audit ding."

"Ohhh, he was *livid*. Carter and D got chewed the fuck out for that mistake."

"So they're involved, too? All of your friends?"

"Well, hold on. Carter and D don't know about the money laundering. What they weren't supposed to do was turn in the paperwork. Rowan or Marco normally head the audits. They're in charge of that small department, and for all intents and purposes, that is intentional. The less hands that touch it, the better."

That's why he wouldn't let Jasmine run it.

"But the auditor emailed the general inbox for Rentals, not Rowan, like they were supposed to. Carter and D took it upon themselves to send the information. Not that they knew they were doing something wrong. On the contrary, they thought they were helping."

"So they sent in paperwork... with the wrong rental amount?"

"Right. Renters are told they only have to pay fifteen-hundred dollars. But Marco and Rowan filter in their own fifteen-hundred and change the documentation to reflect a rent amount of three thousand."

"But don't these renters question why the rents are so low?"

Lorenzo laughs. "You would think they should. But nah, they're usually just content to be able to get a nice place that's affordable for them. If anyone ever asks, they're told there's a grant program that covers the rest. But how many times have you fully read a contract?" He pauses, and when I stare at him blankly, he continues. "Exactly. They don't care enough to look into it. They're happy to pay less, so they don't ask more.

"The money is there. And most of the time, in cash, because then the renters get the 20% off. That allows Marco and Rowan to keep less of a paper trail."

"That doesn't seem to be enough to cover everything they make?"

"Oh, it's not. They have offshore accounts, keep some of it in lump cash. And now we know, they stashed it in hotel rooms. Something *you* discovered."

"Well, not exactly. I didn't see the cash until I was kicking and thrashing, trying to get away from the kidnapper."

His expression darkens. "Tell me, princess. Why were you snooping in Marco's office?"

"I..." The answer is simple, really. Simple and stupid. "I wanted answers."

He shakes his head. "You always do."

"It was fucking weird! All of your relatives and friends secretly working there, the police report with Brad... What role did he play in any of this?"

A pained look crosses his features as he runs a hand through his hair. "Brad was a fluke. An accident. The night we met, right before we got to the bar, we were on a drug run. We had a delivery to handle." A somber look crosses him. "Santi was driving my car, and he was a bit excited for the evening. We were seeing some school friends we hadn't seen in a bit.

"Santi is not the skilled driver I am. We're driving down the main road and he decides to get testy with the speed limit. It was reckless—"

I let out a haughty laugh. "Are you serious? *You're* calling him reckless?"

"He didn't always drive like that. Say what you will, but I've yet to cause an accident. Anyway, he moves to get into the right lane and I start shouting because he's about to hit a car. Santi corrects himself, but too late. I watched Brad's car run off the road and hit that tree. I saw it all.

"Santi didn't stop, and I knew we couldn't. We had pounds of fent in the trunk. Do you know the risk we would take by taking fault? They could search the car if they wanted! If we got caught with that, we'd be arrested. We'd lose all the work we'd put into this investigation. Not to mention, our dad's would have been *pissed* if they found out. We called Ted the next day and he wasn't happy, but he agreed it would have caused more paperwork and headache than any of us needed. Santi and I felt so guilty, we dropped off an envelope with cash at Brad's house."

"Seriously? He didn't mention that to me."

"Yeah, well, Brad Atkins isn't an innocent man. He's not running drugs or anything, but he was doing some insider trading with a previous firm he worked for. I'm not sure how he was able to secure a new job with that record."

"How'd you find that out?"

"Ted pulled the police report and ran his info in case we needed to protect ourselves. In case any witnesses reported us... I begged him for a copy of the report."

"That's why you didn't want me to date him," I say confidently.

"Pieced that together, too, huh?"

I nod.

"That night, on New Year's, when I saw his name, I thought 'there's no way it's the same Brad.' What were the damn chances I'd end up falling"—he clears his throat as my heart skips a beat—"hooking up with the one girl that could be connected to him?"

I shake my head in disbelief. "This world is too small. Imagine if I had mentioned Brad on the night we met? You wouldn't have tried to hook up with me at all."

A strange look crosses his face. "About that..."

My stomach plummets. "What?"

"Kate, I want to come clean about everything. No secrets."

"Okay," I say apprehensively.

"Hooking up with you that night at Rowan's... it wasn't an accident. I mean, I didn't know you'd be working for Valeri Financials when we met the night before. But when I saw you, I saw you as an opportunity. I already had a mission that night. I needed to—"

"The pen," I gasp.

His eyebrows shoot up. "How do you know about the mic?"

"That man who took me, he was waving it at me, demanding to know how I got it in the room."

"Yeah, that's Ron. He was actually in the room with Rowan that night. Remember when we had to hide in the closet?"

"That's why I recognized his voice," I realize.

"Rowan had recently moved into that house. Valeri Financials was finally doing well enough that he could prove a legal income for a new mortgage. That's why Santi and I moved into his old house. I think Rowan got a few drinks in him and decided it was a good time to show Ron around. I didn't know he'd be doing weekly scans of the place," Lorenzo says bitterly.

"The pen... it had a mic in it? Was it from the FBI?"

"Yep. Once Ron found it, Marco and Rowan knew they were being watched. They also knew it was a high likelihood that the person worked at the company because he'd just had the holiday party. That was a huge mistake on our part, one we should have seen coming. But they'd never had a *real* threat before. I had no idea they were so thorough, or I would have told Ted it was a bad idea when he suggested bugging the place.

"Naturally, they didn't suspect me or Santi, but we were always destined to work for Valeri Financials. How better to learn the business if not by working for it?" He laughs humorlessly. "They wanted to move the laundering from Rentals to servicing the mortgage loans themselves. Santi and I taking over, under the guise of managing the Westland Branch, would free them up to focus on expanding distribution. The point is, since I had just started there, he had me monitoring the systems. I set up flags for all types of searches, one of them being—"

I gasp. "Job searches?"

"Yep."

"That's how you figured out my apartment number, too!"

"That's right. Full access to the database."

My mind reels with all of this information. It's nearly unbelievable. And to think, I was in that closet while my future kidnapper—

"Wait... so you never even really liked me? All of that, that night, it was just—"

Bile finally rises in my throat. It's just lie after lie after lie.

"I thought you were beautiful, of course I did. And sexy as fuck. That dress really did make me wild." The ghost of a smile appears on his lips. "But I needed to get in that room. And getting caught hooking up with someone was a lot more explainable than being up there alone."

Every inch of my skin is coated in goosebumps. "You used me." Disgust overpowers all of my tumultuous emotions. I suddenly feel dirty that I allowed him to touch me after all of this. Registering the change, he becomes frantic.

"I didn't want to risk getting close to anyone," he rushes out. "I couldn't even *think* about being with someone. I had a mission, it was all I could—"

"I can't do this." My words of finality strike the air, and the resounding shocks tremor us both.

"I fell for you! I couldn't stop thinking about you. I meant what I said about Sara and trying to forget—"

"This is too much, Lorenzo. Too far. All of it. I lost myself with your words, wrapped up in your dark promises. But I can't, I can't, I can't—"

My lips tremble as tears prick my eyes. My heart is breaking even more than it did before.

Just because he did all of this for a good reason doesn't change the fact that he did unforgivable and selfish things.

"I've been a *wreck* without you! I can't sleep well, I have no appetite. I can't lose you—" He shocks me with tears filling his own eyes. But they only piss me off more.

"You think I've been sleeping well? I've had nightmares every night! Imagining you doing all sorts of terrible things. The difference is, I didn't cause this. *You did.*"

"Please, Kate. Please!"

"You're still a liar! Our entire foundation is rotten, built upon deception. How can we ever move forward with that?"

"We're all liars!"

I scoff. "I am *not* a liar!"

"I want you to look me straight in my face and tell me you meant it when you said you didn't want a boyfriend."

The retort is on the tip of my tongue when he cuts me off.

"You didn't want to get hurt. You were done trying. You were giving up. But you wanted a boyfriend."

I'm done. *So* done. "Me trying to protect myself is totally different, and you know it."

"I didn't want to—"

Tears roll down my cheeks. "Thank you for rescuing me. And thank you for telling me the truth. But I can't do this anymore. Looks like you got what you always wanted. You ruined me."

He appears pained as he opens his mouth to say something, but Santi's voice, accompanied by a knock at the door, interrupts him.

"Zo! We need to talk!"

Lorenzo glances at me. I quickly swipe at the tears staining my cheeks, and Lorenzo does the same. When I nod, he replies, "Come in."

Santi barges through the door. There's no other way of putting it. His hair is unruly, evidencing that he's been through it as well. His eyes wash over me before pinning on Lorenzo.

"Ted just called, they're ready for us. This can't wait. It's only a matter of time before—"

"I know," Lorenzo cuts in, much calmer than his best friend. But I don't miss the hint of worry. "Can you just give us like, five more minutes?"

"I'm so happy you've made up," Santi bites out sarcastically. "But we don't have time for this right now."

Lorenzo and I look at each other awkwardly before averting our gazes. Santi must misread it as vulnerability rather than inaccuracy, because he crosses his arms expectantly, waiting on Lorenzo, who shifts uncomfortably beside me.

Running a hand through his hair, he says, "Fuck. I know." He looks at me, torture etched into his every feature. When he turns back to Santi, that pain is erased, replaced by determination.

"Can you at least let me get changed?"

Santi waves a hand dismissively. "Nothing I haven't seen before."

I can't help myself, I burst out laughing. I think all of the hysteria is catching up to me. I can't catch my breath. I double over as Lorenzo crawls out of bed and into the walk-in closet.

"This is ridiculous, bro," Lorenzo mutters as he tears his gym shorts and boxers off in one go. My laughter turns into a groan at the clothing so haphazardly discarded when there's a hamper a foot away. The mess is quickly forgotten when I catch sight of his tight ass before he covers it with fresh underwear.

"I don't want you getting distracted," Santi says, pointing an accusing finger at him.

I turn solemn with the reminder of what's about to happen. "Where are you guys going?"

"This is it. It's now or never," Lorenzo says evasively, putting on a pair of black jeans.

"What's it? Is this because of me?" My lip starts to tremble as Lorenzo tosses on a fresh black shirt.

"We knew the risk," Santi says stoically.

"We'll have a squad undercover and ready. We should be fine," Lorenzo says reassuringly, sliding his black combat boots on.

"Undercover?" My face pales. Regardless of the fact that I was prepared to break this off and escape, I can't help the anxiety that takes over me.

"Kate." Lorenzo cups each of my cheeks, his warm and calloused hands calming me. "I need you to stay here while we go. Can you do that for me?"

"I—"

"If you don't want to do this, I understand. We can talk about it after. But I can't go into this worrying about whether you're safe or not. They'll never find you here."

"I don't want to stay alone," I whisper.

"Char is here," Santi says. I almost forgot he was standing a few feet away. My eyes dart in his direction as Lorenzo glares at him.

"Dude, *please*. Give me two minutes."

"Fine. Two minutes." He stalks out the door, but I don't hear additional steps once the door is closed. He's probably standing outside like some sort of watch dog.

"Char will stay with you."

"Does she know?"

"She knows some. You can fill her in on the rest."

I nod with an ache deep in my soul, one I see mirrored in his irises.

"Kate... I lo—"

I shake my head vigorously, silencing him. I can't hear it right now; my heart can only handle so much.

He tips my chin up and searches my eyes before planting a kiss to my forehead. I squeeze his forearms before pushing him away.

"Santi's waiting," I say quietly.

He nods, fingers grazing my cheek and dropping to his side. "Come on, Char is downstairs."

I follow him down the hall and staircase, finding Char on the couch. She sits straighter when she sees me walking towards her.

"We're headed to meet Ted," Santi says from the doorway. Lorenzo decisively walks up to me and brings his hand behind my neck, pulling me closer. "Please stay here, no matter what. Promise me."

I nod. "Okay."

"Say it."

"I promise," I agree reluctantly.

His eyes lock with mine. "Think about everything. Process it. Do what you do best. Whatever you decide, I'll understand."

"Okay," I whisper. He closes the gap, pressing his lips to mine for a kiss that says those words I didn't let him say before.

And then he's gone.

Char places her hand on my knee when I drop into the seat next to her on the couch.

"How are you?"

All of my emotions bubble to the surface and I start balling. I'm not sure how long I cry for, Char stroking my back the entire time, before I finally wipe the last tears.

"Did you guys talk?" Char asks. When I nod, she says, "What did he say?"

I recite every last detail that Lorenzo told me, some of which she knew. The details of my kidnapping are hazy and distorted, but I tell her everything I remember from when I arrived at the hotel to when Lorenzo shot my kidnapper.

He shot a man.

I didn't even know he had experience with firearms. I realize that for as many answers as I got today, there are still a fuck ton more.

"This is all just so insane..." Char says when I fill her in on everything. "You said there were stacks of money?"

"Inside the wall."

"I wonder if it's the whole wall. If those are hundreds... damn."

"Yeah."

"You should have grabbed me a stack."

"Char!" She giggles but I can't join her. The repercussions of my actions are starting to catch up with me. When she catches my expression, she sobers up. "Sorry, I shouldn't be joking about this."

"I don't know what to make of any of it. I still don't understand why he didn't just walk away from the business. Why did he have to go to the extreme of involving the FBI? How did that even happen?"

"From what they told me, it sounded like they didn't have much of a choice," Char says despondently.

"There's *always* a choice," I say.

We're quiet for a moment, each lost to our own thoughts. "It couldn't hurt to hear him out, though."

"Hear him out? I've heard enough already. I don't know how this is forgivable!" I say indignantly.

"I just... I mean, it's obvious he's in—" I peg her with a glare so sharp and intense she switches gears. "He obviously cares about you. If only you had seen him, he was *distraught* when we were looking—"

My stomach flips, but I don't want to hear anymore. "Even if that's true, it doesn't excuse everything he's done. Everything *they've* done."

"Running Brad off the road and not even stopping is terrible. I know that. But... I don't know, I can see why they felt the need to avoid arrest. They had bigger fish to fry, so to speak."

"Okay, but what about the pen? He was completely fine with *using* me for this 'greater good'!"

"It's shitty, but I get it. He was desperate! He wanted to stop his dad, and for good reason, it sounds like. But he obviously fell for you unintentionally and now—"

"That doesn't make it better!"

Char looks at me sympathetically. "Look, you gotta do what's best for you, toots. If you can't move past this, then don't. But no one needs a third-act breakup, so try to make a choice and stick to it."

"A third-act *what*?" I ask.

Char sighs. "You really need to start reading romance books."

"I—" My head throbs and I decide I don't care about what it means. "Nevermind. I think I need to lie down." As I move towards the staircase, I suddenly feel like I need to be clean. "Actually, a hot bath sounds nice."

"Go. I'll be right here." She lays down on the couch and pulls out her phone.

I return to the bedroom I was in with Lorenzo earlier, having seen a door I believe was the ensuite. Opening the door confirms there's a luxurious bathtub stocked with soap and towels. There's no shampoo or conditioner, but then again, Lorenzo said he'd only been here once before.

I remove my clothes and sink into the bath, ignoring the sting from the gash in my leg.

I can't deny how much more alive I feel, despite the weakness in my body. The fire lighting me up is returning to my soul and I know it's for one reason only. It's obvious that I'm already hoping for the best, wanting this all to be permissible for some greater good.

But what if I burn alive?

CHAPTER TWENTY-NINE

May 1st

☾

Zo

"**T**ry to get as much information from them as possible," Ted says, pinning the hidden mic into the waistband of my jeans. Santi nods from beside me.

"What if we can't get them to say anything?"

"Between the video footage and the massive amounts of cash we found, we have grounds for arrest. The meet in August was ideal, but the recent... *events* changed things."

I nod, but I can't ignore the sinking feeling in my stomach. This is all my fault. Getting involved with Kate resulted in her being kidnapped, and our ultimate mission potentially being ruined.

"Don't overthink this," Ted says, bracing my shoulders before stepping back. "You're human. You should have never been put into a situation like this to begin with."

"Let's get this over with," Santi says stoically from behind me. I silently thank him with a head nod. I need to get out of this headspace and focus on what we're about to do.

"We'll be parked on the next street over. Once you're in, I'll send the team to surround the perimeter and work on removing the guards. Once I hear the right moment, I'll send them in."

We all nod our heads and he walks towards his office door.

"Ted," I call out. When he faces me, I ask, "Do I have permission to shoot?"

His eyes give away his sympathy. "You've already shot a man. On acceptable and excusable grounds, yes, but it's still murder. We don't have justifiable reason here."

I grit my teeth but bow my head. He's not wrong.

Ted holds the door open for us as we roll out the suitcases stuffed with cash. They were able to efficiently break down the walls of the hotel room, finding hundreds of thousands of dollars hidden within.

Santi and I load up the four suitcases into the trunk and get in the car. As we head to Rowan's house, I call Marco to let him know we're on our way while Santi checks the glocks. While we don't intend to use them, it's better safe than sorry. Our fathers have a lot of means at their disposal, and there's no telling if they know what we've really been up to tonight.

In the same way we're setting them up, they could be setting us up.

Once we park in the driveway, I face Santi—my brother, regardless of blood.

"If, for some reason, I don't make it out of this—"

"Don't talk like that, Zo. We're going to be fine."

I shake my head. "If you make it out, please tell Kate I love her. She has to know that through all this bullshit—all *my* bullsh—"

"Quit talkin' like that, man!" Santi's eyes flash with fear and I can tell I'm freaking him out. "We're both getting out. Point blank."

I nod so as not to cause him any more fear, but I'm not convinced. We're moving forward with this because it's our only chance, *if* we haven't already been discovered.

Rowan's house is one of the safest locations; all of the drugs are stored here before they're transferred for distribution. Rowan and Marco are the only ones allowed to move the product from here to a warehouse, where it's picked up for delivery.

Santi's been here more than me because he visits his mom and brother, but I've only been inside a handful of times, and with limited access. That's why the holiday party was crucial for planting the bug. They have eyes on this place 24/7. There are guards that walk the perimeter, and cameras galore. Unlike the office, they feel safe having cameras here. Since they're the only ones who transfer the initial deliveries, they turn off the cameras at those times.

Marco and Rowan only make appearances for large deals, and they're always armed with their hitmen. Ron was one of them. While they never host meets at Rowan's, they try to keep it on their turf. You maintain more control that way.

Once we exit the car, I pull Santi into an embrace. He pats my back.

"To the stars," I say.

"To the stars," he responds, his voice filled with determination. We pad the front porch steps and knock on the door three times in a row, then wait while I'm sure Rowan checks the camera to clear us for entry.

About a minute later, the door swings open and we're greeted by my father.

For the last motherfucking time.

"Boys," Marco says warmly.

"Sorry we took so long," I say. "It was a pain in the ass getting all the drywall taken down."

"You're right on time," he replies, shutting the door behind us and leading us up the stairs. I spot movement in the kitchen and pray Ryan isn't here to witness what's going to take place. "I knew you two could handle it."

He leads us to the faux guest bedroom, which no one really *uses*. Well, except for me, once. As much as I want to get lost in the memory of the first time I fucked Kate, I need to stay focused.

"Why didn't you tell us about the hotel?" Santi asks. We avoid eye contact and we keep our masks on, nodding to Rowan when we enter the room.

"We didn't deem it necessary," Marco says offhandedly. "You two still have loads to learn about the way we run things."

So you think.

We hand over the luggage and they each unzip one. If they were cartoons, their eyes would have money bags in them when they see the cash stuffed inside.

"I thought you were laundering all the money through the business and off-shore accounts," I say. We need to get them talking. The more we get, the better.

"You always keep a stack, son," Marco says.

"Always," Rowan agrees.

"If you ever get popped, you'll need something they can't trace for bail," Marco says.

"And a lawyer," Rowan adds.

You two will never be free.

"Is the meet still on for August?" Santi asks, switching gears.

"Yes. Thirty kilos of fent so we can expand distribution. We've found some new leads in southern states," Rowan replies as he unzips the second suitcase.

"We might send you two to speak with them," Marco adds. "It's high time you two learned to manage these transactions."

"We could use a break," Rowan says. "And we can't trust anyone else. You two are our blood."

If you trusted us, why'd you hide the hotel from us?

They rezip the luggage and open the closet, stuffing them on top of the many boxes filled with the poison itself.

"We'll get these relocated tomorrow," Rowan says, wiping his hands once they're placed inside.

"Tell me something, father," I say when he closes the closet and turns back to us. Santi stealthily sidles up beside me. "Do you ever feel guilty for killing people?"

"Awww. My son and all of his feelings," Marco taunts. "You always have been an *emotional* bitch, just like your mother. When are you..."

His words are drowned out by the rage consuming me. He's crossed the line far too many times, and it's high time he feels my wrath. I'm sick and tired of this goddamn charade I've had to live through for years on end. It ends tonight, and I don't need Ted or anyone else to do it.

I whip out the pistol tucked into my waistband, cocking it and pointing it at *my father's* face in one swift motion. Santi throws his hand over the wrist at my side in warning, but I shake it free, my gun never wavering.

Marco's eyes are blown out, the surprise evident and sickeningly satisfying. He never saw this coming.

This emotional bitch bested you, motherfucker.

"Do you know how long"—I take in a slow, deep breath—"I've been waiting for this moment?"

There's an eerie silence, and I revel in it. I can taste the victory before it's happened.

"What is this?" Marco says with equally eerie calm. I know this man, I know how his twisted brain works. He's analyzing, searching for any way out of this.

He thinks I've only come to kill him.

I can see it in the way his eyes haven't filled with true fear. He doesn't have an inkling of our informant status.

Movement from Rowan has me diverting my attention. I watch as he slowly shifts his hand to his own waistband, but Santi is quicker, whipping his glock out and taking aim.

"Boys, let's be rational about this. Let's talk it out," Rowan says, raising his hands in mock surrender. He always *was* the more diplomatic of the two.

"Your mistake, son, has always been that you think with your heart instead of your brain. What's got you addled, huh? Have we been too hard on you?" His voice turns mocking. "Expected too much?"

It takes everything in me to maintain control because no part of me wants to. I've been in control for far, far too long. I want to let loose, let him have the fate he truly deserves. The permanence of death.

At *my* hands.

Ted said there's no justifiable reason to shoot him in response to my request.

No justifiable reason?

Letting my mother waste away because he didn't give a fuck, because he had no problem utilizing me in this selfish life he's built for himself—that's not justifiable?

One kilo of fentanyl has the potential to kill five-hundred *thousand* people, and that's not *justifiable?*

The only thing that's not justifiable is letting him—either of them—walk out of here with their lives, imprisoned or otherwise.

No... this is justified. Me pulling the trigger my finger steadily hovers over *is* justified. I can feel Santi's tension next to me, because he knows that I shouldn't be doing this, but he also knows there's no stopping me.

The wrath I've contained for so long is finally free and it refuses to see logic or reason.

It only sees revenge.

I take a step closer to the man who has made my life a living hell for as long as I can remember. "This is for Ma." Another step. "This is for my childhood." Step. "This is for all the people you've stood by and *murdered* because you don't give a damn about anything but your bank account"—I take the last step that keeps me at a safe distance—"and power."

My finger touches the trigger and three things happen at once.

A loud bang sounds from the first floor.

A woman—*Lily*—screams.

A gunshot echoes in this room.

I turned my gun at the last second, shooting the bullet between Marco and Rowan's heads so that it hit the closet.

Footsteps pound on the staircase as a SWAT team of no less than twelve men ready to infiltrate the room.

And that's when I *finally* see it.

The fear in his eyes as he realizes what's happened.

"You..." Rowan says, and my head turns sharply in his direction. For a moment, I'd forgotten he and Santi were also with us.

"That's right, father," Santi says, lowering his weapon. I keep mine pointed between them as a reminder of what I could have done. What I still could do.

"You're no sons of ours," Marco spits.

"DOWN ON THE GROUND!"

Marco and Rowan lower themselves to their knees, bringing their hands to cradle their heads. I still haven't lowered my weapon, even as shouts and footsteps and chaos ensue around me.

"Come on, brother," Santi says in my ear, tugging on my shirt. "It's over now."

CHAPTER THIRTY

May 1st

KATE

I'm awoken suddenly by the sound of the door opening. I squint in the darkness, my eyes adjusting to find Lorenzo's frame walking through the doorway.

"Sorry for waking you," he whispers hesitantly.

"What time is it?" I ask, my voice riddled with sleep.

"Sometime after 3," he responds, kicking off his shoes.

After soaking in the tub for an hour, trying to make sense of everything that happened to me and everything I'd learned, I made my way back to the bedroom. I'd intended on redressing and meeting Char downstairs, but the bed looked so comfortable and inviting, I decided to tuck myself in.

I didn't think I'd have the gift of sleep, but obviously I dozed off. Even with all the reasons I shouldn't care about Lorenzo, I couldn't stop worrying about what was happening. I couldn't stop myself from searching his closet, putting on one of his black shirts, and breathing in deeply, longing to catch a trace of his lingering scent.

"I can..." He nods towards the door, but I shake my head, becoming more alert.

"No, I..." My voice trails off, heavy with implication. "I want to know what happened."

He nods and begins walking towards the bed, then pauses, silently asking for permission. I scoot to the middle, leaving him the spot I emptied. He tugs his jeans off, leaving them in a heap on the floor as he slides into bed and turns on the bedside lamp. His eyes skim my shirt and his pierced brow arches, but he doesn't comment.

"We finally got them," he says. The weight of what he's just been through rolls off him in waves.

"Can you explain how you got involved with the FBI? Why were you involved with this at all if you didn't want to be?"

Lorenzo laughs darkly. "You think I ever got a choice? We were born into this. From day one, it was always the plan that Santi and I would join in their dirty business. And when I was a young kid who didn't understand shit, it felt like an honor."

I stay quiet to see if he'll continue, but he seems lost to his memories. "What changed?" I ask breathlessly.

"My mom died." His eyes pierce mine with that information, the pain in them evident. My own chest aches at the sight of it. Then, his gaze turns surprised. "You knew?"

"Knew what?"

"That she died."

"Yeah... yeah, Larissa told me. At the last party."

He nods and doesn't seem to be upset about her admittance. "The story was that she overdosed. And it's partly true, I suppose. But it wasn't an overdose of the drug she was trying to get high from—coke. It was from the fentanyl laced in it."

My jaw drops. "Your dad was giving her drugs?"

"Not quite. My mom never wanted me involved in the business. Obviously. I mean, what loving parent wants that for their kid? But she was knee-deep with my father. Add in a kid, and she didn't feel like she had an escape. And me—loving my father because he bought me all sorts of presents and acted like father of the year to a gullible child—I wanted to be just like him.

"They met in college, and she liked to party. She used coke and pot, like most kids of the 80's did. But once they graduated and got married, she stopped. And I'm sure she believed he would quit dealing, too. I can't say for certain, I never got the chance to ask her."

His expression darkens, and my heart hurts for him. But only for a moment. After all, he was literally doing coke and selling these murderous drugs.

"I think she just got to a point where she was so depressed, she'd do anything. She was drinking all the time. In my mind, *she* was the shitty parent. I couldn't realize back then that she was just trying to survive the misery of being married to my father... but no, she didn't get the drugs from him. She would buy them from people he sold to, who were cutting the coke with his fentanyl. And ultimately, it killed her."

"I'm so sorry."

A ghost of a smile appears. "Don't be. Not your fault."

"But... how did you figure all of this out?"

"Well, I was thirteen when she died. When they declared it was an overdose, it sort of woke me up to what my father was doing. I never really understood what that meant, as silly as it seems. It was just so... normal to us. We were told not to say anything at school, that they could get taken to jail and we'd never see them again. That sounded like the worst thing in the world.

"Santi and I grew even closer once Ma passed. I would go to his house most days because my house would be empty. Marco was rarely around before, but it got worse once she died. A part of me likes to hope that it was from guilt. But the older I got, the less I believed that. I think he didn't have the only obligation that kept him around."

"That's so terrible. But... how did you figure it out?"

"I told Santi my thoughts. I was so angry, Kate." He looks deep into my eyes and I see that familiar fire. "You know what it's like to lose a parent?" I shake my head. "She wasn't always a drunk junkie. When I was little, she was my best friend. And even in her depressed addiction, I knew she loved me. So, I wanted answers."

Answers.

"Santi is the best man I'll ever know for this reason—he vowed to help me. He agreed that we needed to learn about our fathers—*really* learn about them. We started to act like we wanted to learn about the business. And they were so eager to teach us at thirteen fucking years old. They didn't give a fuck. We made them proud."

I shake my head and cover my mouth with my hand. This is *sick*.

"They didn't allow us to handle any business, but they started teaching us. They explained the ins and outs. Santi and I did research into fentanyl, because they were insistent that it was the way to success. They were still small in it back then; not a lot of drug dealers were using it yet."

"I don't understand. Why would dealers put something that *kills* into their drugs?"

"A few reasons. It's cheaper than the pure stuff, so they cut it just enough. It also makes the drug seem more powerful, so people keep coming back. Gotta have loyal customers," he says bitterly. "But the worst reason—when drug users hear that someone dies off a hit, they want it that much more."

"That's... insane."

"I know. I mean, they don't *want* it to kill people. Not everyone, anyway."

"But Lorenzo... why? Why would you do drugs, knowing all of this?"

The puzzled look on his face surprises me. "I don't use drugs, Kate."

"But..."

"The coke you found in my dresser is shit he gives me to sell. But I don't do it myself! I sell to my friends, and I make sure he gives me the pure stuff. That way I know they won't die, at least."

"Why didn't you just hide it from your friends?"

"By the time we got to high school, our fathers insisted we start selling to other kids. Fresh new market to hit, you know? And at this point, Santi and I wanted out. We tried to say no. You know what they said to us?"

I blink.

"The only life we get is the one they've built for us. That we should be grateful."

My eyes blow out and my jaw slackens.

"Then we tried a different angle. How would we explain it to our friends? But that completely backfired."

"Carter, and D, and—"

Lorenzo nods his head. "They told us to let them in on it. Lou, too. The more people selling, the more people buying. They don't know everything, of course. They definitely don't know the shit is cut with fentanyl. They had no idea about me and Santi's level of involvement, not at the time.

"We couldn't say no. They didn't outright say it, but they've killed for less. Santi and I knew that it was a death sentence if we didn't do what we were told. They could pay anyone off to make it look like an accident, and that's the end of our lives."

"So this isn't just a drug ring... this is some mafia shit."

"No, it's a drug ring. Or was, after tonight. And a tight run one, at that. But who do you think drug dealers run with? It's all the same shit at the end of the day. Different motives, same means. Power, money, and more power are what rules."

"Fucking hell..."

"Yeah."

All of the doubt I had begins to drip away. "I'm so sorry."

"When I was going away to college, the death threat became real. I wanted out. I couldn't live with myself, knowing he was dealing drugs that could hurt people. That literally killed my mom. I went the easy route and told Marco I wanted to pursue an IT career and I wouldn't have time for his business.

"That didn't go over well. Said I was wasting my time. I fought him on it. You know what happened on my first day of college?" He doesn't wait for my answer. "I get a knock on my dorm room door. I recognize the guy immediately—it was Ron. The guy I shot last night."

My brain explodes at this information.

"Ron was Marco's right hand man. He didn't sell drugs, but he did all his dirty work for a pretty penny. Beat the shit out of people, even killed a few, whenever a threat appeared to the business."

I pull the comforter up to my chin. "Why was he at your dorm?"

"He feigned concern for wanting out of the business. But I understood the underlying message. I knew who my father was at that point. It was a threat. A threat on my life. You leave, and you're done."

"This is... insidious. So fucked up."

"I know. I called Marco the next day, told him I was sorry for being so difficult. That of course I wanted to be in the business. His reply: "I knew you'd make the right choice. I'm glad Ron was able to talk some *sense* into you"."

"So you had to continue selling drugs to people?"

"Not *quite.* Naturally, Santi and I went to the same college. The crew did, too. He—"

"Why do you guys call yourselves that?"

Lorenzo shrugs. "Kinda just happened. We're all highly loyal to each other. Whenever we'd be apart someone would say, what's up with the crew? We seeing the crew later? Shit like that. It just stuck."

"Were Melanie and Maria part of it, too? And what about Larissa? Did they all sell drugs?"

"Nah. Larissa hung around with us because she's my cousin, and when she moved here, she had no one else. I introduced her to Maria and Mel, and they eventually joined our group."

I nod, and Lorenzo continues what he'd been saying.

"He—Santi—wanted out as much as I did once I told him about Ron's visit. He realized, just as I did, that our fathers didn't care about us. They cared about their business. They don't care who it hurts. And at this point, fentanyl was becoming more widely used; largely in part because of them.

"Santi and I vowed to find a way to destroy them. To stop the business. We got a bit distracted, livin' the college party life and pretending like our lives weren't shit thanks to our fathers. But we also worked our *asses* off. We hit the gym every day, for hours at a time once we were strong enough. We convinced our fathers that we should be trained in firearms. Essentially, we worked to be able to protect ourselves. And luckily, our fathers believed us at every turn. That it was all for the good of running drugs and being able to protect that. Eventually, our way out arrived."

I turn to my side, nestling into the pillow. "How?"

Lorenzo shifts into a lying position to face me. "On our graduation night, we went out with a bunch of Santi's friends. As capable as I am of putting on a show, of being the social guy, I didn't want to. I hated living all these lies. I slowly grew to hate myself, and Marco more than anyone else. But that hate was what drove me. It gave me direction and a sense of purpose.

"We get to a bar and I pound drinks, wondering how the fuck we're ever going to achieve what we want—out. And termination of the whole thing. A few hours—and drinks—later, a group of cops walk in. They sat in the booth behind us, which instantly made me uncomfortable. I'd been ignoring most of the conversation around me, anyway, so I started listening to them.

"They were discussing an arrest they'd made. A guy had been caught selling dope. You wanna know my first thought? Was it laced with fent? Did these cops save lives by stopping them?

"And I don't know why, but it hit me. Why don't we get the police involved? We know so much. There's no reason to keep it all hidden.

"But I was drunk, and so was Santi. This wasn't the time to discuss it. Next morning, I shared my thoughts with him. He was terrified at first and said absolutely not. That if we ever got caught, we were dead. We went back and forth a lot, but ultimately, I won out. No matter what route we took, we were risking our lives. We didn't have any other choice.

"This was the safest way. We could get *professional* help, and we wouldn't be doing these terrible things for no reason anymore. It was for information. It was a way out that also helped keep the shit off the streets. We went to the library and started looking at how to report this—"

"The library?" I giggle despite the seriousness of this conversation. "You didn't have laptops? Or phones?"

He gives me a look. "Kate, all of that is traceable."

"Oh."

"When you run with criminals, you learn to watch your back, no matter what. You don't know who will look into what, or why. We couldn't risk our fathers finding out. It was a stretch, I know, but you have to understand the types of risks we were taking."

I don't know if I'll ever be able to fully understand that.

"We learned pretty quickly that this was big enough for the Feds. Marco and Rowan deal in many states, and the amounts at which they were profiting, it warranted the FBI.

"We put in an anonymous report and said that if they were interested, they could meet us. We knew it could take weeks for a reply, if we ever got one, so we set the date for a month out.

"A month later, we went to the location we'd outlined. They—"

"Where?"

He eyes me for a moment. "Here. It was the only time I'd been since renting it."

I blow out a breath. "This is all... just—"

"Unbelievable? I know. Ted was the one who met with us. We told him everything. *Everything*, Kate. He was silent the entire time. Just listening. Didn't write a lick of information down.

"He said he'd be willing to help us. If we became confidential informants, he'd clear us of any indictments. It wasn't until a few weeks later that we learned the FBI already had a case open and were planning to send in an undercover. So it was a mutually beneficial agreement."

"Oh my god."

"It would have taken years for an undercover to get to the level of knowledge we had, maybe even longer. And we would soon have access to the entire system at Valeri Financials. Ted couldn't turn us down. Looking back, I think he felt sorry for us. I was desperate at that point."

I ruminate over his words. "But what about Carter and D? And the rest of the crew? They know—"

"No one knew about us working with the FBI. We couldn't risk it ever getting out. In this business, you trust few, but you must trust some. You have to take risks to reap rewards in life. It's no difference with this sick business."

When our silence extends into more silence, goosebumps coating my arm, Lorenzo adds, "When Marco and Rowan wanted to hire some workers for Rentals, because it was expanding to a point that they needed help, he asked me to ask my friends since they were already dealing. Lou's auto shop was in the works, so Carter and D took the jobs.

"They didn't ask questions when I told them not to look deeply into things. Get the tenants, fill out the paperwork, send it to Rowan or Marco. That's it."

"How could they just *not* ask?"

Lorenzo chuckles and tucks a strand of hair behind my ear. The simple gesture sends a tingling sensation across my skin. "I know it's impossible for you, princess. But there are people that can follow orders blindly. Particularly grunt workers. People who deal in shady business understand—the less you know, the better."

No wonder I couldn't keep my nose where it belonged.

"What about the matching tattoos you guys have? Is that like a gang thing?"

Lorenzo laughs. "You think we're going to put physical proof on our bodies of our connection? That's asking for trouble. No. Santi and I did that in our last year in college, when we realigned our vision and decided to get serious about our desire to take down the business. The night we met Ted, we got the ink."

He lifts his shirt up to reveal the tattoo, but it's not what catches my attention. My eyes are popping at another tattoo, one that wasn't there before. It's inked directly over his heart.

A moon.

"Almost like you're the moon and I'm a hatching sea turtle. I just want to follow the path that leads me to you."

I know there are words coming from his mouth, but I can't process any of them. I'm left gaping, unwilling to believe what I'm seeing. It can't be about me... it just can't.

But every part of my heart, which is quickly being pieced back together, knows it's true.

"What is that?" I ask in a whispered tone. He follows my line of sight, and as though he's only just remembering what's there, his eyes shoot back to mine. And he looks scared. Vulnerable. Lit on fire.

"I needed something to remember you by..."

"A tattoo?! That's so permanent! You weren't even my boyfriend!"

"Haven't you pieced it together by now, princess? I couldn't risk having a girlfriend. You were never supposed to happen. I couldn't have any liabilities lying around. If Marco ever caught us, if he ever *knew*, anyone that meant *anything* to me would be dead."

The gravity of his tone forces me to believe him.

"It was killing me not seeing you, not talking to you... and then you moved locations..." His eyes water. "I knew it was for the best. Not because we shouldn't be together, but because I shouldn't have ever put you at risk. I was desperate when I asked you to let me explain. But when you ignored me, and I calmed down, I realized... it's for the best. That one day, I'd be able to explain. Once my father was taken down, and I didn't have to live in fear. I'd sacrificed this long, I could sacrifice a bit longer."

His words trigger a memory from months ago in Santi's garage.

"We don't get to make those kinds of choices, Zo!"

"I'm not stopping. This is the limit for me. I've sacrificed enough!"

I stare at him. Everything... It makes perfect sense. The puzzle pieces fit.

"Say something, princess," Lorenzo whispers. I meet his worried eyes.

"Tell me what happened tonight," I say, needing every last bit of information. He recounts the entire takedown, leaving my mouth hanging open when he explains how close he was to killing Marco.

Once the FBI had hold of Marco and Rowan, they raided the closet to retain the evidence. Their fathers are likely in jail cells already, or enroute to be. Santi and Lorenzo returned to Ted's office to sign paperwork releasing them from their roles as confidential informants, as well as agreeing to testify in court in exchange for pardon of their crimes.

"You're the only reason I didn't kill him, you know," he concludes. "I had to see you tonight."

Is that supposed to be romantic? "I... this is a lot. I don't trust you."

He looks disheartened, but he nods in understanding. "I don't blame you."

"You shot a man!"

"He was prepared to kill you!"

"But you could have just knocked him out or something! Why would you want the man's death on your conscience?"

"Do you really think I'm going to let a man that touched you walk away with his life?" He lets out a dark chuckle. "No one hurts you and gets away with it."

His expression turns murderous, and I'm suddenly grateful I wasn't able to turn in time to see him pull the trigger. It likely would have scared me more than anything, and I don't need that image seared into my brain.

"I..."

"No need to thank me, princess. Having you here—safe—is all I wanted." His eyes soften and my heart turns into a puddle of mush until I remember that he almost killed his father, too.

But he didn't.

"You know," I say with a sudden thought. "It's kind of ironic that you insisted you weren't going to save me, and yet, you literally did."

"Did I? If I would have stayed away from you from the start, this wouldn't have happened. You wouldn't have been looking into any-thing."

"I guess that's true."

"That's what I meant. All that time... I was putting you at risk. I always thought it would be my father finding out and using you against me... in a way, it turned out the way it should have. My father would have ordered a kill for you just to prove a lesson."

I shudder at the thought.

"The true irony is that *you* saved *me*. The only light at the end of the miserable tunnel of my life was knowing that there was an end to all of this. That we were working to take them down. It wasn't life, it was survival.

"But then I met you, and everything changed. The tunnel wasn't quite so miserable anymore. You became the light and gave me a reason to *live*. The moon for this turtle to follow."

He taps his tattoo and suddenly, I'm done with words. I crash my lips onto his, throwing my arms around his neck. All this information, everything that's happened in the last twenty-four hours, is taking a back seat to the sudden need coursing through every tendon in my body, every molecule in my bones. I need to feel him, be consumed by him.

He meets my kiss eagerly, wasting no time in coating my lips with his tongue. Our hands are everywhere. His touch my hips, my waist, my breasts, my shoulders. They tangle into my disheveled hair, pulling at my nape while simultaneously pushing me closer.

My hands roam over his torso, lingering on his new tattoo. He doesn't stop kissing me more passionately than ever, and I'm quickly lost to the feeling of all of this. I want him. Now.

I begin shoving my panties off, but he peels his lips from mine and finishes the job just as hurriedly, careful not to rub them against the gash in my leg. He rips his shirt off, tossing it on the floor with my underwear while my hands work his boxers. He moves them past his knees and kicks them off the bed.

"I love you in my shirt," he says. "I want to fuck you with it on."

I moan in response. He shoves my back into the bed and hovers over me in an instant, lining himself up with my entrance. "I don't have a condom," he says, looking into my eyes.

"I don't care," I whisper. The moment the words leave my lips he thrusts into me and I moan, giving myself completely to this moment. His lips are back on mine, and his hips match the tempo of his mouth. One hand holds him up and the other tangles into my hair, pushing my face into his bruisingly.

"I missed you so fucking much, baby," he says in between kisses.

"I missed *you* so much," I breathe. When his hips pick up the pace, I lift mine to match his rhythm. I want to take this slow, to savor every second, but I can't think past the unfiltered need coursing through me.

"Fuck," he groans. "You feel so fucking good. This is where I belong. This is where *we* belong."

I nod, sweat building on my forehead. He slows down, dropping his chest to mine. My spine feels like it's been zapped by a lightning bolt when my nipples graze his skin. My skin is alight; *everything* is alight.

"You light me up," he whispers. "I—I need you."

"You have me," I say automatically.

"For always? I—" His eyes roll back into his head as I pulse my hips into him and tighten. I can sense where he's taking this and I'm not prepared. I'm not ready. I don't know if I'll ever be after everything.

Instead, I redirect him. "Light me up, Lorenzo. Set me on fire."

His eyes burn into mine and he fucks me harder than he ever has before. I claw his shoulders, cursing and moaning as I come all over his dick. The ecstasy rolls over me as he pulls out and pumps his cock, cuming on my stomach.

With both of us panting, he drops next to me and wraps a leg around mine, scooting me close to him. I close my eyes and savor this feeling. I don't know how much time passes before he lifts his head, forcing me to meet his gaze.

"I'm going to get you a towel," he whispers, placing a tender kiss atop my head before unraveling himself from me and walking off to the ensuite. He returns a moment later with a blue washcloth, handing it to me.

"I'd clean it off for you, but I know you're particular about these kinds of things," he says with an adoring smile.

"You're right in this case."

"In most cases."

I peg him with a glaring look, but there's no true umph behind it. I *am* a bit particular. He waits at the edge of the bed until I'm done, then takes it from me and returns it to the bathroom. Now that the post-sex high is tapering off, the conversation we had comes crashing back.

Was doing this reckless, as I always am with him? Is giving this another chance the stupidest thing I'll do next?

My eyes burn as tears leak out. In the past twenty-four hours, I've been drugged and cut up, hardly eaten or slept, and undergone mental strain from all this information. Not to mention the anxiety of Lorenzo going to meet his sick dad.

That's the hardest part of it all. What if he had been killed?

My heart can't handle imagining it.

The idea of losing him hurts far worse than any of his past actions. Actions I assigned meaning to because I didn't have all the knowledge I do now. And suddenly, the potential of ending things feels like a foreign language I never understood. Just thinking of never being wrapped in his arms, of hearing his voice, of smelling the smoke and cinnamon...

It's not even an option.

He returns to the bed and pulls me to him, wrapping his arms around my waist. I rest my head on his chest, tracing the new tattoo over his heart. I still can't believe he did that, and we weren't even together. If this entire event showed me nothing else, learning that he really did always care for me is enough.

Keeping me at arms distance, refusing to put a title on things, his new numbers and old phones, it all makes sense now.

I can't blame myself for not believing him. And I'm not sure how we proceed going forward.

As long as...

"How are you feeling?" he murmurs, searching my eyes with new-found worry.

"I feel a little weak, but I'm a bit... distracted."

"You need to eat. We can find some food. There's nothing here, but I'm sure there's a place open." He begins to shift, then abruptly stops. "You probably need to sleep more, though."

Food is the last thing I want right now, no matter how much my body needs it. And how am I supposed to sleep when I'm back in his arms after thinking I never would be again? "I thought I lost you," I whisper.

"You're never going to lose me again," he says quietly. Full of *vivid* promise. "It's all over now."

"I'm sorry," I rush out. "I was just scared and I didn't know what to believe and—"

"Hey," he says, pulling back to stare deeply into my eyes. "You don't have to explain. I completely understand. I would understand if you still wanted nothing to do with me."

I shake my head. "Stop. That's ridiculous."

"It's not ridiculous. I was—"

"It *is* ridiculous! I thought you might *die!* I forgive you. There's nothing *to* forgive. It all makes sense now. I just didn't—"

"Kate, please." His voice is so demanding that I snap my mouth shut and stare at him with a deer in headlights look. "I don't want you getting so worked up over me. I don't want you to suffer anymore."

"You don't get to decide how much I suffer," I snap. He's so frustrating; I'm sitting here confessing my feelings and he's trying to tell me what to do?

He chuckles. "There's my fiery badass."

I roll my eyes.

"I have a question for you, actually," he says suddenly, searching my eyes earnestly. "Why didn't you ever turn me in?"

I let out a sigh, unsure how to properly explain. "I don't know... I was so sure you were an asshole that didn't care about other people. And that you were using drugs. I felt so guilty, not reporting it to the police. But... I couldn't bring myself to do it. Brad was okay. And Char said we didn't *actually* know what happened. Oddly, she was right."

He shakes his head. "No matter how understandable this all is, I know I've done some terrible things. I lied to you. I've given you zero reason to trust me."

His words are all true, and yet I can't help that my heart wants to give him one more chance. Maybe it really all was for the greater good. He seems lighter somehow, and I'm not sure how I never saw just what a dark place he was in.

"I'm so glad you're finally free now," I whisper.

"When I returned and saw you were still here... I was so fucking grateful."

"Grateful?"

"You have every right to never want to see my face again. But you're here. And I know why."

I search his eyes, which are filled with that strong emotion I'm afraid to name.

"We always knew what we felt, didn't we, princess?"

I give him a watery smile, my lips trembling with the tears I'm trying to keep at bay. I don't succeed.

"What are you trying to say?" I press.

"I've been in love with you since before I could comprehend it. It didn't truly dawn on me until you left the party with Char. After you knew."

Goosebumps erupt over my skin, both from his confession and the memory.

"But I could never truly appreciate it because I *couldn't* love you."

"Because I'm not capable of loving you properly."

"I wanted to be your boyfriend ever since the night we shared at Rowan's. But I fought myself tooth and nail. Every encounter we shared was a sin, because I was risking you. And you didn't even know it. I was selfish."

"Lorenzo—"

He holds up a finger. "Let me finish."

I snap my jaw shut and stare at him.

"There is no heaven or hell where I deserve you. You were upfront, and honest, and vulnerable from the start. Certainly more vulnerable than me. But if you would please give me a chance, I will prove to you everything that you mean to me."

"I already said—"

"You were always blinded by your feelings for me. My father was right about one thing—I was blinded by emotions, too. If I had known what taking you into that guest bedroom would do to me, I never would have risked it. But something happened that night... something I worked so hard against. And yet, I couldn't stay away from you. I didn't *want* to. And that's my biggest sin yet."

It's hard to care that he did implicate me in any of this because I love all the moments we spent together. If I were in his shoes, I'm not sure I could have resisted, either. I didn't resist even when I knew all along something was very wrong.

"I... I'm not saying I trust you. But I want to try," I say quietly.

"I want to make sure that you know where I stand, clear as crystal. I won't put you through any of that ever again."

"I believe you," I say breathlessly. No part of me can deny the truth in it right now. My eyes roam over him, drinking in what seems to be a changed man. When my eyes land on the nearly full moon etched into his skin, I snap my eyes to his.

"When did you get the tattoo?"

He lets out a breath. "That's a story. You might get mad, but I don't care. No more lies. No more secrets."

My stomach drops; what in the world now?

"After you wouldn't answer my texts, and you stopped going to work, I was a mess. You know," he pauses with a sudden thought. "You said I succeeded, that I ruined you. But what you don't realize is you ruined me, too. You changed my entire world, the way I saw everything. By the time you were gone, I didn't know how to go on without you."

"I'm sorry," I whisper.

"The best kind of ruin. I'd let you ruin me over and over and over again."

Butterflies take flight in my stomach. My heart skips a beat. I don't need to breathe because my lungs are full of the purest air. Every one of those clichés is happening to me, and I desperately need to kiss him.

When I lean in, he raises a finger.

"The truth?" I stand straight and nod. "I got super drunk and showed up at your apartment. The lady next door told me you moved out. I returned home a wreck, and Maria was the perfect distraction."

It takes a moment for the information to process, but when it does, my cheeks flush. He slept with her? After everything?

I can't say he cheated on me because we weren't together. We never were. But once you've been cheated on, you know the feeling of betrayal. And this feels like that.

"We kissed for five seconds before I realized that I didn't want to feel anyone's lips but yours. I sent her away and I had a sudden idea. I was desperate for something to connect me to you. I didn't have a single item of yours, and you didn't contact me. To be fair, I stopped trying because I knew it was risky. I put my head on straight and allowed the space because I knew I shouldn't have gotten near you to begin with.

"So, I dragged Santi to the tattoo shop in the middle of the night. He looked at me like I was crazy when I explained it to him on the ride over, but I think it finally clicked for him. Just how much you mean to me."

His confession reminds me of Gustav, and I realize I owe him the same. "I get it. When I went to Char's housewarming party, I had a similar thing happen with one of her friends. We just made out, but it was enough for me to know I didn't want anyone else."

Lorenzo nods in understanding. "You were always mine."

"I was always yours."

"I was always yours, too."

My mouth parts and I lean into him again. "Lorenzo..."

"Please," he whispers. "Call me Zo."

"Zo," I whisper. That phenomenon happens as we stare into each other's eyes, where it feels like time stops and there's no one else in the world but us. And for the first time, I don't run from it. I welcome the fire. I want us to burn so bright that when people try to look at us, they're blinded.

His tongue swipes his bottom lip and I kiss him, gingerly at first, but he digs his hand into my hair and pulls me closer.

"I'd take any pain for you," he says against my lips.

"The greatest pain would be losing you," I say between kisses.

"You'll never lose me. You have me, for now and for always."

Epilogue

KATE

"Let's see it," Zo says when we step into the sunlight.

I pass him the driver's license, grinning from ear to ear. In the aftermath of everything that happened, taking my driver's test took the backseat. "I did it! I can't believe it."

"I can," he replies, smiling at the ID before handing it back. "I never expected anything less from a badass like you."

He takes my hand in his, clasping his fingers around mine and walking us towards his car. He lets me go at the driver's side and hands me his keys, then circles to the passenger side. I step into his car with no fear of driving.

He quit smoking after the first court proceeding for their fathers indictments, yet the fading scent of smoke that permeates the space invites nostalgia. It brings me a peace I never thought I'd find from it because it reminds me of him.

Smoke and cinnamon.

Once he's inside the car, I tease him.

"Even after all this, you can't open a door for me?" I'm not truly offended the way I was all those months ago. Then again, I was certain he didn't care about me back then.

"Why would I diminish your worth by holding a door open for you? Here's the thing, Kate. I'm never gonna be the guy in shining armor.

I'm not going to fawn over you and treat you as some little bird who's injured and needs my help. I'm the guy that forces you to dig deep inside yourself and embrace the power already stowed in you. Be the fire, princess. Not the ash."

"That feels rich coming from the man who quite literally rescued me and saved my life."

"See, this is where semantics matter. You couldn't get yourself out of that situation. Someone inevitably had to save you, and I want to be damn sure that someone is always me. But when you can do it yourself... why would I intervene?"

He leans across the console, breathing life into the previously stale air. "Especially when you are so sexy when you're badass."

I close the gap, my lips brushing over his. When I pull back, he cups my face with his hand and pulls me closer, deepening the kiss. Within moments, I'm moaning into his mouth.

"Come on," he whispers, nodding his head to the backseat.

"Right here?" I whisper.

"No one's going to care. And my windows are tinted." I stare out of the back seat passenger side window. It still allows some light in.

He crawls past me and into the backseat, unbuttoning his pants. "Now, princess."

I roll my eyes and huff, but I join him in the back.

"Someone's extra bratty," he murmurs, nuzzling his head into my neck and biting down on the sensitive skin.

"Someone's extra risky," I retort. He brings his hand up to my neck and squeezes, the blood in my veins thrumming.

"I've never been anything less, Kate. You know this."

And fuck if I don't love it.

"Mmm," I reply lazily, not giving him the satisfaction of my true thoughts.

He growls like a feral animal, crawling over me and trapping me between his arms. He runs his nose along my throat before bringing his lips to my ear. "Fucking *brat*."

He pulls my shirt off in a quick motion, then pulls the waistband of my jeans so roughly that the button pops off.

I'm equally apprehensive and excited. My clit throbs, aching for more. I lift my hips as he slides my jeans to my ankles. As I kick off my jeans, I unbutton his pants and peek outside.

It's broad daylight.

"Give 'em a show, baby," he says seductively. He brings his lips to mine, his tongue capturing mine provocatively. I bite his lip *really* hard, just as he likes it. I taste the blood on his lip as I suck, and he groans.

"Goddamn, I love you," he says. Once his boxers are around his ankles, I grab his ass and guide his throbbing cock to my pussy.

"So eager," he teases. Then he thrusts into me like it's his sole purpose for living. He pulls in and out slowly, seemingly having no regard for the location of our fucking.

"Zo, please," I whine, both from carnal need and paranoia of getting caught.

"Fuck, I love when you call me that," he murmurs, running a hand across my breasts and pinching a nipple. I bite down on my own lip this time, though not quite as hard. He picks up the pace of his thrusts, bringing his hand to thread my hair.

Pulling on it, he says, "Scream for me, Kate. Let the world hear you."

I moan louder, but I'm too nervous of anyone hearing us.

"I'm not asking," he says with that commanding bite in his tone that drives me wild. He brings a finger to my clit and rubs, bringing me closer to orgasm.

His eyes twinkle with a devilish grin as I shout his name into the car, and a bead of sweat drips onto my chest. "That's my good fucking girl."

He drives into me then, my breath lost to him. *I'm* lost to him. To the moans erupting from both of us. To the confined space and potentially the public eye.

When he senses I'm close, his hand strikes my throat, forcing me into the seat. My face flushes immediately, the blood flow restricted. "That's it, princess. Come for me."

He presses impossibly tighter on my throat, sending me over the edge without a breath to get me through it. He heightens his thrusts, pulling out at the last second and cuming all over my pelvis.

Our ragged breaths are synchronized, and when our eyes meet, our smirks align, too. He drops into the seat next to me and catches his breath.

"I love you, too, by the way," I say.

"I know. I can feel it, just as I always have." His smile turns lazy. "Now let's go get that tattoo."

$$))) \bullet ((($$

I take a sip of my Fireball, enjoying the cinnamon burning down my very *sore* throat after our sex earlier. I've acquired a taste for the cinnamon whiskey now that Zo and I have been pretty much inseparable. Once the Feds took control of the company, Santi and Zo moved into The Getaway. I joined them shortly after, with the approval of Santi, of course.

When we first moved our stuff in, I asked Zo what color we should paint the walls. He admitted that they'd intentionally left the white paint, wanting everything light. What drew both of them into the place was the open layout, the expansive windows, and the overall calming feel of the home. They'd lived in darkness for so long, this was a perfect opposition.

In exchange for their service, Santi and Zo were wiped clean of the things they were essentially forced into doing. Brad was an outlier, but their consciences are clear in knowing it ultimately allowed them to bring their fathers down.

My conscience is clear, too. I'm finally sleeping better, knowing that all of his secrets had a reason. His actions since the day I was kidnapped have made up for all of his shitty behavior, slowly rebuilding my trust. It doesn't hurt that he's an excellent cuddler, either.

"Sorry, princess. Santi needed help with one of the dishes," Zo says, walking through the sliding glass door to our deck that overlooks the bay. He's slowly started incorporating navy blue shirts in his wardrobe.

"I didn't need *help*. You agreed to make it, then left me to do it," Santi bites out resentfully. Char follows him onto the patio, shutting the sliding glass door behind her.

"I never agreed to do it. You told me I had to," Zo retorts.

"Here, toots," Char says, giggling at the two of them as she hands me one of the romance books I'd leant her. I took her advice to heart, branching into the genre. Because suddenly, I believed in love stories and happy endings. "You were right, this one was *so* good!"

I tuck the novel beside my leg as Lorenzo joins me on the white wooden swing with navy blue cushions. His own drink in hand, he holds it up to us. Santi, Char, and I raise our glasses.

"To a fucktastic Fourth," Zo says with a lopsided grin.

"Fucktastic?" Char questions.

"Yeah. Fucking Fantastic," Santi informs her as if this is common knowledge.

"Or lots of fucking, however it works out for you," Lorenzo adds. We all laugh and clink our glasses before taking a drink. Zo watches as I licks my lips, then kisses me deeply.

Char clears her throat. "Well, I think I'll go wait for everyone inside," she says, clapping her hands together. "Santi, you joining me?"

"Of course, doll," he replies. It still takes everything in me *not* to laugh when I hear a guy like Santi using a pet name like doll, but I succeed in stifling it. They re-enter the house, leaving Lorenzo and I alone.

"Everything's ready inside?" I ask, placing my hand on his thigh. The crew is coming over tonight for a Fourth of July party we're hosting. Carter and D were pissed to find out that they were in the dark about a lot of the happenings with Santi and Zo, but they understood the need for secrecy. They've left the dealing game behind and found new jobs at another mortgage brokerage.

As for Zo and I, we decided we'd like to explore our options before committing to new jobs. He was able to save a lot of money while living at Rowan's house rent free. He donated all the money he made selling with Marco to a drug rehabilitation center. I have some money saved, and he and Santi said they'd cover the rent while I look for a new job, which I've been so grateful for.

As much as I've always loved working, this break was much needed.

I told Zo he should become a teacher since he was so good at teaching me how to drive. He laughed and said I was biased, but the look in his eyes told me he was considering it. As for me, I want to stay in finance. Numbers are still a source of tranquility for me.

"Yeah, all good," he says. "Now let's get back to celebrating you. A new driver, and an absolute *badass*."

We both look down at the new tattoo under cling wrap on my left forearm. The word badass is inscribed in typewriter font with a period at the end. The blood is drying along the ink and the skin feels raw, but it's well worth it.

When the tattoo artist asked if I wanted the punctuation, I said no. It wasn't how I originally envisioned it. But as he was tattooing the word onto my skin, I realized a period made sense. It was a point of finality. It means there's no further discussion.

I am a badass.

Period.

I refuse to ever doubt it again.

So I told him to add it, and he smiled in agreement.

"Period," I say to Lorenzo.

He plants a light kiss on my lips, then we stare out at the water. The sun just set, and the stars are beginning to light up the sky with a new moon hanging picturesquely in the corner of my view.

"Do you think we'll ever have kids?" Lorenzo asks suddenly, and I choke on my drink.

"Kids?" I laugh. "We just moved into this place. Slow your roll, buddy."

"What? The future is bright," he says in response, not sharing my humor. "It's foreseeable now."

I squeeze his thigh, understanding his true meaning. He's finally free.

"Yeah, maybe. Or maybe not. We'll see as time goes on," I say.

"Seriously? I'm finally ready to nail things down and talk, and you just want to see?"

I laugh again. "I guess the stars haven't aligned for us quite yet."

He's about to respond when a loud pop sounds in the distance. We face the water, met with fireworks exploding into the sky.

"People can never wait," he murmurs. "They have to start early."

"I don't know, I kind of like it," I reply, watching the sky light up with gold, purple, and red. "They're so excited, they can't help themselves."

He shrugs and we watch as more fireworks explode into the sky.

"In the darkness, seek the stars. You may not see them, but they are always there for you," he whispers suddenly.

My breath hitches. "That's... beautiful."

"My mom always said that to me when I was little."

My eyes water from the overwhelming sentiment. "That's so sweet."

"She was wrong, though."

I peer at him curiously, but his gaze remains on the sky, fireworks reflected in his eyes. "It wasn't the stars."

He faces me, his eyes filled with my favorite twinkle.

"It was the moon."

Author's Note

If you made it this far in Kate and Zo's journey, *thank you.* I love these characters so much, and I'm so sad to say goodbye to them. But as they say, this isn't goodbye, this is see you later. I will *definitely* be jumping back into this world in some form or another. The best way to stay up to date with my new releases is to follow me on Amazon and join my newsletter! You can find the links on my TikTok and Instagram @amandabentleyauthor.

This series touches on a very serious topic—drugs laced with fentanyl. Drug use in general can be dangerous, but with the rise in fentanyl related deaths due to it being laced in street drugs is something I want brought to attention. Zo's story was a way of highlighting its destruction. If you or anyone you know struggles with addiction, there are resources for help. I also encourage you to educate yourself on the rise of fentanyl laced drugs and the harm it brings.

Substance Abuse and Mental Health Services Administration (SAMHSA)
1-800-662-HELP (4357)
samhsa.gov

Also by Amanda Bentley

Drift

For Now (Now & Always Duet Book 1)
For Always (Now & Always Duet Book 2)

Acknowledgements

The end of Kate and Zo's journey... wow. Thank you to everyone who's read this story and fallen in love the way I have. You're the ones I wrote their ending for.

Special shoutout to my husband, who was the only person who knew the entire plan from the start. You know the drug front setup? The business Kate works for? Yep, all his ideas. He would let me talk his ear off with my crazy ideas and patiently helped me find answers to my fictional problems. Alvin, I love you.

A *very* special thank you to Alex and Anne, who let me bounce all my wild ideas off of them before putting them down on paper (and kindly, yet bluntly, telling me when it's a hard no). I may not always listen (Gustav *cough, cough*, Lorenzo crying *cough, cough*) but your guidance is everything to me.

Another special thank you to Kaila and Emily, who gifted me so much dedication and moral support in the final draft.

And of course, my beta readers: Alex, Anne, Ava, Baby, Cassie, Kaila, Emily, Kath, Jordan V, Jordy, and Randi. I always thank you guys, but I wanted to give an extra round of applause with this book. Your honest feedback is what altered this story to become what it was meant to be.

And finally, to you—the reader! Kate & Zo have such a special place in my heart, and it's pretty cool that (hopefully) they have a place in your heart, too. Fictional worlds are where I want to be, and the chance to create them and have other people join them? It's an amazing feeling. It wouldn't be possible without *you*.

Thank you, thank you, thank you.

Amanda Bentley loves escaping into fictional worlds through reading and writing. A typical Pisces, she's as much a mood writer as she is a mood reader. She likes her book boyfriends morally grey, but she'll read any book with romance (preferably drenched in spice and angst).

When she's not writing, you might find her chasing her wild toddler, or on stage, performing improv with her husband. She's a creative, free spirit, and while she loves a fun adventure, there's no place like her bed with a book.

Amanda can be found on TikTok and Instagram under @amandabentleyauthor.

Made in the USA
Columbia, SC
04 September 2023

22411670R00157